W9-AUW-590

The
Not-So-Perfect
Man

NEWBURYPORT PUBLIC LIBRARY
94 STATE STREET
NEWBURYPORT, MA 01950

Books by
Valerie Frankel

THE NOT-SO-PERFECT MAN
THE ACCIDENTAL VIRGIN
SMART VS. PRETTY

The
Not-So-Perfect
Man

 VALERIE FRANKEL

AVON
TRADE

An Imprint of HarperCollinsPublishers

THE NOT-SO-PERFECT MAN. Copyright © 2004 by Valerie Frankel. All rights reserved. Printed in the United States of America. No part of this book may be used or reproduced in any manner whatsoever without written permission except in the case of brief quotations embodied in critical articles and reviews. For information address HarperCollins Publishers Inc., 10 East 53rd Street, New York, NY 10022.

HarperCollins books may be purchased for education, business, or sales promotional use. For information please write: Special Markets Department, HarperCollins Publishers Inc., 10 East 53rd Street, New York, NY 10022.

FIRST EDITION

Designed by Elizabeth M. Glover

Library of Congress Cataloging-in-Publication Data

Frankel, Valerie.
    The not-so-perfect man / by Valerie Frankel.—1st ed.
      p. cm.
ISBN 0-06-053668-3 (alk. paper)
1. Single mothers—Fiction. 2. Dating (Social customs)—Fiction. 3. Mothers and daughters—Fiction. 4. Mate selection—Fiction. 5. Sisters—Fiction. 6. Widows—Fiction. I. Title.

PS3556.R3358N68 2004
0813'.54—dc22   2003058263

04 05 06 07 08 JTC/RRD 10 9 8 7 6 5 4 3 2 1

Dedicated to

Alison, Dan, Howie and Judy.
During the worst of times,
you showed the best of yourselves,
day after relentless day.
You are all true grit. The truest.
And—I'm honored to say—the grittiest.

The
Not-So-Perfect
Man

A woman was walking along a deserted beach when she stumbled upon an old brass lamp. She picked it up and rubbed it. A genie popped out.

The genie said, "I am the genie of the lamp. Make one wish and I will grant it."

The amazed woman asked, "One wish? Don't I get three?"

The genie said, "My magic is so powerful, you only need one."

Unhesitatingly, the woman said, "I want peace in the Middle East." She happened to have a map of the region in her purse. "Look here," she said. "I want these countries to stop fighting with each other now and forever."

The genie looked at the map and said, "But they've been at war for thousands of years. I'm good, but not that good. Make another wish."

The woman thought for a moment and said, "I'd like to meet and marry the perfect man. He should be considerate, fun, gorgeous, warm, affectionate, faithful, drug-free, a social drinker, a nonsmoker, have an interesting, high-paying job, love kids, love to travel, have a big dick and know how to use it, be a good cook and a happy vacuumer, get along with his family but keep them at a healthy distance, look great in jeans, and make me feel like I'm the only woman in the world. That's my wish."

The genie let out a huge sigh and said, "Let me see that map again."

Chapter 1

Thursday, September 5
10:34 A.M.

"I've got the perfect man for you."

"Not another one," said Frieda Schast. "Is that why you came to Brooklyn? To give me the hard sell?"

Ilene, Frieda's older sister by three years, said, "You know I love coming out here. It's practically a trip to the country. I needed the fresh air."

"I'm not a cause," said Frieda.

"You are."

"Why?"

"Just . . . 'cause."

Ilene didn't have to explain further. It'd been a year and a month since Frieda's husband died. The day after the deathiversary, Ilene began fixing up Frieda with suitors she'd located, apparently under a rock somewhere.

Ilene said, "He's an entomologist."

"So you did find him under a rock," said Frieda.

The two women sat behind the counter at Frieda's frame store on Montague Street in Brooklyn Heights. Ilene had taken the afternoon off work in Manhattan to make the visit. Despite her annoyance with the topic of conversation, Frieda was grateful for the company.

Frieda asked, "Does he twitch?"

Ilene said, "Not that I know of."

"The last one twitched."

"A tic is not a twitch," said Ilene.

"A tic is when someone tugs his ear if he's nervous, or twirls his hair. I'd even allow a tic to mean incessant blinking or handwringing. But the last one had full-body convulsions every two minutes. I thought I'd have to rush him to the hospital. Or that the force of his seizures would make his head fly off."

"Just as long as you're not exaggerating," said Ilene.

On the counter in front of her, Frieda held a small triptych of a girl on a swing. The photographer had taken the pictures of his daughter, and had carefully selected a three-quarter-inch cherry-wood frame. The girl's dress was red and pretty, and Frieda imagined herself on that swing. She could only guess which sensation was more thrilling for the girl, zooming backward, her hair floating around her head, covering it protectively, or zipping forward, hair blown back, exposing her to the world of the playground.

Frieda reflexively tucked some of her own brown curls behind one ear, leaving the bulk of it to hang down against her cheeks. She knew she'd have to move forward, that it was impossible to backswing indefinitely. Frieda asked, "Have you met this guy? How many degrees of separation are we talking here?"

Ilene said, "He's the brother of Peter's secretary's best friend."

Frieda calculated this information. "That's four degrees."

"Three."

"Best friend, secretary, Peter, you."

"I'm not counting myself."

"Why not?" asked Frieda.

"We're related," she said. "We shouldn't count Peter, either. You've known him for ten years. He's like a brother to you."

"I'm sure Peter had nothing to do with this," said Frieda of Ilene's husband.

"Peter likes my fixing you up," said Ilene. "He thinks it will distract me from the size of his stomach. But let's not even mention it. Peter's belly is too big a topic to get distracted by."

"It is an immense topic," agreed Frieda.

"It's more than a topic," said Ilene. "It's practically a tropic. Like the tropic of Capricorn. The one that spans the globe?"

"I've read the book," said Frieda.

Ilene said, "His name is Roger. He's a resident professor at the Museum of Natural History. The marriage potential is sky high. He could be The One."

Frieda had already had The One. So Roger Bugman would never be that. At best, he could be The Two. Hard to get worked up about The Two. Nobody ever says, "He's The Two, I just know it!"

Frieda said, "It would be helpful, when we have these conversations, if you could shift the pitch from, 'He's The One' to something like, 'You might have a pleasant dinner with him.' Or, 'He's good practice.' Or, 'He's easy on the eyes.' Or just, 'He's easy.' "

Despite her loss of a husband (which sounded like she'd misplaced him somewhere), Frieda hadn't lost her sex drive. It was just buried in her mental closet. She knew that, at thirty-five, it was unlikely she'd never have sex again. But the idea of getting naked with a complete stranger, having been with the same man for nine years, was intimidating. When she'd met Gregg, she was a dewy twenty-six-year-old. She hadn't any wrinkles then. Nor had her belly been thickened by a pregnancy.

Ilene said, "I can show you his picture."

Frieda felt a sudden flutter of nerves at the threat of coming face-to-photo. "You brought his picture?" she asked. "You're sick, Ilene. There should be a special hospital for people like you."

"His photo and bio are on the museum website," said Ilene. "He's very handsome. And he's the nation's foremost expert on dung beetles."

"No shit," said Frieda.

"Take a look," said Ilene.

"I'm very busy," said Frieda.

"I can see that," said Ilene, pointedly glancing around the store. Not a single customer was among the bins and boxes. Business was slow, but not dangerously so. At the Sol Gallery, Frieda sold original photographs and did custom framing. Photographs were mounted on cardboard, wrapped in plastic, and put in bins for customers to flip through. Frieda priced the photos according to size and subject matter ranging from $5 to $500. Her standard arrangement: The photographer would get 40 percent of the purchase price and she'd keep 60 percent. Retail photography accounted for about 20 percent of her overall business.

Rows and rows of L-shaped frame samples covered the walls by the back counters. They were grouped by medium (wood, metal, etc.), color and size (five-inch gilded ornate maple to quarter-inch fiberglass). Frieda often sold a photograph and then framed it for the customer. That was profitable. But she derived greater satisfaction from framing originals. When a customer brought in a picture, painting, old baseball card, antique needlepoint—whatever—and said, "What do you think?" Frieda knew just the thing, and the customers were always pleased with her choices. She saw borders everywhere, the white rims of stop signs, the black lead of newspaper columns, squiggly lines on restaurant menus. She had the habit of mentally reframing anything two-dimensional, believing that, with adjustments, she could make it better. Images without borders made Frieda feel unhinged, as if the words and pictures in a magazine, for example, would slide right off the page without a neat box to contain them.

The desktop of her iMac, which Ilene had turned on, displayed gray rulers at the top and bottom of the screen. Not enough of a border to satisfy her compulsion, but she could live with it.

Ilene keyed quickly, accessing the museum's site in seconds. "Here he is!" she announced, as if ushering Mr. America into the room.

Frieda looked at the screen and stared at the face of Roger O'Leary, Ph.D. Color photo, thick black border.

"You're right," said Frieda. "He is handsome." He was, actually, quite presentable. Nice big smile, square teeth, kind eyes. Decent-shaped head and neat, cropped hair. His bio bragged that he'd gone to Columbia for his B.A., M.A. and Ph.D. He was a native New Yorker, but had traveled the world to speak about his area of expertise. Roger O'Leary had spent five years in Oslo, consulting on the production and construction of the world's first and only beetle zoo. Apparently (who knew?), Scandinavians were way into bugs.

"Now there's a conversation starter," said Frieda. " 'So tell me, Roger, do the zoo beetles live in cages, or in a free-range habitat that resembles their natural environment?' "

Ilene laughed, too brightly. "So you'll date him?" she asked. "Why wouldn't you? He's good-looking, well educated. He lives on Central Park South. I'm telling you, he's perfect."

At a glance, Frieda knew Roger O'Leary would not be The Two. She looked at his face, and saw, concurrently, what he was and what he was not. Clearly, Roger was an attractive male specimen. But, more important, he was Not

Gregg. Every man was Not Gregg to Frieda. She tried desperately to peek beneath the cloak of Not Gregg every day, on every man she passed on the street. But, much as she wanted to, she couldn't. Or, she should say, she hadn't.

"I think it'll take me by surprise," said Frieda.

Ilene turned away from Roger's webpage. "What will?"

"When I can look at a man and see his own face."

"What are you talking about?" asked Ilene wearily.

"Forget it," said Frieda.

Ilene sighed. She clicked off the website and shut down the computer. "So, can I give him your number?"

Frieda knew that Ilene wouldn't accept a no. If would be easier and less time-consuming to go on a date with Roger O'Leary than to explain over and over again why she didn't see the point.

"Okay." She relented.

Ilene said, "You'll keep an open mind?"

Frieda said, "Oh, yes! I'm optimistic! I'm ever hopeful!"

"It'll be fantastic," crowed her sister. "I have a great feeling about this."

Frieda nodded. "I'm glad someone does."

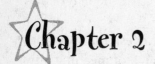

Chapter 2

Friday, September 13
8:56 P.M.

Peter Vermillion's eyes traveled a familiar path, from his wife's lips to her neck and down her slender arm. She was talking (as usual), gesturing broadly, hands flying. He watched her profile, the restaurant's candlelight giving her skin a shifting orange glow. He thought for the millionth time since they'd met that he would never tire of looking at her.

He turned to check her effect on their dinner companions. David Isen, Ilene's colleague and friend, and Georgia, his wife, sat across the table at Il Travatore, a popular East-44th-Street after-work spot for media people. David laughed as Ilene told a story about their boss. Georgia was less than captivated, or just distracted. Peter noticed that she'd checked her cell phone several times.

Georgia interrupted Ilene mid-story and said, "I'm going to step outside and call the baby-sitter." David volunteered to do it, but Georgia had already gotten up.

In the wake of shuffling chairs and the shift in the table's social dynamic from four to three, Peter asked his wife, "Are you going to eat that?" He pointed at the barely nibbled cannoli in front of her.

Ilene gave him a warning with her eyes, and then, her voice calm but packed with the high pitch of meaning only dogs and Peter could hear, she said, "I'm stuffed. Aren't you?"

She didn't want him to finish her dessert, but she wouldn't explicitly say so in front of David. Peter took advantage of the situation. "Enough room for one last bite," and pulled the plate over.

Peter knew he could stand to lose a few, but he maintained that he wasn't too heavy. The weight had come on gradually, a few pounds a year for the last decade. Except for the portly belly, which had the right curve for supporting a beer or a book, he was in decent shape. His shirt buttons didn't pop open. He could zip his pants, although he did have to belt them underneath the swell of his gut, which made his pleats bunch. Peter hoped that women, upon seeing the sag, would assume he was weighed down with an extra-large package. In any event, he had a closet full of double-breasted jackets. He wore one tonight, although he'd had to unbutton the pants after he'd finished his linguini alfredo.

Ilene scowled as Peter's fork moved like silver lightning over the cannoli. She said for David's benefit, "Peter is a man of great appetites."

David, a man of puny appetite, judging from his

marathon-runner body, smiled on cue and said, "I don't think I've ever heard the story of how you two met."

Pussy, thought Peter instantly. What kind of man gives a shit about how couples meet? Or was he just remarking on the disparity in their physical conditions? Peter, plump. Ilene, perfect.

Peter, not wanting to let his mind continue in that direction, said, "We were both covering a Guiliani press conference on the city budget deficit."

Ilene, slender arms aloft again, said, "It was love at first sight."

Peter rolled his eyes broadly. David laughed. Ilene grinned, enjoying the game, relishing her role as the feminine romantic with an audience of men.

She said, "I was working for *Crain's*. Peter was at the *Post* business section then. It was one of Guiliani's first conferences, and the pressroom at City Hall was packed. Peter had a front-row seat. I noticed him immediately. He was gorgeous." She paused, putting her hand on his shoulder and added, "This was ten years ago."

David said, "I thought you've been married for ten years."

Ilene said, "We have."

Peter said, "We had a short engagement."

"How short?" asked David.

"Five weeks," said Ilene. "I told you. It was love at first sight. I introduced myself after the press conference. Peter asked me to dinner that night. And the next. And the next. On the fourth date, Peter proposed."

David asked, "What did you say?"

Peter shrugged. "The standard. 'Will you marry me?' "

Ilene added, "And I said, 'What took you so long?' "

Laughter—bouncy, floating in perfumed air—burst from Ilene. Peter relished it. Her laughter had been the sound-track of the first five years of their marriage, and a greatest hit for the next three. The past year and a half, though, he hadn't heard enough of it. Hardly any of it, actually.

David exhaled deeply and shook his head. "Georgia and I dated for three years before we got engaged. And then we had a two-year engagement."

Ilene said, "When you're sure, you're sure. My parents got married after knowing each other for a couple of months. My sister Frieda and her husband Gregg got en-gaged after three months. It's part of my genetic code, I suppose. Schasts don't hesitate."

"Frieda, the widow?" asked David. "How's she doing?"

Ilene said, "She's fine!"

"No, she's not," said Peter.

"She will be," corrected Ilene. "She's on a date tonight."

Peter said to David, "Ilene is trying to arrange Frieda's next marriage." He looked down with surprise at the empty plate, his fork still moving across it. He'd barely registered a single bite, but he'd masticated and swallowed the entire cannoli. Peter lowered his utensil, and found himself look-ing across the table at the plate of almond cookies aban-doned by Georgia.

Meanwhile, Ilene was still talking. "Frieda's been a bas-ket case for a year, it's true. But she seems to be coming out of it. I'm trying to help her. That's what sisters are for."

Peter bit his lip. Fortunately, he tasted cannoli on it. He was opposed to Ilene's matchmaking. Frieda should be left alone. She had enough to deal with—the frame store, her five-year-old son, Justin, the unresolved issues over Gregg's estate—and didn't need the pressures of dating as well. Ilene insisted she knew what was best for her own sister, speaking with such adamancy that Peter could do nothing but silently disapprove. He did so as loudly as possible.

Peter had spent a decade observing the relationship among the three Schast sisters—Ilene, Frieda and Betty, the youngest. He'd decided they were like the three corners of a triangle, connected by the family genes, each with her own unique angle. The space inside the triangle contained their collective pain and joy. If one was happy, they all were. When one was sad, they plunged. Peter was a fixed point somewhere on the outside. So was Gregg.

The horrible business of Gregg's cancer and death brought out the best in the sisters. Ilene and Betty had been heroic. Peter, an only child, watched with awe as they took care of Frieda, Gregg, and Justin. Anything that needed doing—food shopping, baby-sitting, handholding—his wife made herself available and ready for service. Not that Frieda asked for anything. It'd been year since the death, and Ilene was still available to Frieda. Peter continued to wait for his wife to return to him.

Peter stared at the plate of cookies across the table. Where was Georgia? Wasn't she coming back? And, more important, would she be hungry?

David said, "So, Peter, how are things at *Bucks?*"

"Fine, fine," he said. "Can't get specific, you understand."

Peter was the editor in chief at *Bucks* magazine; Ilene and David were reporters at *Cash,* a competing title. Ilene and Peter were considered the dynamic duo of financial journalism. His field of expertise: bonds. Hers: retail IPOs. Donuts, T-shirts, kitchenware. Bonds and retail were opposites. One investment was safe, secure, simple. The other was dangerous, complicated, tricky. "Opposites attract," was Ilene's line on that subject. Peter wasn't sure what David's specialty was. It would have been polite to ask, but Peter was very ready for this dinner date to end. It'd been a long week. The meal with Ilene's friends exhausted Peter. He wanted to go home and get in bed—preferably with his wife naked and willing next to him.

Georgia returned. "I'm sorry that took so long. David, we have to go. Stephanie's fever is worse."

"What is it?" asked David.

"One hundred."

"That's hardly an emergency," said David. Then, seeing the look in Georgia's eyes, he said, "But we should go."

David took out his wallet, but Ilene said, "I'll expense it."

The couple left Ilene and Peter at the table to await the check. Peter signaled the waiter to bring more coffee, one eye on Georgia's dessert plate.

Ilene said, "Georgia's so beautiful, don't you think?"

"She's dog meat," said Peter. His wife laughed. "Georgia is very pretty. She's nothing compared to you," he added, meaning it.

"Give me your cell," she said.

"Who are you calling?" Peter handed it over. While Ilene busied herself dialing, he sneaked a cookie into his mouth.

"Hello?" his wife asked into the phone. "Frieda?"

Peter shook his head. Ilene couldn't leave Frieda alone even when she was on a date. He listened to Ilene's half of the conversation.

"He *what?* I'm so sorry. Okay, okay. I had no idea. Jesus, *really?* Yes, tomorrow. Okay. Bye." Ilene hung up and handed him the phone. "Well, the bug man did not get under her skin." Ilene looked around the restaurant for the waiter. She said, "The entire date lasted twenty minutes. He brought bug samples to show her, and when he whipped out the jar, she called it a night."

Peter, mouth full, scowled at the horror.

"Frieda has called a reprieve from dating," said Ilene, raising her arm, credit card in her outstretched fingers. "You'd think they'd be all over you to take the money."

Peter tried to chew without moving his lips. He wasn't sure if Ilene had seen him eat his third dessert, but she hadn't said anything. He swallowed as quietly as possible, and said, "A reprieve might be a good idea. She needs a break."

"Frieda needs a man," announced Ilene. "She's always had a boyfriend. Since sixth grade. And I know exactly who she should be with. I can almost *see* him. He's in his early forties, recently divorced. He has a child Justin's age. He's got money. He could step into her life and make everything right again. One look. That's all it will take. I just need to find the right guy for her to look at."

Peter asked, "How come you never fix up Betty?"

Ilene said, "Whenever I mention the joys of married life to Betty, she groans like she's about to give birth. She thinks I'm a marriage nazi. She doesn't want a boyfriend. She's said so explicitly. And, even if she did, she'd have to lose a ton of weight to be fix-upable."

"Betty looks fine," said Peter.

"She's as overweight as you are," said Ilene sharply. "Betty also accuses me of being the fat police."

"I wouldn't say police," he replied. "You're more like the local sheriff."

"I should arrest you for eating three desserts," she said.

To stop her from talking, he encircled her with his arms and kissed her mouth. She leaned into him, kissing back, and then stopped. She said, "It strains my neck to lean over your belly to kiss you."

He dropped his arms. "It pains my ass to listen to you bitch about it." He'd reached his limit quickly tonight. "Every time I touch you, you pull back."

"I do not," she said, glancing around the restaurant to see if anyone could hear them. "You touched me plenty last night."

"Yes, you condescended to grant me sex," he said. "You were a million miles away. Probably calculating how many calories I was burning."

Ilene had her limits, too. She slammed the table with her open palm and said, "Your father had his first heart attack at forty. You're thirty-nine, forty pounds overweight, and you never exercise. As far as I'm concerned, eating three desserts is an act of aggression." She paused, and then finished big. "I *want* to be attracted to you," she said. "But I won't pretend I am if I'm not. And where the fuck is the waiter?"

Peter had closely watched his lovely wife make her speech. He thought, for the millionth (and one) time, that he would never tired of looking at her. Listening to her, however, was getting harder and harder.

Peter pushed Georgia's dessert plate in front of his agitated wife and said, "Have a cookie. You'll feel better."

Chapter 3

Tuesday, September 17
1:12 A.M.

There he was again. Betty Schast had spotted him four
times already in one morning. It was unprecedented. Usually, she was lucky to catch a glimpse once or twice a week.

She sat behind the information desk at the Union Square
Burton & Notham bookstore. She was the branch day manager. From her perch, protective computer monitors at eye
level, she could stare at him unnoticed. He was wearing a
long-sleeve white T-shirt underneath a navy short-sleeved
one and inky-blue jeans. His black hair was an absolute mess,
but *what* a mess! When he absentmindedly tucked some behind his ear, it created a lovely, dark, shiny spray. If she could
only touch that hair. Or that ear. It was large and floppy, with
a hanging, suckable lobe. No earring, thank God. She hated
jewelry on men, except when they wore a shoelace of leather
with a single bead snuggled into the hollow at the base of the
neck. He couldn't be more than twenty-eight.

Betty, thirty-two, studied him as he flipped through the books at the new paperback fiction display table, a mere twenty feet away. She'd noticed that he browsed a lot but rarely bought. Betty assumed he worked or lived nearby and came into the store to kill time on breaks or during bouts of boredom. She'd seen him dozens of times over weeks and weeks of waiting to catch a glimpse. But she'd never spoken to him. She just couldn't.

It would ruin everything. If they spoke, they might become acquaintances, then friends. He'd never be her lover, and a friendship would be too painful for Betty to stand. She far preferred to keep him in his place, inside the carefully constructed fantasies Betty created for the two of them. Her former therapist deemed choosing fantasy over reality unhealthy. Of course it was—but Betty's bad habit was only harmful to herself. And her fantasies were nice. Downright frilly. Lacy, velvety, doilied. She wasn't some nut job who spent hours fantasizing about serial killing, animal torture, and sado-masochism. Plus, her fantasies usually ended with masturbation—the only aerobic activity Betty got. If she were to stop jerking off, she'd probably gain five pounds overnight. Now *that* would be unhealthy.

"What are you looking at?" asked Gertrude, one of Betty's underlings at Burton & Notham. Gert, a Rubenesque forty-five, wore too much makeup and dressed like a thirty-year-old Gap dancer. A natural blonde, she teased her hair up with glittery clips. She was divorced and independently wealthy (family money—her great-grandfather invented the gear-shift mechanism on bicycles). The only reason she took the job at Burton & Notham was the ever-changing, never-waning supply of men who came into the store. Gert stalked them at the magazine aisles on the third floor, hovering by the newsweeklies, *The New Yorker*, car and sport publications and, when she was being obvious about it, the soft-core porn (*Playboy, Penthouse, Maxim*). The strategy worked. Gert got dates.

Betty asked her, "Anything good in the new *Fly-Fishing and Tackle Monthly?*"

Gert said, "He looks dirty." She pointed her rounded chin at Betty's fantasy man.

"I'm just looking," said Betty. "Not smelling."

"Here he comes."

The big-eared guy headed toward the information desk. More peeved than pleased by his approach, Betty knew that her safety zone of twenty feet was about to be violated. Her basic fear, that he would reject her, had a flip side. He could turn out to be such a loser that Betty would have to reject *him*.

He stood two feet away now. Betty asked, "May I help you?"

Gert coughed loudly and sniffed her wrist. She was right. This guy could do himself a favor by browsing in the personal hygiene section. Dear God, the pores, Betty thought. They were massive. He had a trio of pimples on his neck, mingling with several days' worth of stubble. And his hair wasn't shiny, as it had appeared from across the room. It was greasy.

He said, "I was wondering if you had any new books on serial killing, animal torture, or sado-masochism."

Bullocks, she thought. Now it was completely over between them.

Betty said, "True crime and psychology. Second floor."

He said, "I've checked there."

She said, "Then you're out of luck."

"Can't you search the database?" he asked.

Betty looked at him and felt a mixture of sadness and regret. Another fantasy relationship screeching to an end, forcing the usual questions to bubble to the surface. Why couldn't she attempt to meet a worthy man for an actual relationship? Was she really that chicken? She'd have to discuss this with Frieda soon. Her sister would be able to suggest specific steps. She was resolved this time to break the bad habit.

The greasy zit man with the alien Jughead ears pointed at the computer on Betty's desk. "Sometime today?" he asked.

Betty searched the database. Keyword: torture.

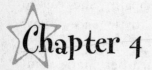

Chapter 4

Monday, September 23
3:03 P.M.

"Mommy!" Justin spotted her and ran toward Frieda, his backpack swinging from side to side. He reached out his arms. It was her cue to brace for impact. He jumped. She caught him mid-flight, his body slamming into her chest, forcing her to step back a pace. Justin was small for his age, only forty pounds, not quite four feet tall. Unlike many of the kids in his kindergarten class, he had yet to lose a tooth. He cried about it at night, demanding answers to life's big questions ("*When* will it happen?" "*Why* hasn't it happened yet?"). Frieda promised him over and over that he would not go off to college with baby teeth, and that if he ate more vegetables they would fall out sooner.

Frieda lowered him to the ground. She waved at his teacher, took his hand and started to leave the garden courtyard at the Packer Collegiate Institute, his private school in Brooklyn Heights. Kindergarten had started almost three weeks ago. Frieda had successfully avoided conversation and eye contact with the other moms at pickup. They meant well with their sympathy. She realized that. But they always looked at her with The Face of Raw Pity. She hated that.

"Frieda! Wait a moment." Justin's teacher, Marie Stanhope, waved and walked toward her. Marie—Ms. Stanhope to Justin—was a cheerful, warm, wonderful teacher who'd been at it for thirty years. She'd seen a thing or two, and had taught fatherless children before. Frieda trusted her as chief ally in Justin's care. He and Marie spent six hours a day together. Almost as much time as Frieda did.

Marie caught up with Frieda, smiling as always. "Justin," she said with her slightly Southern accent, "why don't you go play on the swings for minute while I talk to Mom?"

Justin looked at Frieda, and her eyes told him to go. "We'll just be a minute," said Frieda. Once he was gone, Marie's smile dropped. Frieda sighed. "What happened today?"

"I think we should make an appointment with the school psychologist. Just to talk. Nothing serious."

"Tell me."

Marie's turn to sigh. "We were looking at a book with pictures of the planets and the sun. Justin started talking about his father in heaven, wanting to know where it was in the picture. One of the other boys said that his parents told him heaven didn't exist. Justin insisted that it did. The other boy said that when you're dead, you're dead. And Justin reacted."

Frieda said, "Which kid?"

"It doesn't matter," Marie said. "Justin punched him in the nose."

Frieda asked, "Did it bleed?"

Marie nodded. "I had to notify the child's parents."

Oh, great, though Frieda. Now she was pariah pity widow *and* mother of a violent child. Frieda scanned the court-yard, looking for a kid with a swollen face.

Marie said, "The boy was picked up early."

"Why didn't you call me?" Frieda looked again, trying to figure out which kid was missing. Should she expect an angry phone call tonight from the parents? Probably not, she decided. If anything, the parents should call her to apologize for the insensitivity of their kid.

Marie said, "Justin had a time out. I thought it would be best to let him finish the day."

"Should I call Dr. Schmidt, or will she call me?" Barbara Schmidt. The school psychologist. Frieda met with her briefly when Gregg was first diagnosed, thinking it was the responsible, bases-covered thing to do.

Marie waved Justin back over to his mom. "I'll have Dr. Schmidt call you in the next few days. She may refer you to a therapist outside of school. And talk to Justin tonight. I don't think he'll hit his classmates again if we both make him understand how wrong it is."

"Should I punish him?" asked Frieda, relying on Marie's experience and judgment. She often felt like she had no idea what she was doing. At times, Frieda feared that one good tug would unravel her completely and the contents of her life would spill onto the ground like lipstick and quarters from an overturned pocketbook.

Marie said, "He's already been punished with the time out. Tell him that hitting is wrong, and that if another child says or does something to upset him, that he should tell me or my assistant. We'll handle problems. He doesn't have to."

Justice was the purview of grown-ups. What a comforting idea to present to Justin. Frieda stared at his blond head as he loped back to her, smiling, the incident compartmentalized.

She said, "Home, Justin."

Chapter 5

Friday, September 27
1:00 P.M.

"How's the salad?" he asked.

"It's fine. Good," said Ilene. She'd been picking. Not hungry. Nor had she been an entertaining lunch date. She looked across the table and gave David Isen a radiant smile. "It's wonderful. This is my favorite salad in the entire city of New York."

They were at Café Centro, a midtown two-star restaurant. She'd ordered her usual mixed field greens with olives, cranberries, sundried tomatoes and raspberry vinaigrette—the sight of which usually filled her eyes and heart with desire.

He said, "Starving yourself won't make Peter lose weight." David cut a juicy piece of steak and popped it in his mouth with an audible moan of pleasure. *This is a man who loves meat,* she thought. With his metabolism—and the marathon training—David could eat anything. She'd seen him shirtless a couple of times over the years. His body could have been drawn from an anatomy textbook. Hard shoulders, long legs, chiseled six-pack. Peter had never had a six-pack. His belly looked more like the cooler.

Ilene dropped her fork to rub her temples. "I don't know what I can possibly do," she said. "I've tried talking to him, and he rebels. I've tried not saying anything, and he responds by eating everything in sight. He claims to have no vanity issues about it, but I don't understand how that's possible."

David said, "Give him a break."

She asked, "Sticking up for your gender?"

"Women have no idea what they do to men."

"Explain."

David continued eating, not looking at her directly. "A man considers his love relationship to be the only area of his life that is personal. I see women in the office get upset about some slight from a colleague. Or a snide comment from Mark"—their boss, the editor in chief of *Cash* magazine— "and they fall apart, run crying to the ladies' room. You've run crying to the ladies' room."

"I have not," she said.

"Last year, when he killed your feature on Krispy Kreme."

She blushed. "I had something in my eye."

He laughed. "You had big, salty tears of self-pity in your eye. Mark was embarrassed for you. So was I."

Ilene stabbed an olive. "This talk is really helpful. I feel much better now."

"Mark wrote it off—as I did—because you're a woman.

When you've been insulted, you think it means you're worthless. I saw a woman get upset when a stranger on the street told her she had a fat ass."

That would ruin Ilene's day. "Ridiculous," she said.

"A man takes any kind of insult or criticism, assesses the remark's value, and then takes it for what it's worth. Not for what *he's* worth."

"Any insult."

"Anything."

"You, David," she said, "are an asshole."

He thought about it. "I'm not taking that personally. I've assessed your comment, and rejected it. I don't believe I'm any more of an asshole than I did five seconds ago."

"How convenient for you," she said, a glint in her brown eyes, which she knew were luscious and wanton, having been told so by every boyfriend she'd had since high school. "How convenient for men, how ingenious, to have license to dismiss the opinions of others, people who might know better. For example, if some construction worker, sitting on the curb, eating his lunch from a pail, has a butt-eye view of a woman's behind, he can more accurately judge the size of it than she can—even if she painstakingly examined the area in the mirror while getting dressed. His opinion *does* have value, and a woman values all opinions."

"Giving equal weight to her boss, a construction worker, the manicurist, her friends, and her husband, diluting her own opinion."

"Now you're just being silly," she said. "My manicurist doesn't speak English."

He smiled. His crow's feet appeared like magic. On *his* face, somehow, they made him look younger. Just part of the miracle of David, the physical glory of male. Thank God they were both attached, safely within the protective walls of marriage.

David said, "A man cares, emotionally, about one other person's opinion. Just one. Not his barber or his golf partner. He cares what his wife thinks."

Ilene frequently underestimated her affect on Peter. She wondered, as she often did, whether Peter would take the health risks of his weight more seriously if they had a child. Ilene said, "How's Stephanie's fever?"

"You're changing the subject," said David. "She's fine."

Ilene remembered when David's daughter was born. The whole editorial department of *Cash* visited Georgia and Stephanie at the maternity ward at NYU. Georgia looked exhausted but still beautiful, with her cheekbones and flawless skin. After seeing the joy at the hospital, Ilene went home and announced to Peter that she'd like to get pregnant. Peter confessed that he'd been waiting for her to be ready. That was six years ago. Neither one of them had brought up the subject of fertility treatments.

David said, "I've always liked you, Ilene."

She blushed. She smiled and said, "I've always liked you, too." She took a taste of Sauvignon blanc.

"Georgia and I have been separated for a month."

Ilene choked on the wine, initiating a coughing fit that lasted a solid two minutes. The whole while, David sputtered, "Are you all right? Can I get you anything?"

"What about the other night? You still go out to dinner as a couple?" She didn't understand.

David said, "We made the dinner date before we agreed to separate, and I wasn't ready to tell you the truth. But after that night, we decided to go public. That's been harder than I expected."

Ilene didn't know what to say. Should she offer condolences? Congratulations?

David said, "Mark knows."

Of course, he'd had to tell Mark. She said, "You moved out?"

"I'm living in a furnished apartment on East Thirty-fifth Street. It's small, temporary. Georgia wants to move to Vermont," he said.

"With Stephanie?" asked Ilene. That would be devastating for David.

He nodded. "She can write anywhere"—Georgia was the author of a best-selling book on closet organizing—"and she thinks a country upbringing is healthier for Stephanie. I can't say unequivocally that I disagree. Once she finds a house, we'll sell the apartment." David and Georgia owned a duplex on East 17th Street. A real find. They'd lovingly restored the apartment room by room. It took years. They'd thrown a party to show off their labors not six months ago.

Ilene's mind spun. He moved out, but she was moving to Vermont? What did Stephanie know? Would it be rude to ask for the whole story? She said, "I had no idea anything was wrong."

"I thought for sure you picked up on the tension at dinner," he said.

Ilene hadn't. But now that she was clued in, she did think David looked drawn, as lean and vulnerable as the meat on his plate. She felt a twinge. A tiny hammer with the softest blow struck her in an unlikely place. She crossed and recrossed her legs.

"David," she said gently, "If you'd like to unload on anyone, unload on me." Ilene worried that sounded vaguely sexual. "I mean, if you need to get off on my chest . . . I mean, if you need to get anything off of *your* chest, you can always come on me. *To* me. Come to me. Please. I'm here."

He nodded and said, "Thank you."

"Whatever you need."

"Don't tell anyone at work. I want to do it myself."

"Not a soul."

"You can tell Peter," he said.

"Okay," she said.

"I feel much better," he announced, and dug into the rest of his steak like he hadn't eaten in days. The meat made his lips shiny. Ilene drank her wine. David was a good man. He deserved a good woman. He'd need to meet people, get fixed up. Instantly, she thought of the perfect woman for him. They could start as friends. And see where that led. Unless, of course, they fell in love at first sight, which was not outside the realm of possibility.

David Isen, brother-in-law? It could happen.

Once he'd cleaned his plate and drawn a large mouthful of wine, Ilene said, "So, David. Are you ready to date yet?"

Chapter 6

Wednesday, October 2
11:59 A.M.

Peter returned to his office and sank into his chair. It was a dirty job, firing someone—especially in this dismal economy. Peter felt a wave of acid rise in his gullet. Even in the chill of early October, his collar was damp with sweat. He had issued warning after warning. But at a certain point, when alarm bells don't resonate, and begging failed (literally begging: "Please show up on time, please meet deadlines, please don't fuck up"), Peter had been forced to act.

He hit the intercom on his desk phone. His secretary, Jane Bambo, came in, closed the door behind her, sat down in the chair opposite his desk, and asked, "How'd it go?" Her face—open, features small and scattered—reminded him of a finch. She was a flitting thing, harmless, loyal. Finches returned to nest in the same place, every spring. Jane had been his secretary, seated at the same desk, for five years.

He said, "What's going on out there?"

"Everyone is gathering around Bruce's desk."

"Why is it always the popular ones?" Peter would be distrusted by the staff for a while. Meetings would be tense. But, eventually, things would return to normal. Work was work. Deadlines had to be met.

Jane said, "Bruce was accustomed to getting by on his looks."

"I suppose that happens a lot," he said.

"Don't worry, Peter," said Jane. "It'll never happen to you."

He laughed. Jane smiled at his approval, letting herself giggle a bit, too. The burning sensation in his esophagus dulled. The laughter of a kind woman was potent medicine.

Jane said, "I have menus."

Fanning them like a poker hand, Jane held them out across the desk, silently asking him to pick a menu, any menu. He took them out of her hand, and flipped through the stack, perusing. He said, "Comforting me with food?"

"I'm hungry!" Jane was always hungry. She couldn't weigh more than a hundred pounds and she ate like a horse. She could eat an entire horse every day and not look like one. He envied her. And feared her. Her appetite was part (an extra-large part) of the reason Peter could not reduce.

"What do you know about this Atkins diet?" he asked.

She cocked a thin dark eyebrow. "It works. My friend Linda lost forty pounds in five months."

"Eating what?"

"Bacon, pork chops, steak, eggs, hamburgers, chicken. No pasta, rice, bread, cookies, cake. Some vegetables, but no fruit, juice or alcohol."

"I can manage without fruit," he said. "But no alcohol? No bread? How can people live without bread?"

"Exactly!" she said. "What do you use to sop up the cream sauce?"

The day was shot. Peter was too rattled to do any real work. He had a long list of phone calls to return and a pile of articles to vet. After the strain of the firing, he couldn't focus on anything.

"Did you use the 'three strikes' line?" Jane asked.

He had. "I delivered the speech exactly as we rehearsed. Bruce cut me off right after the 'not my call' part, and started snarling that it *was* my call, that I'd never liked him, that his firing was personal."

"He did not," said Jane.

Peter nodded. "He thinks I was threatened by him. For questioning my judgment in front of other people."

She said, "You did hate that."

"It was the *way* he did it. Not *that* he did it."

"Tone is important."

"Tone is everything," said Peter. "If you speak with respect, you can say just about anything and it'd be okay. I am the boss. Undermining my authority is not to be tolerated."

"Before I forget," said Jane, "your wife called."

Peter said, "Okay."

"What else did Bruce say?" she asked.

"Why did you bring up my wife just then?" Peter asked.

Jane seemed stymied. "What?"

"I was talking about the way Bruce tried to undermine my authority, and you said my wife called."

"She did."

"Jane," he started, "I want your honest opinion. I want your brutally honest opinion. I'm not asking as your boss. I'm asking as a friend. There will be no repercussions or consequences to providing your opinion, which is something I have grown to respect and value deeply."

She said, "Grown to respect? You didn't always?"

He pondered that one. "I have to get to know someone before I deem her trustworthy, intelligent, and insightful. It takes years, decades maybe, to fully appreciate another person's intuitive and analytical . . ."

"Just ask your question," she said, cutting him off.

"Do you think my wife's behavior toward me has changed?"

"Yes." Jane did not hesitate.

"How?" Peter asked to clarify.

She shifted in her chair, trying to get comfortable. It must be a torture to sit on a hard plastic seat, hour after hour, on her bony ass. This was a benign observation, not meant as a criticism. Peter preferred an ass that had some flesh. A rump. Ilene's ass had a nice shape. Curvy, slappable. He recalled one of the mental snapshots of Ilene that had burned themselves into his corneas over the years. He'd returned from the bathroom to find her sleeping nude on her belly, her tush round and sleek in the moonlight. She looked so supernaturally beautiful, he thought she'd disappear in a cloud of smoke if he took one more step toward her.

Jane said, "It's been a gradual change. Over the last year, I guess. She made me swear not to tell you, but she wants me to e-mail her whenever you have something to eat."

He was outraged. "Do you?" he asked.

"I tell her you have a salad every day for lunch, and an afternoon snack of yogurt and strawberries."

Peter said, "She believes that?"

"She wants to," said Jane.

He sighed. Deeply. Hungrily. "I am starving to death."

"Since you value my opinion so highly, I'm going to give it to you straight, Peter," said Jane. "You don't have enough sex."

He laughed. "You're telling me?"

Jane shook her head. "You need to seduce her, romance her."

"I do try to romance her," he said lamely. "I guess I could buy some candles or something."

"Oh, man, have you got a lot to learn. Most women wouldn't care if you bought out the candle department at Pier One. They want oral sex," said Jane. "When's the last time you went down on your wife?"

Peter stammered, flummoxed. The honest answer: He wasn't sure. "As usual, your thoughts are as precise as they are valuable," he said.

She shook her head and said, "Conversation over?"

"And then some," he said. Then, "Take a peek out there." Bruce's desk was only ten feet from Peter's office. He could hear the staff, milling, murmuring. There was a conspiratorial, muffled lowness to their voices.

Jane cracked Peter's office door and peered out. She closed it immediately. "They all looked up when they heard the door open."

Peter sighed. "Let's go with Big City Deli. Pastrami on rye. Fries extra crispy, gravy on the side. Lemon meringue pie. And a diet Coke."

"I'll have the same," said Jane.

Chapter 7

Wednesday, October 9
8:30 A.M.

"Just coffee, thanks," said Betty to Frieda. Her sister loved to push a big breakfast on her, but Betty refused every time. She just couldn't eat in the morning. She'd read a million times that having a solid morning meal would prevent excessive afternoon snacking and/or 10 P.M. pig-outs. Betty once calculated that she consumed 50 percent of her daily calories in the two hours before bedtime: the absolute worst eating pattern. If one cared about that sort of thing.

Betty had spent the night in Brooklyn Heights to help Frieda with Justin. She spent a night a week at her sister's. Made her feel useful. Frieda clearly enjoyed the company and the extra pair of hands for cooking and picking up toys. Betty didn't know how Frieda got through her days as a single working mother. With all the life insurance money, Frieda could afford to hire a regular baby-sitter. She refused, saying that the last thing Justin needed right now was to be foisted off on some stranger who didn't love him, and that he liked hanging out at the framing studio after school. Betty thought both mother and son needed play dates with like-aged friends. Their family of two was already too small, too isolated.

Betty would never voice her concerns to Frieda. It was not her business. She downed her coffee and put her mug in the sink. Frieda's kitchen in the Henry Street brownstone co-op was full of light, the orange of autumn morning. Out the window, from where she sat at the fifties-diner style green linoleum-topped table, Betty stared at the fiery red leaves of a maple tree. The tree was turning, some leaves hanging on, struggling for another day. In two weeks, they'd all be gone, and Betty would look out that window at bare-naked branches. She turned toward Frieda, who was rinsing cereal bowls and putting them in the dishwasher. Justin was complaining about the content of his lunchbox. Frieda promised him they'd go shopping after school to get the good kind of peanut butter.

Betty said to her nephew, "Don't you have therapy after school on Wednesdays?"

"That's right," said Frieda. "I'll do a food shop during lunch."

"Therapy again?" asked Justin. "I went last week."

"You go every week," said Frieda.

"For how long?" asked Justin.

"Until the insurance runs out."

Betty asked, "Do you like your therapist?"

Justin shrugged. "She's okay. I just sit there and draw. She tries to get me to talk about my *feelings*." He said the word like it was covered in slimy mucus.

Betty, marveling how early emotional retardation started in men, asked Justin, "You don't like to talk about your feelings?"

"Do you?" asked Justin in return.

Frieda laughed. "Insightful little beast, isn't he?" she said.

The three of them left the apartment, and went to school. After drop-off, Betty accompanied Frieda on the short walk to her shop. Betty noticed that men on the street looked at Frieda. Men had always looked at Frieda.

Betty said, "You've got a birthday coming up."

"The big three six," said Frieda, nodding.

"Can I take you to dinner?"

"It's not for a couple of months," said Frieda. "You might have a hot date that night."

Betty scoffed. "You might, too."

"Right," said Frieda.

They arrived at the gallery. Frieda fit the key into the lock and said, "Can you come in for a few minutes?"

Betty checked her watch. She was supposed to be at Burton & Notham in an hour. A guy was coming in from corporate to start working on audio-book-sample machines. It was a new initiative for Burton & Notham. Taking a cue from music retail superstores like Tower and HMV that had freestanding kiosks with earphones to hear sample cuts from CDs, her store, a flagship in Manhattan, was among the dozen nationwide to set up booths so customers could listen to five-minute snippets of books on tape. Betty was irked by the intrusion. She had no idea where these booths were going to go, and annoyed by the invasion of strange personnel.

"I've got five minutes," said Betty. "And, actually, I've been wanting to talk to you about something."

Frieda held open the gallery door. Betty entered, and took her usual seat in front of the counter. She looked around the shop first, admiring the work of a new photographer.

She said, "You wouldn't think a fresh perspective of the Brooklyn Bridge was possible," pointing at a hanging print.

Frieda said, "It's for sale. Two hundred bucks. But I'll give it to you for one ninety-nine."

"One-dollar discount for sisters?"

"I'm not in business to lose money," she said. They both laughed. The Sol Gallery was usually in the red. But money wasn't Frieda's problem.

"What did you want to talk about?" asked Frieda as she took a seat behind the counter. "I have *got* to clean this place up. Look at this dust." She dragged a fingertip along the top of her computer monitor.

Betty steeled herself for complete honesty. "I haven't had a boyfriend in three years."

Frieda nodded. "We've noticed."

"Let's leave Ilene out of this," said Betty. "I don't think her full-court-press approach works for someone with my subtle needs."

"I'd say your needs are as subtle as a sledgehammer, but I'm happy to keep this conversation between us," said Frieda.

Betty paused. "You don't know how lucky you are," she said finally. "Okay, not so lucky with the dead husband. But you must realize that you attract men by breathing. You could have your pick, even now in your low-grade depression. After Gregg's funeral, I jokingly told Gert that you'll probably remarry before I manage to get a date. And then I realized: That's no joke. It's a fucking travesty."

"So you want me to stop breathing?" asked Frieda.

"I want you to breathe some of that good stuff on me," said Betty. "Teach me your magic ways. Give me the list of ten things I need to do to win the perfect man. I've got a pen in my purse. Let me dig it out. Okay. I'm ready. Go."

Frieda stared at Betty. She didn't like the look in her older sister's eyes. It verged on the weepy. A Gregg-reflection warning. Betty put her pen down, and said, "Go ahead."

"I can't help it."

"Just go," said Betty.

"I'm thinking about the first time I met Gregg. At his friend's cousin's roommate's party."

"Continue," said Betty, hurrying her sister along.

"We were introduced by the cousin's roommate," she said. "And didn't leave each other's side for nine years. I can't tell you how to win a perfect man. But I do know what it feels like to meet him."

Betty said, "Heat, passion, desire. I feel that all the time when I see hot guys. But nothing ever happens."

"Because you do nothing about it," said Frieda correctly. "When you meet the right guy, you won't have a choice."

"My legs will walk toward him, driven by a power I can't control, arms raised with hunger, eyes gleaming."

"You won't turn into a zombie," said Frieda. "But you will be compelled to act."

Betty asked, "How will I know I'm compelled?"

Her older sister shook her head. "You've never felt compelled?"

Not that she could recall. "Of course I have," said Betty. "Just refresh my memory of that unforgettable feeling."

"When you meet a man who compels you, you feel a slap across the face," said Frieda. "Not a real slap. It's figurative."

"The slap of lust?" asked Betty. "That's what you're giving me? For that, I expose my vulnerabilities to the light of day and will be twenty minutes late to work?" Betty felt lust all the time, and had never been compelled. "I am sorely disappointed in you, Frieda. I'm not coming to you again for any of this so-called wisdom."

"Did you really tell Gert I'd get married before you got a date?" asked Frieda.

"That makes you feel better, doesn't it?" asked Betty. She stood, gave Frieda a hug and left.

The subway was crowded, uncomfortably so. Betty hated being pushed and jabbed by backpacks and briefcases. By the time she got to Burton & Notham, her mood was black. The store was busy, as always, people milling around, messing up the neat stacks of books. She took the elevator to the third floor.

Gert was in her office, answering the phone. Betty closed the door, put her purse in the bottom drawer of her desk and locked it. "Thanks for opening," Betty said. "Did the audio-books-booth guy show up?"

Gert, radioactive in pink angora, said, "Not yet. Your brother-in-law called."

For a split second, Betty thought she meant Gregg. He used to call her regularly to order books and CDs. Betty got a 30 percent discount on all titles, and for Gregg, she was always glad to exercise her perk. Every month, when he came in to pick up his order, he'd take her to lunch or out for a drink to thank her. They'd talk about Justin, or mock Frieda's fastidiousness (her love affair with Ajax, her obsession with nesting bowls). They complained about their jobs (Gregg had been a vice president at a direct-marketing firm; he proudly referred to himself a "pur-veyor of high-quality junk"). The hour would fly, and then he'd have to go, always pressed for time between work and family. Betty would leave the restaurant or bar with him, and watch him jog toward the subway on his long, bowed legs.

Betty said, "Peter called? What does he want?"

"He left his cell."

"I have it somewhere."

A knock on the door. Betty said, "Come in."

In he came. The air in the small room ionized on contact with his body, as if all the microscopic floating particles of dust stood still, and then sank paralyzed to the carpet. He put on a friendly salesman smile, clearly accustomed to introducing himself to strangers. And he spoke. "I'm Earl Long. Are you Betty Schast?"

She nodded silently.

He waited for a reply, but not too long, before he said, "You knew I was coming today, right?"

She said, "Audio-book booths."

"I'm the man."

Gert introduced herself. He held out his hand to give her a shake. Earl Long's fingers were long; his hands square and clean. Gert asked him if he needed coffee. He reached into his wallet, took out two dollars and said to Betty, "You look like you have some loose ends. I'll get coffee and give you few minutes before we talk, all right?"

Betty nodded, as helplessly paralyzed as the dust on the floor. Gert gave her a mystified look and offered to usher Mr. Long to the store's café. They left together, blessedly closing the door behind them.

Alone now, Betty shook herself loose of the spell. So that was the sting of a compelling slap. Now she knew. Betty could hear the sound of it reverberating in her ears. And she would have to work with Earl Long every day for a couple of months. She'd have to talk to him. Get to know him. Spend time in his compelling presence.

It would be agony.

# Chapter 8

Wednesday, October 9
10:19 A.M.

Betty had left a half hour ago, and Frieda hadn't moved. She couldn't get her mind off that night, when she had met Gregg for the first time. The unfairness of his death never let up. Her happiest memories had become her most painful ones. She had to admit, the sadness had lightened as the months passed. These days, she could think back on his illness and not feel completely devastated. She believed that, one day in the future, she might be able to reflect on that time without feeling any pain at all. Although it would probably be a relief to block it all, she was duty-bound to remember. Justin would want to know every detail. Perhaps the worst of it for Frieda was that Justin wouldn't have a father. It put him at a terrible disadvantage. Maybe she would remarry, and Justin would have a stepdad. But she couldn't imagine that happening for years.

The gallery door opened. A welcome distraction from

her thoughts. She looked up and smiled at the man who'd entered. He smiled at her. Friendly enough. He walked among the racks and bins of photos and posters, casually looking, but without the intention of buying. She didn't want to make him feel self-conscious, so Frieda turned on her computer and checked e-mail, headlines, movement in the Dow.

After about three minutes, she looked up. The man continued to browse. She let herself examine him, slyly, out of the corner of her eye. Medium height, slim build. He was young. Not yet 30, she guessed. Chocolate-brown hair with eyes to match, dark brows, and sideburns were a striking contrast to his fair skin.

He caught her looking and smiled again. Flustered, she immediately looked back at her computer screen. Thinking the better of it—he was a customer and she needed business—she said, "May I help you?"

Grateful for the invitation, he stepped toward her at the counter. She could appraise him openly now. He wore a black fleece pullover, loose khakis and engineer boots. His dark hair was a bit wild. He needed a haircut, but she liked the way it stuck out wildly as if he were a mad scientist. His hands were in his pockets, fists, she could tell by the way the khaki material protruded. His eyes were so dark, she couldn't see his pupils. They looked almost fake, like doll's eyes, until he smiled, and then they came fully to life. His skin, tight and springy, pulled snuggly over the bump of cheekbone and sharp slice of jaw. Not a sign of wrinkles. His nose was prominent, aquiline, distinctive, a centerpiece. His mouth was red with a faint line running vertically on the bottom lip. She gazed at it, following that line from the top to the bottom and back up again.

He said, "Do I have something stuck in my teeth?" He smiled, showing her his incisors. "You were staring at my mouth."

She was? "What can I do for you?" she asked, slightly embarrassed.

Reaching into his backpack, he removed a newspaper page and laid it on the counter.

Frieda read, "*New York Times*, October eighth. Yesterday. The theater review?"

He nodded. "I'd like it framed. Something simple. And when I say *simple*, I mean inexpensive."

She picked up the paper and quickly read the review. It was of a production of the musical *Oliver!*, playing at City Center, a medium-size theater/concert hall in the East mid-50s. According to the review, the show's run would end in three weeks. The notice was positive. Just the facts (who plays who, when, and where). Only about four hundred words—several column inches—written by a man named Boris Graves.

"Are you Boris Graves? The writer?" she asked. "Your first piece in the *Times?*"

He said, "I'm in the show."

Frieda glanced again at the short review. The critic had made special mention of the actor playing Billy Sykes. Betty read aloud, " 'Lester Showfield as Bill Sykes is a bastion of masculine aggression: enthralling, captivating and animalistically sexy."

The man said, "Lester Showfield is a bastion of queenly gayness. I'm not him."

Frieda looked again. The only other actor to get particular notice played the part of Fagin. A guy named Sam Hill (poor bastard). She read aloud, "Sam Hill uses his considerable talents to accentuate the thieving Fagin's grubby, sniveling wretchedness. He gives a stand-out performance, the most despicable and filthy portrayal since Ron Moody's Academy Award-winning turn in 1968."

The man said, " 'Despicable and filthy.' It's like music to my ears."

"You are Sam Hill?" she said. She couldn't imagine this handsome, immaculate young man playing the part of a sniveling, grubby wretch.

Sam bowed slightly. "Now tell me what you recommend. In the decidedly simple range."

Frieda showed him a modest black wood frame, a half inch thick. She recommended a gray mat, a shade darker than the newspaper. He seemed to think it looked good. She gave him a quote.

"*Fifty bucks?*" he asked.

"You can't get a custom frame for less, I'm afraid," said Frieda. He bristled at $50? *Off-Broadway acting must not be terribly lucrative,* she thought.

Sam said, "Okay. I'll do it. Can I pay later?"

"I'll need half now," she said.

He frowned and said, "I can give you twenty."

"That's fine. Should take a week or so. I'll get in touch with you when it's ready. If you'll please give me your address, phone number and birth date."

He asked, "Why do you need my birth date?"

"So I know how old you are," she said. She'd felt compelled to ask.

Sam Hill smiled broadly. He squinted at the same time, obviously wondering if he'd walked into more than just a frame store. She blinked a few times, giving him the eyelash treatment. The old reflexes were kicking in.

"I'm at a loss," he said.

"Frieda Schast," she said, introducing herself.

"And your birth date?" he asked.

"You first."

"I'm twenty-eight. Nearly twenty-nine," he said.

"Thirty-five. Nearly thirty-six."

"We're one year apart," he said.

"One dog year," she said.

He grinned at her for getting it. She loved his mouth. She could suck the line off that lip.

"You're flirting with me," he said, "I'm flattered. From the waist up, you are an extremely attractive woman."

Her cheeks flushed bright red instantly. "That's a courageous statement," she said. "From the waist down, I could be monstrous."

"Show me," he said.

Frieda took the challenge, acutely aware of only one thing: She didn't want Sam Hill to leave. She was having the most fun she'd had in over a year. The only fun she'd had in over a year. She stepped out from behind the counter and stood in front of this Sam Hill person, and allowed him to inspect her.

"Twirl, if you please," he said, his finger making a circle in the air.

She did. The sleeves of her shirt ruffled, her hair lifting off her shoulders. He watched her, taking as much pleasure in her performance as she did in giving it.

Sam said, "Stand still, please."

Doing as she was told, he walked a circle around her, clucking along the way. Finally, he stopped in front of her and said, "You look good." And then asked, "Shall I?" He made a circle with his finger again.

"Once around," she said.

He turned slowly, giving her a good two seconds to check out his ass, which was, most definitely, not a day over twenty-eight years old. He made it all the way around, and they stood toe-to-toe.

He asked, "Have you had coffee yet?"

She said, "I have."

"Breakfast?"

"Yes."

"Lunch?"

"It's ten in the morning."

"I can come back in a few hours."

Frieda wanted to say yes. "I have to do a food shop at lunchtime."

"Dinner?" he asked.

A date offer. One she wanted to say yes to. But she

wouldn't feel right unless he knew what he was getting himself into. Then again, revealing her personal history might kill his interest instantly. It was a risk she'd have to take. If he couldn't handle her circumstances—kissable lips or not—he wasn't worth her time.

She said, "I can't have dinner on such short notice. I'm not sure if I can line up baby-sitting. I have a son. Justin. He's five."

Sam paused. Considering. She watched him closely. He didn't seem to shrink back in horror.

"Divorced?" he asked.

She took a deep breath. "Widowed."

"I'm sorry to hear that," he said.

Frieda realized suddenly that this was the first time she'd thought of Gregg since Sam Hill walked into the gallery. She looked hard at his face, at the dark hair and eyes, the skin.

"Oh my God," she said.

"Is something wrong?" he asked.

"You're not Not Gregg."

"Pardon?" he asked.

He was not Not Gregg. He was Sam. She stared into *his* face, and saw *his* features, and wasn't thinking about Gregg. She felt a cracking in her mind, a field of ice breaking, calving, fresh air rising from the fissure. Frieda took a deep breath.

"You have a very strange expression on your face," said Sam.

She was all pins and needles, the physical result of waking up from an emotional coma. "Strange how?" she asked.

He said, "You look like you've been slapped across the face."

"You don't say," Frieda intoned.

"I do say," he responded.

She examined him, this man who'd just walked into her life and changed her outlook in minutes. She'd been right about being taken by surprise.

Frieda said, "I know we've just met, and that my circumstances are probably intimidating to you. This may seem like a preposterous suggestion, especially so early in the morning. You haven't had your coffee yet. You may think of me as an ancient crone."

"Actually, you're quite the fox," he said. "And, to be completely honest, which doesn't endear me to most women, I'm not afraid of you because you've had hard times. I'm afraid of people who haven't."

Frieda was impressed. Not many young men—not many men—would like the fact that she had a son and a dead husband to contend with. Sam interrupted her thoughts, and said, "So what was your suggestion?"

"Let's kiss."

He stumbled back in mock horror. He laughed at his own theatrics. "You widowed mothers don't waste time."

She shook her head. "We don't. Wasting time falls under the category of 'Have I Learned Nothing from Gregg's Death?.' "

"That must be a long list," he said.

She nodded. Sam stepped toward her, lowered his head and very sweetly pecked her on the mouth. Frieda licked her lips afterward, to grab the taste on her tongue. Sam watched her.

She said, "More, please."

He put his hands on her shoulders, and leaned in for a real kiss. It knocked her socks, shoes, and pants off. Would have, anyway, had they more privacy.

He broke away for a breath and said, "There is one thing you should know about me before we go on," he said.

Dreading the worst, she asked, "You have cancer?"

"I am in perfect health," he assured her. "And I have great medical insurance through Actors Equity."

"What then?" she asked.

He said, "I'm from Maine."

Chapter 9

Tuesday, October 15
5:44 P.M.

Peter should have worn a heavier jacket. New York went from summer to winter overnight. What happened to fall? When had the middle ground given way to extremes? He wrapped his suit jacket as tightly around his girth as he could, feeling the tug across his back, fearful he might tear the seams. He had to rush, having promised his sister-in-law, Betty, that he'd get from his office in midtown to the Union Square Burton & Notham by 6 P.M. to pick up his order of books, namely *The Zone* and *Dr. Atkins' New Diet Revolution*. He would attempt a life without bread for a week, but first he would read all about it.

He walked quickly out of his office building on Madison Avenue and 45th Street, past the Cosi sandwich shop, the Sugar 'n' Spice pie shop, and the seven street vendors outside of Grand Central Station selling hot knishes, beef on skewers, pralines and hot dogs. The scents shot into his brain like bullets, hitting all his hunger receptors. With superhuman strength, he avoided the temptations and pushed through the revolving doors into Grand Central.

Blessed warmth. The relief made him shudder. He hurried along a passageway, intending to take the escalator (past Michael Jordan's Steakhouse and the Cucina takeout) to a subway platform. But first, a quick stop at the Hudson News. He loved New York newsstands, especially this one. It was massive, selling hundreds, maybe thousands, of journals, papers, and magazines. When he'd been promoted to editor of *Bucks,* he'd come to Hudson News every lunch hour to watch if people bought the magazine. If they flipped through it, he wanted to know which articles made them stop. Good research, he thought. More useful than the contrived focus groups where housewives were paid $50 to bash his hard work while he watched behind a two-way mirror.

He did a quick scan by the financial journals. Miraculously, a fantastically attractive woman—the whole package: blonde, tight as a tiger in a leather skirt, black boots up to her knees—was reading his magazine. It was like the opening to a *Penthouse* "forum" letter. He could approach her, introduce himself as the editor of *Bucks*. She'd be impressed, worshipful—an aspiring young business writer looking for her break into publishing. She'd be eager to please, and who was Peter to discourage her?

He leaned against the wall of sports and fitness titles, pretending to read *Shape,* and let his imagination take over. She was incredible, legs as long and curvy as a river. And she'd stopped flipping to read an article on municipal bonds that Peter himself had written. A hot woman, reading his words (not moving her lips), with the crease of concentration on her otherwise unlined forehead. He had to arrange his shoulder bag to hide a growing erection.

Beautiful women, they had to know men stopped to stare. How could they not? With the sweep of his eyes, Peter realized he wasn't the only man at the newsstand pretending to read a magazine for the momentary pleasure of beholding this woman. In fact, three others, dressed just like Peter, were rearranging their shoulder bags in front of their trousers. As he made this deflating (literally) discovery, the blonde turned a page of the magazine, her eyes rising to find him in full gawk. Peter could have caught his heart in his hand when she winked at him.

Logically, he knew the wink meant "Busted!" But, with eternal optimism, Peter let himself believe she wanted him. The thought was both emasculating (was he man enough to make a move?) and exciting. His erection doubled in size, lifting his bag off his hips.

He really needed more sex.

"Excuse me, Mr. Vermillion?"

He turned toward the small voice that came over his right shoulder. She was petite, brunette, vaguely familiar, not altogether unattractive. He glanced back to see the blonde tiger put the magazine back in the rack and click off in her man-killer boots toward the elevators.

He said looked down at brunette and asked, "Have we met?"

"Forgive me for interrupting your *reading*," she said. He realized with an embarrassed start that he'd been holding *Shape* upside down.

"It's quite all right," he said, fumbling to close the magazine.

She said, "I followed you from your office. We've met a few times. I'm Bruce McFarthing's wife."

Wife of the man he'd fired. "Mrs. McFarthing," he said. "Of course I remember you."

She smiled ruefully. She knew he'd forgotten her. "I'd like to speak to you about my husband."

Peter said, "I have to get downtown."

She said, "Bruce is threatening to sue you for discrimination."

"Have his lawyers call our lawyers." Talk about climatic extremes: His mood went from red hot to ice cold in seconds.

She said, "He said you were jealous of him. He feels he's been discriminated against because he's fit and handsome."

"I don't have time for this," said Peter. This woman followed him from his office to threaten a lawsuit and call him an insecure egomaniac? Discrimination on the grounds that Bruce was too attractive? Peter felt a tightness in his chest. He wondered if he were having a pre-heart attack, if such a thing existed.

She put her hand on his elbow, stopping him from clutching his chest. "Bruce said the same thing about his last three bosses."

Bruce was insane. Peter had been right to fire him. God

knows what kind of trouble the magazine would be in if he'd let Bruce stay on staff. Peter said, "If Bruce wants to pursue legal action . . ."

"I'm not threatening you," she said. "I just want to know the truth."

He said, "I fired him because of the quality of his work."

"You read his clips when you hired him," she said.

He didn't want to get into the detailed explanation. Good clips could mean good writing—or good editing. You could never be sure. Peter said, "His clips were not extraordinary. He came across well. I thought he could fit in at the magazine. He had great references."

"So you hired him because he made a good first impression. So why did you fire him?"

Grossly aware that any word out of his mouth could come back to him in court, Peter said, "I can't say anything."

Mrs. McFarthing (he tried desperately to remember her first name) started to cry. At full volume. Her face reddening with each rattling wail, she teetered in her low heels and leaned against Peter's bulk for balance. Arms limp and impotent at his sides, he allowed her to wipe her wet eyes and nose against his tie. The contact was excruciating.

He said, "Please, Mrs. McFarthing."

"I'm beginning to wonder if the man I married is all style, no substance," she said through her tears.

"How long have you been married?" Peter couldn't help asking.

"Fifteen years."

That was a long time to begin to wonder. His style was, apparently, good enough for the first fifteen years. Peter thought instantly whether his own substance had a shelf life to Ilene. Was there a point when a woman—any woman—started to want what she didn't think she had?

Peter said, "Look, Mrs. McFarthing, I'd be happy to make some calls on his behalf."

"Don't bother," she said, lifting her face off his tie. She brushed the tears away with the back of her hand. When she looked up, shamed by her outburst, confused about what she'd do next, Peter saw a vulnerability that was, actually, quite terrifying.

She said, "My name is Peggy."

He shook. "Peter."

"I know," she said, sniffing. "Sorry about your tie."

"Bruce will find a job," he lied.

"I'm sure he will. For as long as that one lasts." Peggy took a mirror out of her purse. She looked at her eyes. She snapped the compact closed, startling Peter.

"I look terrible," she said.

"You're fine," he said.

She *was* fine. A fine-looking woman, but not beautiful or sexy. Bruce had chosen Peggy over what must have been an endless supply of sexy women. Maybe Peggy was brilliant, or rich.

Peter asked, "Are you also a writer?"

Peggy said, "I'm a nutritionist."

"You help people diet?"

"Yes," she said, regaining composure.

"My wife would like me to lose twenty pounds."

Peggy said, "I'd say forty."

Okay, he really had to go now. "Good luck with everything," he said.

"You, too, Mr. Vermillion," she said. "You're going to need it."

Chapter 10

Thursday, October 17
8:12 P.M.

The three sisters sat together at Bouillabaisse, a tiny bistro near Ilene's apartment in Chelsea, for their monthly dinner/ agenda meeting. The restaurant's menu changed nightly and was written in script on a chalkboard that the waiter had to lug from table to table. No liquor license. Diners could bring their own wine. Ilene had selected both the vintage ('01 Shiraz) and the place. Betty noticed that whenever it was Ilene's turn to choose, she always picked a place in her own neighborhood.

They all met at Ilene and Peter's expansive Chelsea apartment first. Betty came up from the East Village with Peter's package of books. He'd apologized again about blowing her off last week, and asked if he could take her to lunch to make it up to her. Betty had never had a solo meal with Peter. She hesitated, wondering what the two would say to each other for an hour. But Peter had insisted. Betty was stuck. She thought he was decent enough, but they'd never had much of a bond.

Frieda and Justin arrived next from Brooklyn. Peter and Justin settled in to watch the World Series. Betty had to admit, Peter was brilliant with Justin. He'd offered to step up after Gregg died, and he had, taking Justin to Knicks games, accompanying Frieda to parent-teacher conferences. Ilene must like seeing him with Justin, too. She kissed her husband on the forehead, and the sisters took off for Bouillabaisse.

Everyone was in a good mood tonight, thought Betty. She smiled across the table at Frieda in a blossom pink sweater. Ilene was in her usual black, but her dress was flirty linen. Betty considered her own baggy T-shirt and jeans. Not flirty. But comfortable, as was her aim.

Ilene took the lead. "Shall I read the minutes from our last meeting?" she said.

Betty groaned. "For once, can we just sit down to dinner without the framework of a social-club agenda?"

"I have an announcement to make," said Frieda.

Ilene and Betty turned toward her. Frieda was smiling so hard, Betty feared her jaw might unhinge.

"I've met a man," said Frieda. "He's from Maine!"

"Maine?" said Ilene. "How masculine. He must know how to build a fire and trudge through ice in snowshoes."

"He came into the store," said Frieda. She told them the story of meeting Sam Hill, reciting the *Times* review from memory, giving some biographical details.

"He's Catholic?" asked Ilene.

"Oldest of six," said Frieda. "Non-practicing. Disdainfully so."

"Thank God for that," said the oldest of three.

"I like it," said Frieda. "It's different."

"Well, we can't all be New York Jews," said Ilene.

"Of the disdainfully nonpracticing variety," Betty said. "Can we get back to the kissing part?"

Frieda blushed. "It started with a peck. And then moved to a full-blown, slobbering kiss. He grabbed me, squeezed the pulp out of me, and then mauled my mouth. He totally took me over, which was such a shock because his first kiss was just that little peck. I thought he might be shy or passive. Boy, was I wrong. We went at it like that for fifteen, twenty minutes. And then someone came in and we had to stop."

The way she punched each word—*went at it*—made Betty jealous beyond measure. She doubted that, in her fumbling sexual encounters, she'd ever *gone at it* with ferocity.

Betty said, "He walks in to get something framed, and inside of ten minutes, you're making out? Why does this never happen to me?" Betty felt Ilene watching her dip a piece of baguette into a dish of garlic-infused olive oil and pop it into her mouth.

Frieda said, "I am floating on a cloud. I see rainbows in street puddles. I have been sprinkled with magic dust. He is absolutely adorable! I keep thinking of what Mom told me the night before I married Gregg. She said, 'At the end of the day, only one thing matters in a marriage: When you sit down to dinner and look across the table at your husband, you think he's cute.' "

Ilene laughed. "She told me the same thing."

"I always thought Gregg was cute," said Frieda.

In unison, Betty and Ilene said, "Very cute."

Frieda nodded. "Sam Hill is of a different order. He has a face people pay to watch. A quick look and he seems almost ordinary. And then, if you look again, he's stunning."

"Did he go from ordinary to stunning before or after the mouth mauling?" asked Betty.

"I'm thrilled for you, Frieda," said Ilene. "You need to have fun. And the timing couldn't be better. Sam Hill is the ideal transitional man. Totally inappropriate marriage material. He's like a trial run. And when you're ready to get serious, I have the perfect man to fix you up with. He's a guy from work, recently separated but not ready to date yet. In six months—you'll have had your fill of Sam Hill by then—my guy will be raring to go. I could not have planned this better myself."

Frieda said, "I wouldn't say that Sam Hill is inappropriate marriage material."

"Of course he is," said Ilene. She laughed. "You can't honestly say that you have high hopes for a lasting relationship with him. Just enjoy the hell out of it for what it is. And when you're ready for more, I'll set you up."

Betty watched the frown appear on Frieda's face. Clearly, Frieda was smitten, regardless of Sam Hill's marriage worthiness. That must have been some kiss.

Betty said, "You don't know what's going to happen,

Ilene. I'm sure Frieda isn't thinking about Sam Hill's future prospects. She's living in the moment."

"Exactly," said Frieda. "I'm focused on right now. Six months down the road, who knows? That was the amount of time between Gregg's diagnosis and death. None of us has any idea where we'll be in six months, who we'll be with, what we'll be doing. But right now, all I want is to see Sam Hill again."

Betty said, "When will that be?"

Frieda answered, "Next week. He has performances every night."

Betty said, "That seems like a long time to wait."

Ilene said, "Waiting is the downside of living in the moment."

"I can do it. I've waited over a year for someone to make my heart beat faster. I can go for one more week. I do worry, though. He might get a load of me naked and think, 'Am I fucking my mother?' "

"You're seven years apart, not seventeen," said Betty.

Ilene added, "A penniless itinerant actor? He's lucky to stand next to you on line for the bus. Besides which, if *you're* old, what does that make me?"

Betty said, "Older."

Ilene said, "Let's drink to that."

The women drank. They refilled the glasses, killing the bottle—and they hadn't even ordered their entrees. This happened every time. Frieda offered to run to the wine store a half block away. She grabbed her purse and hurried to the door.

The oldest and youngest sisters remained. As soon as Frieda was out of earshot, Ilene said, "You know Sam Hill isn't going to last. He's nothing like Gregg. Where's the compatibility?"

Betty dipped another crust of bread into the olive oil. She knew Ilene was watching her soak up the golden puddle of fat and calories. Betty said, "The whole stepfather thing. I don't see this twenty-eight-year-old filling Gregg's shoes there. He's just too young to deal with that kind of responsibility."

"Exactly," said Ilene. "So you agree with me."

Betty nodded. "I agree that Sam Hill won't be around in a year. But we disagree about . . ."

"We'd have to disagree about something."

"Let this run its course," warned Betty. "If you try to steer Frieda away from Sam Hill, she'll cling even tighter to him. It's all premature anyway. She hasn't had a date with him yet."

"But she's set on him," said Ilene. "She wants him, so she'll have to have him. But I know enough to be discreet. There are ways to dissuade her without overt criticism. Planting seeds, that kind of thing."

"Evil gardening?" asked Betty.

"How's *your* love life?" asked Ilene.

Frieda had rushed back in, bottle in a brown bag, able to catch that last part. "How *is* your love life, Betty?" she asked.

The conversation now focused on her, Betty drained her glass before speaking. "Okay. Here's the thing."

"The thing is . . ." prompted Frieda.

"The thing is," said Betty, "I like a guy."

Ilene and Frieda pounced on the morsel of candor. "Who is he?" asked Frieda.

"His name is Earl Long," she started. "He works at Burton & Notham, but only temporarily. He's setting up audiobooks booths. I guess he's in his mid-thirties. I have no clue about his religion, background, status, financial standing."

Betty tried to sound casual about it, even though she was obsessed with Earl Long. Her thoughts chased him around Burton & Notham like a panting dog. If he stepped into the bathroom at work, she imagined following him in, locking the stall door, and assaulting him. If he sat down at the café for a sandwich or coffee, Betty pictured joining him, sneaking her fingers onto his thigh for a squeeze.

Frieda asked, "Does he know you like him?"

Betty nearly laughed. "No way." She avoided him whenever possible. Their conversations were terse, businesslike. Betty's attraction overwhelmed her, and she couldn't muster a degree of warmth in his presence. She'd been aware of the tendency since high school: Out of fear, she treated the boys she liked with disdain. In return, they hated her. Their rejection emptied her of confidence, a void she filled with Ring Dings. She had put on five pounds since Earl appeared in her office. Despite the mini-chats she had with herself (e.g., *"You know you're eating this Big Mac because Earl Long pays more attention to Starr, the eighteen-year-old cashier, than he does to you*), Betty was powerless to stop herself.

"Does he like you?" Ilene asked.

"How should I know?" In the two weeks he'd been on site, Earl had touched her once, to get her attention. She'd been supervising a delivery at the store's 17th-Street rear entrance, clipboard in hand. His touch on her shoulder had surprised her so much that she dropped the clipboard, alarming the delivery man, who asked if she was having a seizure. She couldn't meet Earl's eyes afterward. He apologized five times for surprising her, forgetting, in his embarrassment for her, what he'd wanted in the first place. And he hadn't dared touch her again.

Ilene said, "Are you set on him?"

Betty was afraid to say yes. If she admitted it to her sisters, the risk of failure and rejection tripled, quadrupled in a mere second. Frieda could plunge into a relationship with Sam because she had an excellent track record with boyfriends. She seemed unafraid. Then again, after what she'd been through with Gregg, what could be worse? Betty had a long history of failure. But only experience could change that.

She would take inspiration from Frieda. Betty said, "Yes. I'm set on him."

Ilene slammed her hand on the table and declared, "Then you'll have to have him. Do you have a plan?"

God, no. "My plan," said Betty, "is to do absolutely nothing."

Ilene shook her head. "That won't work."

Frieda said, "Have you considered asking him out?"

Betty choked on her wine at the question.

At that moment, the waiter appeared, dragging the

chalkboard menu with him. He described the night's fare, and the sisters placed their orders: Frieda asked for the salmon steak; Ilene, grilled chicken with rosemary; Betty, filet mignon with pepper cream sauce and mashed sweet potatoes on the side.

Once the waiter was gone, Ilene said, "If you truly want this man, you should rethink your order." Betty felt the blow in her solar plexus. After laying herself belly-up and vulnerable, Betty couldn't believe Ilene would give her shit. Then again, when it came to the subject of weight, Ilene was relentless.

"Ilene, don't," said Frieda.

The oldest sister said, "Isn't the whole point of these dinners to help each other? To lay out our problems and work as a team to solve them?"

Frieda said, "It's been the unspoken objective, but now that you've described it like that, the whole idea seems contrived."

Betty said, "We haven't dissected your problems, Ilene. What can we help you with? How's Peter? Your marriage? Any luck getting *him* to lose weight?"

Ilene said, "I'm sorry that I've upset you, Betty. But if you would stop being so defensive and sensitive and just listen to me, you'll be glad you did. It's nearly impossible to look at your own life objectively."

"What makes you think you're being objective when you look at my life, or Frieda's?" asked Betty.

"Can we please change the subject?" asked Frieda, playing referee.

"And, thanks for asking, my marriage is perfect," said Ilene. "Peter is perfect. He's working very hard on his diet and appreciates my support."

"Objectively speaking," said Betty, "bullshit."

Chapter 11

Ilene turned on the shower full blast. Hot. Hotter than Peter could take. He'd asked if he could join her. She said, "I'm not sure you can stand the heat."

He glared at her and said, "Is that your way of telling me to stay out of the kitchen?"

"Not at all," she replied, and then hopped into the steaming stream of water, effectively ending conversation.

Ilene had been awake since nine. She bounded out of the bed to make herself breakfast, read the paper, and checked any after-the-bell financial news on FNN. She was eager to get started with her Saturday. First, she'd head over to David Isen's new bachelor pad at noon to help him unpack until fourish, then go to the gym and pound the treadmill into submission for an hour. Steam, sauna, and then she'd get her six o'clock Swedish massage at the club spa from Renaldo. After which she'd come home, make herself a giant salad, and watch at least three hours of the BBC six-hour production of *The Singing Detective*. Ilene wasn't sure what Peter had planned. She should have checked before she'd scheduled her day. But then again, Saturday had long been the one day of the week they both reserved for personal use.

She stepped out of the shower, towel dried her long, straight hair, and walked into their bedroom in her silk robe.

"Surprise," said Peter.

Curtains down, the room was dark. Peter lay nude beneath the sheets. Candles lit the room, around the perimeter of the bed, the mantel, the bookshelves, the dresser, and night tables. Some were fat, some thin, a spectrum of colors. The scents were a bit much. Ilene nearly recoiled from the commingled fragrances.

"Did you buy up the entire candle department at Pier One?" she asked. Her eyes and nose fully occupied, the music took a moment to register. "Is that Ravel?"

Peter, grinning, patted the space next to him on the bed.

Ilene stood, frozen, at the threshold of the bathroom.

He said, "Come, wife."

"You lit all these candles while I was in the shower?" asked Ilene.

"Obviously," he said. "Are you coming over here or not?"

Ilene was touched he'd go to such effort—not much; in fact, hardly any—but she was running late. She was expected at David's in a half hour. How to get out of this without hurting Peter's feelings?

She cinched her robe more tightly around her waist and walked over to him. She sat on the very edge of the bed. He scooted toward her, keeping himself fairly well covered, and put his arms around her waist.

Ilene let him touch her, but she didn't allow him to pull her down. She said, "Sweetie, this is so nice of you."

"I'm glad you like it. I have other surprises in mind."

That's when her eyes lit on the small tin on his night table. It was black with a gold ribbon wrapped around it. "What's that?" she asked.

Peter was kissing her wrist. Between smacks, he said, "It's chocolate body paint. I thought I'd smear some on you and, you know. Lick it off."

She laughed. "Only you could turn sex into a high-calorie act."

He stopped kissing her. But then started again, speaking between smacks. "I thought we could spend the day together, in bed. It *is* Saturday, after all."

"Sweetheart, we haven't spent a Saturday in bed since 2001." They used to, every week, each choosing to use their personal time to administer to the other's personal needs. It had been a ritual. Sex, breakfast, sex, lunch, sex, dinner, sex, snack, sleep. Now that she thought of it, maybe it was all those Saturdays of indulging themselves that had instigated Peter's post-marital weight gain.

He said, "Then we're long past due."

She said, "You're very sweet, Peter. Really."

He dropped her forearm. Her hand hit the bed and bounced gently on the down-covered mattress. " 'Sweetie, sweetheart, sweet Peter, really,' " he said mockingly. "You obviously want to leave. So get dressed and go."

She felt terrible. But she did have to get dressed. "I'll make it up to you later, I promise."

He said, "Glad I went to all this trouble. I want it on record that I tried."

"Noted," she said, standing.

"And that you are not meeting me halfway."

She was starting to feel annoyed. He'd sprung his little seduction at the worst possible time. Why couldn't he have waited until tonight? Besides which, as she suddenly felt compelled to say, "What trouble? You lit a bunch of cheap candles, put on a CD, and bought some stupid condiment. If you really want to interest me, you could go to the honest effort of getting in shape. That would mean something. Not this unoriginal, low-rent, porn-inspired crap." She flung open her closet door and added, "Every time we have sex, I'm half-convinced you're going to have a heart attack. Not exactly fun for me."

He wasn't listening. He'd already bunched up the covers, wrapped them around his body and gone into the bathroom. She dressed quickly and left.

"David, it's gorgeous!" said Ilene. The apartment was lovely. David, himself, looked pretty good, too. In the six weeks since he'd left his wife, he'd taken off ten years. Separation was like all-natural Botox. David could appear in an advertisement for breakups: "In no time, you'll have healthier, younger-looking skin. Guaranteed!"

"Come look at the kitchen," he said. "I can fit a decent-size table in here. These cabinets will have to go. I don't need the shelf space anyway. I tell you, living alone has been liberating. Much less stuff."

They walked in circles, admiring David's EIK in the sprawling West Village apartment he bought yesterday. Ilene had been getting daily updates on his apartment search over the last few weeks. He'd looked at dozens of properties before deciding to buy this "modest charmer" on Minetta Lane, near Sixth Avenue. Modest indeed. It was at least sixteen hundred square feet, probably in the seven-figure neighborhood. The actual neighborhood was noisy and crowded. Full of head shops, tattoo parlors, leather emporiums—and the legion of tourists who came to shop at them. David said he'd always wanted to live in the Village. Ilene could not fathom why.

Ilene was dying to ask about the financial details. He and his estranged wife hadn't sold their duplex yet (they'd make a huge profit on that sale, enough for Georgia to buy a twenty-acre farm in Vermont if she wanted to). Did David have $200,000 lying around for the down payment, as well as enough liquid to pay two mortgages concurrently? Plus alimony and child support?

"Your third move in a month," she said. "You seem unfazed."

He said, "I'm fazed. I miss seeing Stephanie every day. But I have a good feeling about this apartment. I'm relieved to get out of the Roosevelt."

David had been living in the East-Side luxury hotel.

Must have cost a fortune, thought Ilene. David had to have family money. Working at *Cash* would give him a middle-class income in New York. Nowhere near enough to handle his expenses. And look at him! His was not the face of a man who was worried about paying the bills.

She said, "I wouldn't mind living in a hotel. Room service, housekeeping."

He shrugged. "That goes old fast."

"You missed the comforts of home," she said.

"My home hadn't been comfortable for a while," he said. "You have such a great marriage, you probably can't understand."

Ilene's turn to shrug. "All marriages have ups and downs."

"My marriage fell down and it couldn't get up," he said. "Let me show you the master bedroom." He grabbed her wrist and tugged her toward the back of the apartment, through the large living room, past the bathroom off the hallway. His fingers burned on the same skin Peter had kissed an hour before. Only then, she'd been ice cold.

"This is it," David said. "Are you okay? Your face is bright red."

"I'm fine." She coughed. "Something caught in my throat."

"What?"

"My throat."

"What got caught in your throat?" he asked.

Her thudding heart? "I swallowed my gum," she said.

"You chew gum?" he asked as if he could more easily

80

imagine her gutting a trout. He swung the bedroom door open and said, "What do you think?"

She approved. The space was nearly bare, just a platform bed with navy sheets, shams, and duvet, some stacked moving boxes, a nightstand with an alarm clock. The door to the closet was open. Ilene saw the suits on hangers, arranged by color, exactly as she ordered her closet.

"It's bright," she said. "If you need help shopping for furniture, I'd love to join you. Really. It's the next best thing to shopping for myself." He nodded noncommittally. She added, "Once you've settled here, you should go out. Have some fun. You must let me take you to dinner. With Peter. I'll ask my sister Frieda to come, too."

"Frieda the widow."

Why did he insist on calling her that? "Frieda's really much better now. She's never looked more beautiful. She's a devoted mother. She owns a gallery in Brooklyn Heights," pitched Ilene. She didn't want to push too hard. She carefully turned the soil, keeping it moist. Planting seeds.

"You have two sisters, don't you?" he asked.

Ilene said, "Betty is the youngest."

"I met her once," he said.

Ilene didn't remember that meeting. She said, "I don't think Betty's ever come to the office."

David said, "We ran into her on the street. We'd had a lunch at the Blue Water Grill and ran into her in Union Square afterwards. She was wearing a huge down coat. It looked like she'd wrapped a comforter around her body."

Ilene was drawing a complete blank. "Less than a year ago," he prompted.

"You have an amazing memory," she said.

"I never forget a coat," he said.

Ilene looked out David's window, at his view of Minetta Lane. The block was curved. Most of the buildings were a 150 years old or more. If one could delete cars from the picture, the street would be straight out of an Edith Wharton novel.

David opened one of his moving boxes and pulled out books. "Betty looks a lot like you," he said.

"She does not!" said Ilene.

"She has your face."

"On a size fourteen body."

"I haven't told you everything. About Georgia," David said suddenly. "Let me get this off my chest right away: Georgia had an affair. With a teacher at Stephanie's school. It's over between them. I don't know the full story, and I don't want to know. Georgia denies it, but I bet she wants to move to Vermont just so she can take Stephanie out of that school and get away from him."

Ilene's mouth went dry. This affair complicated matters significantly. His emotional recovery might take longer than the six months she'd planned for.

"Forgive me if this is too personal," started Ilene.

"If it's too personal, I won't answer," he said.

"Has the affair destroyed your faith in women?"

"I thought you were going to ask me how I feel," he said.

Ilene hated asking a man about his feelings. She preferred men kept their feelings to themselves. Nothing was quite as unappetizing as a quivering heart on a plate. The sight of a man crying? It could make a person sick.

Ilene said, "You can keep your feelings to yourself."

David said, "I hate it when people ask me to open a vein and bleed all over them."

She nodded. "The context is always so negative."

"No one ever wants the update on your unbridled happiness," David agreed. "Help me with these books."

Ilene walked toward him. He dumped a stack in her arms and pointed at the bookshelf against the wall. "I'm sure I'll trust a woman again, but next time, I'll be more careful," he said.

"How?" she asked.

"I've made a mental list of qualities I'd like to find in a woman," he said. "Emotional strength, some sign that a woman can handle obstacles and hardships. She has to be optimistic, too. No more always seeing the dark side, like Georgia. Someone with kids would be nice. And some experience with marriage so we'd both have a history to improve on."

Ilene smiled. Had he not just described Frieda exactly? Don't push, she reminded herself. To keep her tongue silent, Ilene looked at her book pile and found a five-volume series on World War II. "Are you a Hitler freak?"

"I was a history major," said David. "Thesis on America's point-of-entry in nineteenth- and twentieth-century wars. You should see the Civil War series. Thousands and thousands of pages. The war lasted five years. It took me six years to read the books."

"Now that's commitment," Ilene said, admiring his love of history.

"Did Georgia read these, too?" she asked.

He shook his head. "She read romance novels," he said. "She liked hearts and loins, not arms."

"Funny," said Ilene. "So the Civil War series took you six years. How long did you say your marriage lasted?"

He laughed. "The marriage followed the path of the Revolutionary War series. Two years to get through, with a great start and a withering finish. But I had to see it to the end."

"Once you hook onto something, you stick with it," she said.

"Until the last word," he agreed.

Chapter 12

Wednesday, October 23
8 P.M.

"You're right on time," said Sam Hill as he opened the door.

"I walked around the block so I wouldn't be early," said Frieda.

"You should have just come up," he said.

"Next time, I will."

Frieda shed her pea coat. Sam Hill hung it on a hanger in the closet by the door.

"You look good," he said.

She wore a black A-line miniskirt, black tights, and a lavender stretch T-shirt, three-quarter sleeves. She'd changed outfits several times before the babysitter arrived, and would have continued the fashion show of her entire wardrobe had she not felt the urge (the urgent urge) to sprint to Sam Hill's sublet, a universe (eight blocks) away from her apartment. She'd been thinking of nothing else—had for days—ever since they'd made the date. The laundry had gone unfinished. There was no food in the house. She'd missed a couple of delivery dates on frames. Who had time for work when she could, instead, lie down on her bed to think about kissing Sam Hill? Five minutes would turn into two hours. Time evaporated in thought. She'd lost mornings. Afternoons. Entire evenings after Justin went to bed. To stare at the ceiling in her bedroom and drift.

What would it be like? she asked herself repeatedly. The first time with Gregg had been lovely. Perfect. She'd had a number of lovers by then, but hadn't been shown much generosity by them. Gregg was so sweet and worried about her having a good time. Along with other things, she enjoyed the trust she felt with him. Over the years, they'd learned together. She'd grown up with Gregg, in so many ways. Naturally, in a marriage, she thought they were each other's final sexual destiny. She had been his. But he wasn't hers. Not that Sam Hill would be the last man she ever slept with. She wasn't thinking of this as a first date that would lead to a second and, eventually, to the altar. Having the goal of marriage was laughable. She'd been married. She had a child. Her life experiences made the single- (and simple-) minded goal of lifelong commitment irrelevant. Tonight, with Sam Hill, Frieda was looking for a good time.

He'd been forthright when they'd made plans. "Would you like to come over to my apartment?" he asked on the phone.

"What about dinner and a movie?" she replied.

"You have to pay a baby-sitter, right?"

"Yes."

"What's the going rate?"

"Ten dollars an hour."

"Dinner and a movie would be a poor use of time and money," he said. "Wouldn't you rather be alone together for four hours instead?"

It was a naked invitation to come over and have sex. For four hours. He hadn't even offered to cook her dinner. Is this how people dated these days? Frieda wouldn't be able to eat anyway. Nerves. If she'd Learned Nothing from Gregg's Death, Frieda believed that formalities were often useless—especially if the formality at hand was getting to know a man before she fucked him.

Despite the clarity of her prime directive, Frieda was still anxious. Much of the edginess was forgotten when Sam opened the door. She hadn't seen him for over a week. But when she beheld him again, she couldn't believe how beautiful he was. He wore jeans, a faded red T-shirt. No shoes. He hadn't agonized over his wardrobe choices. She focused on his face, anyway. Something about him, the skin, in particular, and his dark brown eyes and dark brows instantly drew her complete attention like a loud clap or the pop of a balloon. She was staring. How rude.

He said, "I love the way you look at me."

She loved the way he looked at her. Like she were a magnet, as if she could draw him to her and he'd do exactly what she wanted without her having to say a single word.

"You really look good," he said it again.

"So do you," she said. "Here."

Not wanting to arrive empty-handed, Frieda had brought Sam a gift. He unwrapped the present.

"Hey! Look at that," he said, appreciatively. His framed review had turned out perfectly. "It looks awesome."

She said, "Forget about the bill. My treat."

"I accept, and thanks," he said. "Would you like to sit?"

He gestured toward the couch. She could see it plainly from the doorway. She could see the entire studio from the doorway. She knew it was a sublet, and hadn't expected much. Her expectations weren't quite as low as the reality. A stove and refrigerator, a bed on a frame in one corner, the couch in the another. Kitchen, bedroom, and living room within four gray walls. The gray carpet on the floor had stains (but seemed clean, well vacuumed at least.) A TV, cable box, VCR, and stereo were arranged on a long console near the bed. Pots and pans hung from hooks in a peg-board over the stove. Like the carpet, the stove was clean of surface dirt, but marred with burn marks that couldn't be washed away. The couch, where she was to sit, was pilly and frayed.

He put the framed review on the table and asked, "Would you like a Scotch?"

She hated Scotch. But coming out of Sam Hill's mouth, in this dumpy sublet, a drink sounded like just the thing. She sat on the lumpy, orange couch. He solicitously poured, making sure he put in adequate ice, and brought the glass to her.

He sat next to her, his shoulder touching hers. The contact was sublime. Warm, like hot bread. She said, "Toast?"

"I'll drink to that," he said. He held up his glass. "A toast to toasting." They clinked and drank.

The Scotch was awful, burning. "Tastes like lighter fluid," she said.

"I've never had lighter fluid," he said, nodding. "So I'll have to take your word for it."

"Refill?" she said.

He poured her another shot. "Are you nervous?" he asked.

Frieda said, "Yes. About what might happen. I've been thinking about this constantly."

"Me, too," he said.

"Are you nervous?"

He said, "No. Just excited."

Fearless, this Sam. "Who, or what, is Sam Hill?"

"He was a farmer from somewhere in New England who ran for public office in the late eighteen hundreds, but no one knew who he was or where he'd come from," he said, finishing his drink. "He didn't win."

"Never ran again."

"Faded further into obscurity," he said. "He has a famous name for being an anonymous person."

Frieda, draining her glass, decided she was wrong. She loved Scotch. It was her new favorite drink. She said, "I haven't had sex in a year and four months, and that wasn't real sex. You can't have real sex with someone in the final stages of terminal cancer. I hope you're not shocked by that. I never know how much people can take, which is why I talk about my husband's death so infrequently. Hardly ever. In fact, never."

She paused, noting his perplexed expression. Not repulsed. But definitely puzzled. Where was she going with this? She said, "My point is that it's been forever since I've done it with any degree of abandon. And I need more Scotch, please."

He said, "You've had enough," taking her glass and putting it in the sink. It was only four paces from couch to kitchen. Ilene would plotz if she saw this place. Frieda was to have sex, for the first time in forever, in a shit hole.

"How long has it been for you?" she asked.

He didn't answer, rinsing out the glasses and putting them in the drying rack by the sink. He didn't let dishes sit. That was a good sign. The place *was* clean. No dust bunnies or lint. The kitchen orderly. She hadn't yet seen the bathroom. It could be ugly in there.

Frieda repeated, "How long for you?"

He said, "I'm thinking."

Didn't seem like a question that required much thought. Frieda wondered if he were thinking about how to get this tipsy widow with a hard-on out of this apartment before she attacked him. Finally, Sam said, "The short answer is six months. But you gave me more information than a number. I want to do the same. The long answer would be that it's been a couple years since I had sex with someone I cared about. I've had short-term relationships with a few women between her and you, but I could see the ending from the beginning, so the sex part wasn't very satisfying. The last time was with the actor who's playing Nancy in *Oliver!* It started after a party. She didn't want to go home alone, so she took me with her. I never thought she liked me. To tell you the truth, I felt used."

He said the "I felt used" part with mock sarcasm. Like he'd been mortally offended. A woman using a man? She couldn't have been using him for money, or jobs. If she'd been using him for sex, that was promising.

"What's her name?"

"Lynette," he said. Seeing her reaction, he added, "I know. Bad name. But she's a nice person. We're on good terms."

"Who was the woman you cared about?" she asked.

"That was Zina. She's an actor, too. We were best friends, and decided to try a sexual relationship. That one didn't work out because, frankly, she was too gross for me. She loves fart jokes, and burping in public. It's hilarious in a friend. But not in a girlfriend. We're still close. She's got a chorus part in *Oliver!*"

"Have you ever had a long relationship?"

He said, "I lived with Deborah for two years. She's a Jewish doctor's daughter. A musician, a flutist. She wanted to get married and have a kid, but I was only twenty-four, and the sexual attraction wasn't intense enough for me to want to commit for life. We're still friends, too."

"Let me guess. She's playing in the orchestra at *Oliver!*"

"She is indeed."

"I've got to see this show. It's a cavalcade of your ex-girlfriends."

He laughed. "There's another one in this production, too. The 'ripe strawberries, ripe' woman."

Frieda knew the part. In the movie, it was the first scene after the intermission. She sang the line in her best operetta voice. Sam cringed. He said, "I guess we know one thing for sure."

"That is?"

"If I fall in love with you, it won't be for your singing."

Frieda said, "Another wee dram of Scotch?"

He demurred. "You seem drammed already."

She was, and she liked it. "Why haven't you been with anyone in six months?" she asked. "No available women left in the cast?"

Sam, still at the sink, poured her a splash and walked back over. He sat next to her again. His body leaning on hers was inebriating enough. She put the glass on the table.

He said, "The dry spell." Silence. Sam Hill clearly liked to think before speaking. A good quality. Frieda bet he hardly ever said anything in haste that he regretted later. But it was unnerving to have to wait for an answer. Frieda had been raised to blurt. As a rule her family members spoke without thinking.

Sam said, "As you said, I've pretty much dated anyone I had an interest in within the company. And, with all the traveling we do, I just haven't met anyone on the outside."

She'd have to remember to ask him about 'all the traveling,' but she wanted to get to something else first. "You said, 'between her and you.' Meaning, you hadn't been with anyone you cared about between Zina and me. So you're saying you care about me."

"I am."

"You don't know me."

"I don't?" he asked. "Don't I?"

"Why should you?"

He said, "Unless you've completely misrepresented yourself, you're kind, smart, and funny. And you frame beautifully."

She said, "I don't feel like I know you at all."

He said, "But you're comfortable with me."

"Yes."

"You're attracted to me."

She smiled.

He said, "You can't see the ending from the beginning."

Here, she had to pause. She flashed back to Ilene's speech at Bouillabaisse. That Sam would be fun for a few months, a reinitiation in romance, and then Frieda would wake up, realize how inappropriate he was for a husband and stepfather. That Frieda would end it to find a suitable suitor, someone stable, with money.

She said, "Sing for me. Something from *Oliver!*"

"No," he said.

"Recite some lines," she said.

"I'm not giving you a performance, Frieda."

She said, "Come on, Sam."

He said, "You'll have to pay to see it, just like everyone else. But I will show you something."

He went to the closet and took her coat off the hanger. Rummaging on the table near the couch, he found a handkerchief, his wallet, his keys. He stuffed the items in the pockets of the coat.

"Put this on," he instructed. She put it on. He said, "Go to the far corner."

The room had only near corners (it was that small). But she went to the corner by the platform bed. He stood diagonally across from her, in the corner by the door. "Now," he said, "come at me. Slow."

Frieda walked toward Sam. He walked toward her, whistling, checking his watch, pretending to stare at the sky. They were just about to pass each other, when he bumped into her shoulder, knocking her off balance. He grabbed her under the arms, his hands rubbing the outsides of her breasts, steadying her, helping her get solid footing.

He said, "Forgive me, madam," and bowed slightly.

Frieda said, "Not at all," with an English accent. Not sure why.

He said, "Good evening," and walked past her. She walked past him. When they were at opposite corners of the room, they turned to face each other.

He said, "Check your pockets."

She reached into her coat. The handkerchief, wallet, and keys were gone.

Sam said, "Looking for these?" He held up the items, tossing them one by one on the bed.

She was awed. Honestly, she hadn't felt a thing. She said, "Let's try that again." On the table, she found a *Newsweek*, a pack of gum and a MetroCard. She put them in the pockets of the coat. "This time, you're not going to distract me by feeling me up."

He smiled. "You noticed that."

"Only a lot."

"Shall we?"

They walked toward each other again. He bumped into her shoulder the same way. This time, instead of steadying her and copping a feel, he snared her around the waist, hugged her tightly against his chest and started kissing her.

They leaned into each other, kissing madly. He held her with both hands, cupping her jaw, controlling the movement of her head, rotating it to the left and right, inhaling the kiss. She'd laced her fingers behind his neck, loving the feel of his skin. His skin! It wasn't particularly hot or soft. But it was alive with an energy that made touching him exquisite. His skin was one more mystery about him, like being from Maine, and being an actor, and his long silences. The kissing went on and on. She couldn't stand for it any longer. She had to lie down.

He broke the contact and whispered in her ear, "You like the pickpocketing?"

She said, "Yes."

"I can also take off all your clothes without you noticing a thing."

"Show me," she said.

Chapter 13

Tuesday, October 29
3:33 P.M.

"Peter Vermillion? This way, please," said the fetching nurse. Was she a nurse? he wondered. Did nutritionists, who weren't really doctors, hire trained, licensed nurses? Hardly mattered. She was sweet and cute, and obviously ate well. He could tell by her tasty body. How many women could pull off the white polyester uniform and look sexy?

He followed the nurse through the waiting-room door, down a white-walled corridor and into a small examination room with a table, a chair, a sink, a scale, and several cabinets. The inner sanctum of nutrition. The locked compartments under the sink had to be where they stored the supplements, the pricey powders in cylindrical plastic tubs. Within five minutes of the consultation, the nutritionist would start hawking. He reminded himself that cynicism might not be helpful in this process.

The nurse said, "Please remove all your clothes and put on the gown." She pointed at a cocktail-napkin–size square of paper on the exam table.

"This?" he asked, picking it up. It unfolded into a tissue-weight tunic that was designed to fit the body of a junior-high-school anorexic.

She said, "Hmm, that might be a bit snug. Let me look for something larger for you. Meanwhile, why don't you get undressed and I'll let the doctor know you're here."

The doctor? Doctor of what? Not an M.D., thought Peter. Maybe the nutritionist had earned a Ph.D. in the philosophy of snacking.

Peter stripped. He hung his suit on the hook of the door. He folded his shirt, socks, and undershirt and placed them in an orderly pile on top of his shoes. The boxers would stay put. He wasn't baring his ass along with his soul to this guy. Peter had summoned a great deal of courage to seek help to change his eating habits. Ilene didn't know about this. He wanted to keep it a secret. When he did lose weight, he wanted her to be impressed, surprised, grateful. If she knew he hadn't done it on his own, it might not have the same impact.

He'd made the appointment a few days after his embarrassing encounter with Peggy McFarthing at Grand Central. She was a nutritionist. Although she was emotionally unstable that day, she didn't seem like a scam artist or whack job. He asked Jane to get referrals for nutritionists in the area. Preferably—unequivocally—a man. Jane made an appointment for him with Eric Belittler at an office only a few blocks south on Madison from *Bucks*. Jane assured him Belittler came highly recommended.

Peter climbed up on the table. He looked around the room for something to occupy him while he waited. Nothing. Not a single copy of *Eating Fit* or *Cooking Light*. He circled the space with his eyes for the tenth time. They kept returning to the scale, black and imposing. He wondered if the nurse automatically reset the weights back to zero after a patient stepped off. What mortification to know that the next person in the examination room would see what the previous one weighed. With bravery and determination, Peter approached the scale. He stepped on it defiantly. An inanimate piece of metal wasn't going to intimidate him. Unless it was a gun. Or a knife. Or a lead pipe. Whatever, the point was that he would face off with the scale. Face it down. Down to the ground.

Thunk. The silver pointer slammed upward. So he didn't weight zero pounds. He pushed the bottom measure from zero, past 50, 100 and 150 to rest in the 200 slot. The pointer hadn't budged. He began moving the upper measure, past 5, 10, 15. At 223 pounds, the pointer dropped a hair.

He stepped off the scale: 223 pounds. He never would have believed it if he had not seen it with his own eyes. He figured he weighed 200—210 tops. He *was* a big-boned man, just an inch or two under six feet tall. Peter exhaled deeply. The cold, hard metallic slap of reality was what he'd needed, and now he had it. Maybe Ilene was right. He was close to the danger zone.

Now he felt jumpy. Uneasy. He sat back on the table, his feet dangling. That felt ridiculous, so he hopped off. Restless, he checked the unlocked cabinets above the sink. Sure enough, as he'd suspected, Peter found tubs of Metabofire and Protein Blast, and chromium picolinate. The plastic containers were priced. For sixteen ounces of Metabofire powder: $56. Protein Blast: $78. Chromium picolinate: $109. What was he getting himself into?

Peter decided, then and there, that he would get dressed and get the hell out. He'd seen the number on the scale. That was motivation enough. He'd think *223* whenever he reached for something fattening. And he'd stop. The pounds would melt off, and he wouldn't have to burn through hundreds of dollars in the process.

Peter had one leg in his trousers when the door swung open. He looked up to see a woman with curly brown hair, black-rimmed glasses, upturned breasts (even under the white coat, they stuck out like they had something important to say). He'd caught just a glimpse of her, though, because he'd instinctively tried to turn away in his one-leg-in, compromised position. In shifting, he lost his balance and fell to the floor in a jumble of trousers and near nudity. Who the hell was this woman? Didn't she know how to knock? He untangled himself and rose to his feet, holding his pants against his underwear, his pulse slamming in his ears. He closed his eyes and clutched his chest, gripping what had to be a pre-heart attack.

She said, "I'm sorry to startle you . . ." she had to pause to check the name on his chart. "Mr. Vermillion? Peter?"

He opened his eyes and took a look at her. *"Peggy Mc-Farthing?"*

She smiled. "What a surprise to see you here! You should have told the nurse that you know me."

"I was expecting Eric Belittler," he said meekly.

"My partner. He's out of town at a convention in Switzerland giving a paper on ephedrine. I'm taking his appointments this week."

"My secretary, Jane, made the appointment. If I'd have known that this was your office . . ."

"You wouldn't have come?" asked Peggy. "You don't have to be afraid of me, Peter. I was only seeking clarity when we spoke at Grand Central. I won't cry on your suit again. Scout's honor. Now, why don't you tell me why you're here."

"Maybe I should wait for Belittler to get back from Europe."

She said, "You're a busy man, Peter. You're here now. I promise you that my credentials are as good if not better than Eric's. Please sit down and we can start the consultation."

Jane was in deep trouble. You could start at trouble, drive all night, and still not reach where Jane would be when he got back to work. "Don't you see that there's a conflict?"

She said crisply, "Please don't question *my* professionalism."

Resigned, he said, "How do we start?"

"Why do you feel you need a nutritionist? You're an educated man. You know which foods are healthy and which aren't."

He said, "I'm seeing this as an experiment. To join forces with an expert. To have a supportive partner." A supportive partner? Sounded like he needed a wife.

Peggy said, "Are you interested in psychological help as well?"

He didn't want to get into *that*. "Can we move along?" he asked. "Get to the part about meal planning and, uh, supplements."

She said, "Step on the scale, please."

"I already weighed myself. Two twenty-three."

"I'd like to see for myself. Just part of the exam."

He said, "If you insist."

He stepped back on the scale, still on 223. The silver pointer slammed back to the top. Peggy said, "Let's move this just a bit."

She moved the upper measure to 224. Then 225. The silver pointer was still just a hair closer to the center. Two twenty-six. And then, at 227, the pointer leveled.

She made a note on the chart. She then took Peter's blood pressure and temperature, and asked him a series of questions about his eating habits. How many vegetables did he eat per day? Which kinds? Did he have a sweet tooth? Did he eat chicken skin? Red meat? Pretzels? Croissants? Did he practice nighttime feasting behavior? Had he ever had an eating disorder? What was his high-school weight? How much had he gained in the last twelve months? The list went on and on. For twenty minutes, he sat in his underwear and answered highly personal questions about dairy and doughnuts.

She finally put down the clipboard and said, "I'll be honest with you, Peter."

"Please," he said.

"You're an emotional eater."

"You mean I really love food?" He laughed.

She didn't. "Emotional eaters use food to compensate for what's missing in their lives," she said. "You're using food as a substitute for love and affection."

He examined Peggy McFarthing, in her white lab coat, with her perky breasts and black glasses. She was as skinny as a bow, clearly not an emotional eater despite her much-fired husband.

Peter said, "I *have* love in my life. Deep, abiding love."

"Of cheeseburgers." She laughed.

He didn't. Did she talk this way with all her patients? It was offensive, cruel. She was making fun of his weight problem, and calling him a loveless loser as well.

He said, "What do you recommend? A diet or a divorce?"

"Let's start with an eating plan, all right?" she said in a condescendingly calming voice.

"Fine."

"We like a high-protein, low-fat, low-carbohydrate diet," she said. "To make specific food choices, we use a system based on traffic lights: 'go' foods, 'caution' foods and 'stop' foods. We color-code them on a chart: green, yellow, and red. I'm going to give you a packet that details food in each category, and the chart. Ninety percent of what you can eat will be 'go' food. But you may have two 'cautions' a day, and one 'stop' a week. The packet also details portion size and restrictions on 'gos.' For example, you'll find grilled chicken breast on the 'go' list. I had a patient who ate a dozen of them every day, and wondered why she wasn't losing weight. The 'gos' are broken down into two categories, unlimited and limited. Unlimited 'gos' may be eaten in any quantity. You may have three limited 'gos' per day. It sounds complicated, but when you see the packet, you'll figure it out."

Peter wondered what an unlimited 'go' was. Iceberg lettuce? Broccoli? She might as well give him unlimited license to run naked down Fifth Avenue. He said, "I like a good system."

She smiled encouragingly. "Let's set a goal weight of one eighty-five."

"Doable," he said, gulping. Forty-two pounds? That sounded like a ton.

"You can get dressed now. We'll see each other once a week for as long as it takes," she said. "When you break two hundred, we can move to phase two of the program. You need to keep an exercise chart. Thirty minutes of aerobic activity, five times a week."

Shit. Now this? "Okay." He quickly put on his pants.

"And one last thing," she said. "We expect fledgling patients to have lapses."

"I won't."

"You will."

"I won't," he said adamantly.

"Okay, you won't," she said, the super smooth on. "But

if you do, when the dust settles in the kitchen, I'd like you to write what you were doing in the hour before the lapse in what we call a 'food journal.' "

"If you insist," he said.

She said, "You can learn a lot from a lapse."

"I'm sure you can," he said. Peter put on his undershirt and shirt. He pointed a thumb toward the cabinets. "What about the supplements? Aren't you going to make me buy some of those?"

Peggy shook her head. "They're for fine tuning. You're nowhere near that point."

"Got to learn to walk before you can run."

"In your case, we'll work our way up to a crawl."

Whatever her professionalism amounted to, she hated him. And now, he was stuck with her for months. Or not. He could blow off the whole thing. Or find another nutritionist. But then he'd have to go through this humiliation again, the weighing-in, the questions. The $300 initial office-visit fee.

Peter slipped on his socks, tied his shoes. He asked, "How's Bruce? He find a job yet?"

Peggy's smile didn't fade. "He's fine. In contention for a few spots. Your references will help, I'm sure."

"Glad to hear it."

She left as he arranged his jacket. He scheduled his next appointment and paid for the visit in cash.

Chapter 14

Thursday, November 14
4:21 P.M.

"He did *what?* For an *hour?*" asked Betty into the phone to Frieda. She was at Burton & Notham, in her office with the door closed.

"Sex with Sam," said her sister wistfully, "is everything I never dared to hope sex could be."

It had been two weeks since her sister's first date with Sam, and Frieda was a different person. Betty was still reeling from the change. The same woman who'd been nearly catatonic for a year had emerged from her bereaved slumber with a sudden, big bang. The biggest bang of her "entire life," she'd said. Betty was always wary when people used the phrase "my entire life," as in "That was the best hamburger I've had in my . . ." or "I've never been so excited in my . . ." Gross exaggeration showed a lack of perspective that Betty found irritating.

Betty said, "Look, I'm really busy." She could listen to the fabulous sex report for only so long.

Frieda said, "I'm going to *Oliver!* on Saturday night. With Ilene." What's this now? Ilene had been invited, and not Betty? Before Betty could complain, Frieda added, "Ilene surprised me with tickets. Isn't that decent of her? And they're not cheap. She got hundred dollar seats."

Ilene couldn't have gotten three tickets? Had Betty been excluded intentionally? If so, that could only mean Ilene had an agenda, something Betty wouldn't approve of.

A knock at Betty's door. "Enter," she called.

It was Gert. Her blonde hair was teased sky high today. "Earl needs you," she said.

At the mention of Earl's name, Betty's heart beat the Morse code for S.O.S. In the phone, she could hear Frieda saying, "Earl? Go talk to him! Ask him out! Do it!"

Betty covered the earpiece with her hand. To Gert, she said, "Be right there." To Frieda, she said, "Hanging up now." She clicked off before Frieda had a chance to pep talk her. She didn't need the cheerleader routine. Betty hated pep. She despised vim.

That said, she sprang out of her chair and trotted down the stairs to the main floor to find Earl Long.

Even though every conversation with him was like hearing a chorus of angels, Earl was kind of a pain in the ass. Ten times a day, he sought her out with questions and niggling problems about the store's electrical system and square footage. He seemed to enjoy wrenching her from the serious demands of running a gigantic retail store, just so he could send her on a quest for sales statements about CDs and instructional videos.

At the moment, she suspected he wanted to talk again about placement of the audio-book booths. They'd been around the bend on that one a few hundred times, trying to figure out where the store's dead space was, if indeed it had any. Betty believed the booths should be near the audio-book section on the third floor, but Earl wanted to move audio books to the main floor, to showcase the booths at street level. This would be a massive job, a huge headache for Betty to arrange, especially for an experimental outing. But corporate had big plans for these booths, hoping to increase audio-book sales tenfold, and Earl had been given the deciding vote.

She found him on the main floor, in the back, by the CD section. This would be a good spot for the booths, thought Betty. He'd actually set up a booth in the corner. He had on a pair of earphones. She tapped him on the shoulder.

"Earl," she said. "You need me?"

Gert had followed her downstairs and into the back of the store. Betty wasn't sure where her assistant was lurking, but she could smell the Eternity. She scanned the area, and spotted Gert unloading some new DVDs. Whenever Betty was in conference with Earl, Gert was sure to be in the vicinity.

Earl removed his headset. He said, "A compromise."

"I'm listening."

"We have two booths here," he said, "And one booth where the new nonfiction table is in the front. A temporary

109

Valerie Frankel

position, just to increase awareness, and then we can move the third booth back here, too."

Betty hated to lose the table. But she could squeeze in a vertical shelf by nonfiction on the second floor. She said, "Okay. The booth can stay in front for one month only. We'll have to figure out what to do with the loss of all this shelf space back here. One tight aisle of racks might fit over there." She pointed in Gert's direction. Sure enough, Gert was watching, not bothering to be shy about it.

"Should we shake on it?" asked Earl. His smile made her bowels twist, it was so wrenchingly hot. She felt a fantasy coming on, the one where he came into her office after hours, closed the door, and took off all his clothes, piece by piece, until he stood in front of her stark naked, one hand gripping a gigantic erection.

"Just hurry up and get it over with," she said.

Earl shrugged and put the earphones back on. Betty turned to go, relieved to be done with another interaction with him. She hadn't taken three steps when Gert appeared at her side.

"Come with me," her assistant instructed.

Betty, still weak from her flash of fantasy, hadn't the strength to protest. When Gert had something to say, the flow of her words was a force of nature—like a tornado or hurricane—that couldn't be stopped had Betty tried.

Gert escorted her behind the checkout desk in the CD section. Uncomfortably close to Earl. He was well within Betty's eye- and ear-shot. When he coughed, she could hear it.

Betty said, "How can I help you?"

"You can help yourself," said Gert.

"To what?"

"You are rude, condescending, and outright hostile to that man," said Gert. "That's no way to treat someone you're interested in. Don't give me the innocent look. I can tell you like him *because* you're bitchy to him. You're always mean to the men you're attracted to. It's the kind of thing girls do when they're in high school. Junior high. They don't know how to handle their feelings, so they react with hostility."

"Where'd you dream that up?"

"I didn't dream it. I lived it," she said. "After my divorce, I wasn't very trusting, as you can imagine. I did the same thing. You, on the other hand, don't have a divorce to hang your stupidity on. But you do have inexperience. You're still in high school, romantically speaking. Oh, don't be embarrassed. And don't scoff as if this doesn't matter. You have to face your self-destructive tendencies, Betty. We all do. Otherwise, we'll suffer for them, every day, until we die."

Betty was impressed. She liked Gert, but hadn't thought of her as a particularly insightful person. "Thanks for the advice," said Betty. "And now, you're fired."

"I am not."

"You are."

"Go over there and be nice to Earl," she said. "Give him a reason to ask you out, and I bet he will."

Betty shook her head. "I can't do it. It's too hard."

Gert gave her a soul-sucking look of pathos. She said, "I've been watching the two of you."

"I've been watching you watching us."

"I can tell that he likes you," she said.

Betty laughed scornfully. He could never. She'd been nothing but dismissive. She wasn't a crisp wafer of blonde hair and tits that men like Earl gravitated toward. Betty wouldn't listen to this drivel. It insulted her intelligence. It offended her sensibilities.

She asked, "How can you tell?"

Gert smiled, warmly, motherly. "He chases you around the store. He asks you dozens of useless questions to get your attention. He looks you right in the eye when you talk to each other. I hate to say it, because I'm trying to discourage your adolescent behavior, but your meanness may have intrigued him."

"So, by that logic, I should continue on the same path." Done, Betty thought. Back to familiar, comfortable ground.

Gert shook her head. "The time has come to surprise him. You can be a bitch for only so long before intrigue turns into boredom. That's right," said Gert, nodding, teased hair floating above her. "The truth hurts. Here's what you say. 'Earl, you've been working so hard. I really appreciate it.' He'll run with it."

"That's it?" Betty asked.

Gert nodded. "I don't think he'll need much encouragement. Look at it this way: He's been in town for a month. He doesn't seem to have a lot of friends in New York. He works all day, and then, according to my covert intelligence, he goes to his hotel each night after work. This guy needs to get out, be with people. Most people need social interaction and regular sex."

"So you're saying he's desperate for company, so he might as well use me," said Betty. "And what's with the 'covert intelligence'?"

Gert said, "Just go over there and be nice. I know it might kill you to smile, but a date is worth the risk."

Betty said, "I'll sleep on it and get back to you."

"You'll do it right now," said Gert. She raised her arm and started waving. "Earl!" she called. "Come over here for a minute."

Betty was trapped. Gert had blocked her exit from behind the checkout counter. And Earl was walking toward them, easy and slow, like an ambling, moseying cowboy, wrapping the long black cord of the earphones around his hand like a lasso.

He stopped in front of the counter, leaning against it so his belt make a ting sound when it came into contact with the glass. He said, "What's up?"

Betty froze. She couldn't move, nor speak. Gert nudged her. But Betty's nerves had taken control of her voice box, wrapping themselves around it, choking her.

Finally, Gert opened her mouth to speak. She would break the ice. Betty could have kissed her.

"I've got to run," said Gert. "Later!"

Betty could have killed her. She attempted to smile at

Earl, and she felt a shot of pain rip through her forehead. Aneurysm? Stroke? She might die after all. Gert was right: It would kill her to smile.

Earl said, "Gert wants you to ask me out, right?"

"You'll have to excuse me while I go throw up," said Betty. She tried to escape the trap behind the counter, run to the bathroom where she could easily surrender the contents of her stomach.

"No, wait," he said. "I'll save you the trouble."

"The trouble?" she asked, not comprehending his meaning, her cement-mixer stomach having usurped the blood flow to her brain.

He said, "I'll take you to dinner tonight. And then we can walk around the East Village. You live in Alphabet City, right?"

"Only tourists say Alphabet City," she said. Why was she being dismissive, even now, when he was asking her out? She said, "Sorry. I don't intend to be rude."

"Be as rude as you want," he said. It was like a dare. He was asking her to give him her best shot, and they'd see who was still standing at the end of the night. If they made it that far.

He said, "So? Tonight?"

"Why are you doing this?" she asked.

He said, "It's obvious you don't think much of yourself, Betty. I know it must mean something is fucked up about me, but I find your low self-esteem appealing. I like the humility of it. And the challenge to make you think better of yourself. I can do it. I'm sure I can."

She drew in a breath and said, "You're absolutely right."

Earl said, "I am?"

"Yes," she said. "There is something fucked up about you."

Chapter 15

Saturday, November 16
9:30 P.M.

"Yes, Frieda," said Ilene. "He's very good."

"More than good," said Frieda. "He's awesome!"

Ilene regarded her younger sister, the beaming face, the excited flutter of her hands. They stood outside the theater during intermission. It had to be 40 degrees on the street. Frieda hadn't bothered to button her coat. Ilene said, "David seems to be enjoying the show."

"David?" asked Frieda, transfixed by a six-foot-high poster of Sam Hill as Fagin hanging from the theater's canopy.

"My friend," prompted Ilene. "The man sitting next to you in the aisle seat?"

"Of course," said Frieda. "I was surprised when you showed up with him. And Peter."

Ilene had said nothing about bringing Peter and David to *Oliver!* When she'd called the box office to order the tickets, she planned on getting just two. Then, she thought Peter might want to come. If nothing more, it would get them out of their increasingly claustrophobic home environment. And why get three tickets when she could even it up with four? She'd promised to take David out once he got settled. And this could be the perfect way to introduce him to Frieda. Ilene assumed that when Frieda saw Sam Hill onstage in his grubby costume with this shaggy fake beard and wig, she would come to her senses about him. As an alternative ideal, David would be sitting right next to her.

But things were not proceeding as planned. As soon as Frieda laid eyes on that huge poster of Sam Hill, she began talking about how exciting it was to see him in his element, and hadn't stopped since. His element, much to Ilene's dismay, wasn't a rinky-dink off-Broadway showcase basement. City Center, a three-thousand seat theater, was opulent and well maintained. Glittering crystal chandeliers hung from a pressed-tin ceiling. The red velvet curtains and red carpet were lush. Overstuffed seats were covered with still more red velvet. She'd expected a card-table set-up for selling T-shirts and Cokes. Instead, she found a full-size mahogany bar staffed with three bartenders in tuxes serving champagne cocktails, large boxes of peanut M&M's and a cast recording CD ($25!) The theater was sold out. The patrons represented a cross-section of New York: young and old, black, white, elegantly dressed matrons, and students in jeans. Thousands of people had come to see this show. Sam Hill was the star. It *was* impressive.

But nothing could change the basic truths of who Sam

Hill was and what Frieda needed in a partner. Ilene would press her agenda, presenting David as a stable alternative to Sam.

Frieda said, "I had no idea Sam could sing like that. And so loud! Sam told me they're not miked. Not even the child actors. That boy playing Oliver. He's doing well. His mother must be proud. Sam told me he's actually thirteen. And the Dodger is really sixteen, but he looks like a ten-year-old. I guess, to be a child actor, you've got to be tiny."

Ilene said, "Small body, big head."

"Sam was so funny in the pickpocketing scene, wasn't he?" interrupted Frieda. "And he was wonderful in the 'I'd Do Anything' part. I felt like he was singing directly to me! I'm totally in awe. He's so composed up there. So professional."

"It *is* his job," said Ilene. "Interesting, isn't it, that Sam can have this degree of success as an actor, be this talented, and still have no money. Imagine what it'll be like when he's out of work."

Frieda narrowed her eyes at the direct insult to Sam. "Imagine what it'll be like when he gets even better work."

And where would that leave Frieda? Ilene said, "All I'm trying to say is that the life of an actor must be hard. He *is* very good. Highly entertaining. We should enjoy him for his entertainment value."

"Entertaining is where you *start* to talk about Sam," said Frieda. She was bristling. Ilene had overplayed her hand. Stupidly. She should have realized that Frieda was nursing a serious infatuation, her defensiveness exacerbated by criticism.

Ilene should never have bought these tickets. Certainly not spent the additional $200 for Peter and David's. The men seemed to like the show, but both were quiet tonight. She looked at the poster of Sam Hill in his red wig and beard, his huge, brown eyes riveting her attention despite the garish makeup and fake hair.

The lights under the marquee flashed. Intermission was over. Time to find their seats and rejoin the men. The sisters walked back inside, Frieda rushing to her seat like her pants were on fire (they were, actually). Ilene followed more slowly. She hoped to catch David on his way out of the bathroom to ask him what he thought of Frieda. She scanned the crowd, searching for her tall, handsome colleague.

Instead, her gaze settled on a barrel-chested man at the bar. He was trying to get the bartender's attention, failing, even when he raised his arm and waved. The motion of his arm made his jacket pull tightly across his shoulders, the seam threatening to split. She cringed inwardly. If only Peter could see himself from across a crowded room, she thought.

She strode toward the bar and stood next to her husband. Peter was still trying to flag down the bartender. She leaned toward his ear and whispered, "Where's David?" The men had gone off to use the restroom together during intermission.

Peter startled at her voice and grabbed his chest. He said, "How long have you been standing there?"

She said, "The show's about to start."

"One second."

By now the crowd had thinned at the bar. Peter caught the bartender's eye and waved him over. He said, "I'll take the CD."

Ilene said, "You're not buying that."

"Why not? It's a great show. Frieda's boyfriend is fantastic."

Ilene snapped, "Come to the seats now. And forget about the CD. It's overpriced and the performances are horrible."

The lobby lights flashed off and on again. Peter looked at her, confused, his face dark, light, dark, light with the blink of the theater lights. She felt shapeless anger pulsing underneath her skin. Peter must have sensed it. He frowned and said tightly, "I'll be there in a minute."

She spun on her heels and left him at the bar. She was about three paces away when she heard his voice again.

"Yes, one CD," he said. "And a box of M&M's."

Chapter 16

Monday, December 2
9:30 A.M.

"Have a seat on the couch or the chair," said Denise Bother, Ph.D.

"Thank you," said Frieda, choosing the straight-back chair with thin metal armrests. It seemed conspicuously spartan, and Frieda wondered if the choice between the soft, inviting couch and the hard, unforgiving chair had been a psychological test, that she'd be sending a message to Dr. Bother about her opinion of therapy, this process, Justin's progress.

"On second thought," Frieda said, rising. "I'll take the couch."

"Good, good," said Dr. Bother.

In another context, Dr. Bother (referred to Frieda by the school shrink) looked like the kind of woman Frieda would be drawn to as a friend. She had long, tawny hair, unceremoniously down, free of barrettes or ponytail holders. She wore a light white cotton shirt and an ankle-length denim skirt with brown suede boots. The doctor was free of makeup and jewelry, except for the modestly sized diamond studs in her ears. Frieda found her nonthreatening to look at, yet she was ominous nonetheless. If she was any good, Dr. Bother knew the inner workings of her son's grief. He confided in her. They had private confidences. Justin never told Frieda, although she asked each week, what he and Dr. Bother talked about.

Denise said, "I called you in because I've noticed a change in Justin."

Frieda's lower back muscles clinched. She said, "A positive change?"

Denise said, "He's a fantastic child, Frieda."

Should Frieda take credit for that? "He is," she said.

"Can you tell me what you've noticed in the past month?"

Frieda tried to think. She hadn't been scrutinizing her son's mental health lately. Frankly, she'd been wrapped up in her own life, in her increasingly passionate and consuming affair with Sam Hill. She was sure she'd pick up on any conspicuous red flags. "He's eating well," she said. "Sleeping soundly. He hasn't gotten into any fights at school. Hasn't been crying."

"Anything else?" asked Denise.

This was like a pop quiz Frieda hadn't studied for. She said, "He had a good time at Thanksgiving. We went around the table at my sister's house to say what each of us was thankful for, and Justin said he was grateful for me, his aunts, and a father watching over him in heaven."

"What did you say you were thankful for?" asked Denise.

Frieda said, "Justin, my family, my health."

"Are you thankful for anything else, something you couldn't talk about in front of Justin?"

Was this woman a witch or an inquisitor? She said, "I have a boyfriend. I haven't told Justin about him yet. It's too soon."

Denise said, "Justin knows already. Children are more perceptive than adults realize. He told me that you've been going out often at night, leaving him with baby-sitters. He's heard you on the phone talking about a man. He overheard some of your family members discussing your relationship."

"A happy parent makes for a happy child," said Frieda, spinning this as best she could. But she was blindsided by the wallop of guilt. Was her affair causing Justin pain?

Denise said, "Usually I agree with that philosophy. Please don't misinterpret me. I'm glad that you've found someone to spend time with. It's crucial for your sanity. I don't mean that colloquially, either. The state of your mental health has improved dramatically. It's obvious." *Okay then*, thought Frieda, her back muscles relaxing with relief.

Denise continued, "Understand a couple of things about Justin. Of course he wants you to be happy. He far prefers it to the way you'd been. The change in you reminds him of the way you used to be, before Gregg got sick."

Frieda said, "Why hasn't he said any of this to me?" She felt insulted that Justin had confided in Denise and not her, proud of her son's powers of perception, guilty for not being as observant about him, plus the fresh slap of grief about Gregg and the way things used to be.

Denise, treading slowly, said, "You were wonderful with Justin during the illness. You've told me that you made a point of being honest with him every step of the way. You never lied or kept anything secret from him."

Frieda said, "Until now."

The good doctor nodded. "The two of you have been partners. Your having a new friend, especially a man, will be threatening to him no matter what, but less so if Justin's allowed into the relationship. Not that you should bring him on your dates. But Justin has to feel like he's involved in some way, or else he'll be afraid he's losing you."

"What am I supposed to do?" asked Frieda.

Denise said, "Tell me about your relationship."

Frieda said, "What do you want to know?"

"What do you do together?"

"Well, I go to Sam's apartment, we drink a little, and then we have sex for hours."

"Sounds like you're having a good time," said the doc slowly.

Frieda said, "It's more than a good time. It's the best time. The best time I've ever had. I could go into detail, but we don't know each other that well. I'm sure a lot of your patients come in and talk nonstop about their sex lives."

"I work exclusively with children."

Frieda said, "Let me reel that last comment back in."

"Do you think that Justin and Sam would get along?" asked the doc.

Frieda pondered that. "Well, they're both young. They both like to play pretend. Sam's an actor. He's very talented. He's at an audition today for a beer commercial."

Denise raised her eyebrows inquisitively. "Do you see this as a lasting relationship?"

Frieda said, "I don't want it to end. But I don't want it to change, either. I like going off at night, entering the parallel universe with Sam. He knows so little about my life before, it's bliss to rediscover myself with him, reinvent myself. I'm not Justin's mom or the tragic widow. I'm this sexy chick, and he's the ultimate hot date. I think about him obsessively. Every spare thought is about him and what we've done, or what I'd like to do. His apartment—where we spend all our time—is this ratty studio, but it's a sanctuary to me. I walk up the stairs a woman, step inside and transform into a goddess."

Denise's eyes widened. Frieda must have seemed unhinged. "The feeling you describe has a psychological term," said the doctor. "It's called limerence, the early stage of infatuation. The obsessive thought and passion is caused by a flood of chemicals in your brain—dopamine, norepinephrine, testosterone. Limerent subjects have described the feeling as walking on air, being on cloud nine. Sensual input is more intense, lights are brighter. Music is sweeter. Colors more vivid. Researchers have done brain-chemistry analyses of the syndrome. Interestingly, the hormonal activity is similar to people with obsessive-compulsive disorder. The hormonal flood lasts for about six months to a year, and then levels off. Once the rainbows and stars fade, couples move into the attachment stage—a committed relationship, a marriage—or they go the other way."

Frieda said, "It's not about hormones for us."

"No?"

"It's magic."

That stopped Denise's recitation. She said, "I'll just float this out there. Most people who've suffered a major loss need two years to pass before they're on solid ground emotionally. Before that point, they're susceptible to erratic mood swings and can place inflated importance on relationships formed within that time. Gregg died, when? A year ago."

"A year and three months."

Denise nodded. "Have you and this man ever talked about leaving the 'parallel universe' and entering the daily reality of each other's lives?"

Sam had asked her, a couple of days ago, if he should meet Justin. They were on the bed (as usual) in each other's arms after their first session (of many) that night. Frieda was surprised by the question. She didn't want to share Sam with anyone. And if she brought him home, he'd see another side to her. The mother. The one who had to pay attention to Justin, to the cooking, the dishes, the lunchboxes. Goddesses don't pack lunchboxes. Goddesses don't clean ovens or scoop poops out of the cat litter.

Frieda had said to him, "I'm sure Justin would love you, but I'm not sure how you'd react to me when I'm around him."

Sam asked, "You're a different person at home?"

"I'm the same person," she said. "But when I'm with him, I have to pay attention to him. I have to listen to him and draw monsters and beg him to eat broccoli. I wouldn't be able to focus on you."

"What makes you think I'm such an attention hog?" he asked.

He was an actor. His choice of profession was all about look-at-me. His age made him naturally egocentric. Frieda said, "I don't think that about you."

Another of Sam's long silences. Finally, he pushed her flat on her back and started kissing her neck and face. She reflexively reached for him. He moved her hand away and said, "No. Let me pay attention to you for a while." And he did. For a long, long time, until the back of her head exploded. Twice.

Denise said, "Frieda?"

"Yes, I'm here."

"We have to stop now."

"Okay. Thank you for being honest with me." Frieda stood and started to button her coat.

Denise said, "If you aren't ready to introduce them, at least tell Justin about your boyfriend."

"I will."

"And, Frieda?" said Denise. "In the same spirit of honesty?"

"Yes?"

"Be careful."

Chapter 17

"It took two months, but here we are," said Peter as he sat down to lunch with his sister-in-law Betty. "Love this place. Jesus, look at the waitresses."

They sat in a window booth that the glorified coffee shop called Coffee Shop, one block west of the Union Square Burton & Notham. Betty said, "All aspiring models and actors." She admired the young hopefuls. "Nice to look at, depressing to contemplate," she added.

"Look at that one," said Peter, pointing at a six-foot-tall redhead by the bar.

Betty glanced over the top of her menu. "I could have come to midtown," she said.

"Not necessary," he said. "I walked from my office. I needed the exercise." Peter dabbed at his forehead with his paper napkin. He had enjoyed the cold air, the movement of his legs and hips as he trudged down Broadway. He'd walked a total of thirty-two blocks—one and a half miles—in just thirty minutes. He'd been walking the twenty-plus blocks to work from Chelsea each morning, too. The day's total: nearly three miles.

"I'm taking the subway back," he said.

"How can you be away from the office for so long?" Betty asked, putting her menu, folded closed, on the table.

"We do a double issue in December, and then don't publish again until February. This is my annual downtime," he said.

She didn't look at him directly while he spoke. Her eyes darted to the bar, out the window, across the aisle. Did he make her nervous? He had no idea why. Peter had always liked Betty. She was wryly funny, tart, like biting into a green apple. He found her pretty. She and Ilene closely resembled each other, except for the difference in body size. Betty was the most guarded of the sisters. Hard to get to know. Purposefully distant.

Peter scanned the menu. The lunch was a nice idea, to repay Betty for all the discount books she'd gotten for him over the past couple of months. But now, as they sat together without the buffers of Ilene, Frieda, or Justin, he had to wonder why he had pushed for this. He could tell she didn't particularly want to be there, but was willing to take the free meal.

He said, "The grilled-chicken salad is speaking to me."

Betty said, "It's clucking your name?"

"What are you getting?"

She said, "I'm torn between the cheeseburger and the

Ruben. So I'll probably order the garden salad and a diet Coke."

"Are you dieting?" he asked. She *did* seem slimmer, now that he took a moment to look.

Betty, suddenly self-conscious, pulled her sweater around her chest. She said, "Hearing that word 'diet' is a mental trigger to order the cheeseburger."

He laughed. "I know what you mean. That's called the rebellion reflex. I'm seeing a nutrionist. I've got a thirty-page eating plan. I'm keeping a food journal."

"Whatever you're doing, it's working," she said.

Peter beamed. In the last six weeks, he'd taken off fifteen pounds. Peggy said that the first ten pounds were water weight (whatever that meant), and not fat. But his clothes were looser. Water or not, that counted for something.

He asked, "Did you know that a pound of fat has the volume of a quart of liquid?"

She shook her head. "So you're down what? Ten quarts?"

"Fifteen," he said.

"Impressive," she said. "I'm down seven."

"I can see that," he said. They were having a fat chat. Dishing about dieting. Peter loved it. He hadn't been able to talk to anyone about his weight-loss program. It was a secret from Ilene; Jane hated that he refused to order deli food anymore; Peggy was his guru, not his comrade. Maybe Betty would be his diet buddy. How did one set that up? Was it like proposing, or going steady?

Peter asked, "What made you decide to diet?"

Betty said, "Let's not get too personal."

"What does dieting have to do with your personal life?" he asked, perplexed and, frankly, hurt to be shut down when they'd just started to bond.

Betty said, "Your decision to diet probably has everything to do with your personal life. I bet Ilene goes with you to your appointments."

"For your information, my wife has no idea about the nutritionist. It's a secret," he said. "I'd appreciate it if you don't tell her about it."

"Scout's honor," she said, cocking one eyebrow. How did she do that? It was bewitching. He couldn't help smiling at her. She added, "I'm still not telling you about my boyfriend."

"I know about him already," he said. "His name is Earl. He works with you. He's from Chicago. You've been on a handful of dates, but you haven't—"

"Stop there," she said, holding up a hand. "Your information is accurate. I'm sure Ilene has done a lot of editorializing about him."

Peter said, "Ilene is thrilled for you. She wants you to be happy. That's all she wants for everyone. The problem, which Ilene and I have discussed, is that her concept of what makes other people happy might not jibe with theirs. You've known her longer than I have. Has she always been like this?"

Betty said, "More or less. Less before."

"Before what?" he asked.

"Before Gregg died, of course," said Betty.

Peter got a sudden hit, a flash of understanding. The day after the funeral, the shivah gathering was at Frieda's house. Ilene had spent hours and hundreds of dollars on deli platters. They were extraneous, considering the volume of food people brought. Ilene took charge of the incoming. Dozens of casseroles and scores of white bakery boxes were piled high like mini-skyscrapers in the kitchen. Peter was an assistant stacker, building their city of food while Frieda and Justin accepted condolences in the bedroom.

Peter nipped at the pastry. He sampled the cookies. He took bites of the casseroles and did his part to put a dent in the deli platters. His wife had been laboring steadily for hours, and Peter offered to make a sandwich for her. After all she'd done for Frieda that day, he wanted to do something for her. She responded to his offer of kindness by saying, "For one goddamn minute, can you think about something besides food?"

Their marriage had gone straight downhill from there.

The waitress, a rail-thin blonde with low-rise jeans that barely concealed her pubic hair, took Betty and Peter's order. That business concluded, Peter said, "If anything, Gregg's death made our marriage stronger."

"Ilene says you guys are at the pinnacle of connubial bliss," said Betty. "A shining beacon to single women everywhere." He thought he heard sarcasm in her voice.

They were, he told himself. Underneath all the arguments and lack of sex, they had a foundation of love. If he didn't believe that, he couldn't possibly handle the rest.

"Frieda and Gregg hardly ever fought," said Peter. "They were the shining example."

"And look at Frieda now," said Betty. "She's marching straight up Sam Hill."

"He was fantastic in *Oliver!* He got a standing ovation. Frieda jumped up and down for him like she'd been called to be a contestant on *The Price Is Right.*"

"Frieda told me," said Betty. "He's all she talks about. She hardly ever mentions Gregg anymore. It's like he got swallowed up by the earth, and Sam Hill sealed the seam."

Peter said, "Do you miss him?"

Betty nodded. "More since we talk about him less," she said. "Gregg and I used to have lunches once a month. Like this. I really looked forward to them. He was the man in my life for a while there. Platonically, of course. Pathetic that my sister's husband was the only date I had for years. I know how you've stepped in to take Justin to any father-son functions. I thought you were making a similar overture to me."

"By asking you to lunch today?" Maybe he had. He couldn't honestly fathom why it had seemed so important.

Betty said, "You're the last man standing in this family."

Peter and Gregg had always gravitated toward each other at Schast family functions. The two men among the women. Peter had been so focused on Frieda and Justin's loss, he hadn't contemplated his own. He was the last man standing. He had a responsibility to his family which, consciously or not, he was gasping to meet.

He said, "Ilene thinks I'm going to go next. Death by heart attack."

Betty said gently, "It's not inconceivable, considering your family history."

The skinny waitress with the sexy stomach brought their food. Peter looked down at his salad, a beautiful creation of field greens, avocado and grilled chicken, and felt not a single spark of hunger. He couldn't image what power on earth could get him to lift his fork and attempt to eat a single bite.

He said, "This is the most unappetizing lunch I've ever had."

Betty laughed. "Maybe we should do this again," she said. "At the very least, we'll depress each other too much to eat."

Peter said, "Will you be my diet buddy?"

Betty lifted her eyebrows and said, "I thought you'd never ask."

Chapter 18

Wednesday, December 18
6:40 P.M.

"Let's go shopping," said Earl to Betty as they walked out of Burton & Notham and into the icy city at night.

Betty had already decided she would sleep with him after dinner. It was their sixth date. They'd barely kissed. Her fault. It had been so long, and each time he leaned in to plant one on her mouth, she froze. He stopped quickly, not wanting to suck face with a statue, albeit a soft one with a jiggly belly. She knew that if she didn't relax soon, if they didn't get physical, he'd lose interest in her.

Her relaxation strategy was one-pronged. She would drink. Heavily, if necessary. Lower her inhibitions by raising a few glasses. She would suggest dinner at a sushi place near her house, and order copious carafes of sake, then take him home and sake to him.

But he had another idea. "You always wear clothes that

are a size too big and not terribly flattering," he said. "You can do better than that. I'm taking you shopping."

The nightmare of it. He'd hand her a pile of clothes (sweet Jesus, she'd have to tell him her size), she'd model them for him. They'd all look like shit, she'd be mortified, stripped of her camouflage (he'd been right about her buying garments that were too big). He'd see her true shape, the one she'd taken pains to conceal, and he'd make a run for it while she changed in the dressing room. If they were naked and alone in the dark, though, he might overlook certain flaws.

He said, "Don't be afraid, Betty. I'm good at this."

"You want to play dress-up," she said. "I'm a life-size doll for you?" Make that plus-size.

"Daffy's is just around the corner," Earl said definitively.

The store was a huge discount chain that sold designer clothes that (a) were faulty in some minor way, (b) went unsold in finer retail stores, or (c) had fallen off the back of a truck. Betty spent a significant percentage of her clothing budget at Daffy's because it was close to work and cheap. He took her hand and led her there.

Despite her familiarity with the store, as soon as she and Earl walked inside the glass doors and stood among the circular racks of clothes, Betty panicked. She turned on her heel and went back outside. Earl followed.

He grabbed her by the forearm of her puffy down coat. She shook him loose and said, "Every time we've gone out, you've ordered for me. And now you want to dress me."

"That's right," he said.

"You're trying to change me," she said. "If I'm not good enough for you the way I am, fuck off."

"I want you to curse less," he said. "It's crass."

"I'll fucking curse as much as I fucking want to," she said.

He shook his head. "Okay then."

"Okay what? I can do what I want, or you're taking off?" she asked.

Earl dug his hands into his overcoat pockets and said, "I'm taking off." Before she could recover from the sock in the gut, he continued. "You think you've given me an ultimatum, but the choice is really up to you, Betty. You can indulge me, or resist me. Let me take control of the situation, or continue the way you've been."

She said, "The situation? Which is?"

He said, "How you've let yourself go."

That phrase. The one that cropped up in Gert's women's magazines. She loathed it. The implication that she'd willfully surrendered to gravity and the call of Mallomars infuriated her. She'd always felt conflicted about the social demands for thinness, youth, and beauty. She didn't have time to exercise or sit in front of a mirror for hours at a time, blow-drying her hair or putting on makeup. Nor had she the inclination. Vanity was for bubble-headed, superficial morons. Apparently, that's what Earl wanted her to become.

Betty inhaled as a prelude to shouting, "FUCK OFF, BASTARD COCKSUCKER." That's when Earl put his hands on her shoulders and kissed her. The surprise didn't give

her time to freeze. In fact, she was so red-hot with anger, she couldn't have iced over had it been the will of God.

For a second, Betty wondered if Earl had purposefully distracted her with this fight for the sole purpose of kissing her. But then all thought stopped, and she kissed him back.

Before it got over-the-top impolite (they were on the street, in a mass of feverish Christmas shoppers), he broke contact. He said, "When's the last time you gave in?"

"Gave in?" she asked.

"Let yourself go—in a completely different way."

"You want me to surrender to you," she said. To relinquish her power to him, allow him to lead her around like a dog on a leash. What was the destination, anyway? She doubted she could find love at the end of a leash. But, then again, she hadn't found it roaming freely, either.

"I don't want you to surrender," he said. "We're not at war, Betty. I just want to buy you a new outfit, one you'll feel sexy wearing, and then take you to dinner to show you off."

"Where you'll order for me," she said.

"If that's all right."

"As long as you order a large cocktail," she said.

Earl took her gloved hand and tugged her back into Daffy's. True to his word, he did have an excellent sense of what would look good on her. She told him she was a size 14, but Earl brought back size 12s, which fit pretty well, actually. One pair of slacks shaped her nicely, slimmed her middle and emphasized her legs, which weren't that bad. He opted for a few shirts that had low cleavage. Showy ruf-

fled things, the kind of hyper-girlie gear she previously wouldn't have been caught dead in. Except, she had to admit, the soft fabric and the frills did go well with her straight brown hair. The low front drew the eye toward her breasts, which, like her legs, weren't terrible. Earl left her to stare admiringly at herself in her new slacks and blouse, and returned with high-heeled ankle boots—shiny leather, very sexy.

Betty laughed when she saw them. She hadn't worn heels since her college graduation, and only then because her mother, out of some ridiculous notion of formality, had objected to her sneakers. She said, "You can't be serious."

He said, "Just try."

She took the boots. They were the right size. She squinted at him, questioningly. He said, "Lucky guess. Come on, Betty. If they feel uncomfortable, forget it."

She grudgingly put them on. They didn't hurt at all. She hoped they wouldn't prove to be murder as the night wore on. More important, at the end of her not-terrible legs, the boots looked like dynamite exploding from a keg. With the extra height, Betty felt like a tower of strength. The heels forced her to think about posture. The result: She stood upright, not slouched. She had to lean back slightly, which further de-bulked her belly and highlighted her rack.

Earl came up behind her and kissed the back of her neck while she watched the action in the full-length mirror. She closed her eyes, sinking into the moment. He touched her on the ruffles, right there, for all to see in the Daffy's women's department. He touched her new slacks, too.

Dropped his hand inside them. And Betty let him. The truth was, she would have died had he stopped.

He'd been absolutely right. She did feel attractive in the outfit. Like the heels, sexy was a foreign feeling, one Betty would have to get used to. She hoped it wouldn't prove to be murder as the night wore on.

Chapter 19

Thursday, December 19
2:29 P.M.

Ilene loved the cold. The blast of wind on her face, the softness of the faux-fur collar of her coat, her hair flying
around her cheeks. She felt like an arctic princess. Her
blood temperature seemed to rise to counter the chill.
Lesser mortals hugged their coats closer, fighting the ele-
ments that were, for Ilene, friendly and welcoming. With
the slightest regret, she walked into the Citibank on the
corner of Madison and 42nd, out of the brisk air and into
the overheated ATM vestibule.

She had shopping to do. Frieda's pre-Christmas dinner
was coming up, and her gift list was long. Justin would get
toys, Betty and Frieda clothes. For Peter, Ilene had ideas
but nothing she was completely happy with. She would
poke around a few stores and wait for inspiration to strike.
She'd decided to buy generic and impersonal accessories
from Brooks Brothers for Sam Hill and Earl Long. In short,

ties. Not that she was trying to be symbolic. She didn't believe her sisters' boyfriends would have lasting ties to the family. She didn't expect to see either of them at next year's dinner.

The pre-Christmas dinner was a family tradition going way back. Their parents, not wanting their daughters to feel left out, had done gifts and a turkey on Christmas Day since they were little girls. As adults, getting together for Christmas got complicated with travel plans and spouses. Plus, as their collective consciousness rose in the age of terrorism, gathering on the birthday of the baby Jesus felt like a betrayal of their Jewish heritage. The family began a new tradition: the pre-Christmas dinner, held earlier in December during Hanukah, another in the long line of Jewish holidays commemorating how their ancestors were almost killed by enemies but managed to kill the enemies instead, after which point they noshed for three days. L'chiam.

Frieda wanted to host this year, to arrange the night as a coming-out for Sam. This would be the first party at Frieda's since the shivah for Gregg. Ilene had offered to help, but Frieda wanted to handle it on her own. Unsatisfied to do nothing, Ilene contented herself with shopping. She'd come bearing gifts, if not food.

Ilene took off her gloves and put her card in the ATM slot. She usually hated paying cash, but she didn't want Peter to see where she'd gone shopping if he checked the action on their Visa card. The holiday season, combined with his weight loss, was rapidly thawing Ilene's heart to him. Peter must have dropped close to twenty pounds. She noticed every ounce of the shrinkage, but didn't say anything to him for fear of jinxing it. She had no idea what had finally inspired him to diet. What it something she'd said? She wished she knew. She was proud of him, and relieved. His risk of heart attack decreased with the numbers on the scale. Her knot of anger was unraveling. His diet was proof of his feelings. She felt loved again, and safe.

Relationships are 90 percent perception. Ilene's current perspective was sunny and clear, brightening her mind, the day, the season. She checked her face in the mirror above the ATM. She looked good. She felt good—and she'd show Peter just how good in bed tonight. Remarkably, she was looking forward to it.

She punched in her PIN number to access the joint checking account, and hit "Get cash." She'd take out $1,000, the most she could withdraw from the account on a single day. When she tried to extract the money, the ATM told her that $200 had already been withdrawn from the account that morning, and she could only get an additional $800, until tomorrow. Peter had taken out $200? Or was it a bank error? Ilene went to "Account information." Scrolling down the transaction summary, she noticed a pattern. Apparently, Peter had been withdrawing $200 each week for the last six weeks.

"Twelve hundred dollars?" she said to herself. Where had the money gone? He hadn't used it to pay any bills. Ilene wrote the checks in the house. He hadn't been shopping for groceries. For budgeting purposes, Ilene used her credit card at the supermarket.

After withdrawing the $800, Ilene tucked the cash in her wallet, crammed the wallet into her purse, slung her purse on her shoulder, and marched out of the ATM. No longer feeling the cold nor enjoying it, Ilene stormed straight up Madison Avenue to 45th street. The shopping would have to wait. Before she could do another single thing, she wanted to know what Peter was up to. They had an agreement, that all large cash transactions would be discussed first. Two hundred at a time wasn't large, but the six withdrawals added up to a significant amount.

The lobby of Peter's office building always reminded her of a giant bathroom. The walls and floor were lined with marble tiles, and there were huge corn plants arranged every few yards. She hated the décor. The sight of it made her irrationally angry. She stopped at the security desk and signed in. The guard recognized her, but he informed her that the building had a new security policy. Every visitor had to be announced before going up to any of the offices.

Ilene gave him Peter's extension. He dialed on the security phone, whispered into the mouthpiece, and then hung up.

"I'm sorry. Mr. Vermillion is out of the office."

"Give me that phone," she said.

The guard saw the look in her eye and gave her the phone. She dialed Peter's extension. Jane answered.

"Hello, Jane. It's Ilene. Would you happen to know where Peter is? I need to speak with him. It's urgent," she said.

"Ilene, hi," said Jane. "He stepped out. He should be back in about an hour."

"Stepped out. For an hour. At three o'clock on a Thursday?"

"Can you hold, please?"

"I'm afraid not," said Ilene.

Jane paused. "The other phone is ringing."

"Let it ring."

"Is there something wrong, Ilene?" asked Jane in an exaggeratedly solicitous tone. Ilene laughed when she heard Jane disarm Peter that way. She wasn't laughing now.

Ilene said, "I'm waiting."

Jane said, "He had an appointment. I'm not sure where or with whom. If you want more information, you'll have to ask Peter yourself. But, frankly, I don't think he'll want to talk to you when you're in this kind of mood."

The lip! "How dare you . . . Why are you protecting him?" asked Ilene. The security guard seemed anxious to get his phone back. A line of people had formed behind her. She closed her eyes, ignoring them all.

"Have you tried his cell?" asked Jane.

"Miss? I'll have to ask you to hang up," said the guard.

"No," said Ilene to Jane and the guard. She dug into her purse and found her cell. She dialed Peter's number. Voice-mail. Ilene said into the landline, "It's turned off."

Jane was silent. The guard stood and walked around the security desk to take the phone from her by force. Ilene could hear other phone lines ringing in Peter's office.

"What is he up to?" demanded Ilene, dodging the security guard.

"I have no idea what you're talking about," said Jane.

"Please, miss," said the guard.

"Is he buying me jewelry?" asked Ilene with holiday hope.

The guard said, "I'm going to have to call security."

Ilene said, "You *are* security!"

"Jewelry?" said Jane. "Don't bet on it."

Ilene pulled the phone away from her ear to look at it. Had Jane been possessed by demons? Ilene said, "Just tell Peter to call me." She threw the receiver at the security guard. The line of people behind her applauded.

Ilene hoofed it back to *Cash,* only a few blocks up Madison Avenue from *Bucks.* She ignored her assistant, slammed into her office and slid the door closed tight. Sitting down in her desk chair, Ilene tried to get a grip on herself, to think rationally. Approach this like an article. She took out a pad of paper and wrote at the top: "What costs $1,200?"

She proceeded to make a list of what Peter could be buying with that amount. Ilene could make an infinite list of items she'd buy with $1,200, including the entire lamp department at ABC Carpet and Home. She crossed out her first question, and tried a new one: "What would Peter need to keep secret from me?" And then, she wrote out a list, including only scary, bad things.

1. *Drugs*
2. *Pornography*
3. *Botox (other beauty treatment? liposuction not that cheap)*
4. *Gambling*

5. *Debt to Mafia*
6. *Blackmail*
7. *Hookers*
8. *An affair*

He had lost a lot of weight, possibly aided by chemicals. But she knew from her own college experiences that Peter hadn't been exhibiting the signs of cocaine use (fidgeting, nonstop talking, smoking cigarettes and frequent trips to the bathroom). If he'd started smoking pot, he'd have gained weight. Heroin? She didn't know much about the drug personally. But, as she understood it, that would cost more than $200 a week. And he seemed energetic lately, not in a morphine-induced stupor. Could be pharmaceuticals. She added "Prozac?" to the list, and moved on.

Porn. Hard to imagine he'd spend that much on magazines and videos. She scratched that off. Okay, beauty treatments. Men were senselessly embarrassed to admit to getting help from trained Russian facialists. His skin seemed the same. No sign of UVB exposure from tanning booths. No injection marks from Botox. He couldn't very well hide the crackling red burns of a fruit-acid peel. Cellulite suction treatment? He couldn't stand the pain.

Gambling, Mafia debt, blackmail. Unlikely, she thought. But who really knew about such things? Had Peter hit a kid in the Bronx while driving drunk—like in *Bonfire of the Vanities*—been seen, and had to pay off some wise guy? Wouldn't the blackmailer ask for a larger sum, probably lump?

Debt? On what? Not drugs. Gambling? He'd never shown any interest. The one time they'd tried roulette on a vacation in the Bahamas, Peter nearly wept when they lost $50. Hookers? Peter would be terrified of catching a disease.

Which left an affair. Ilene put down the pad. Two hundred, once a week. The price of a two-star hotel room in Manhattan, plus a bottle of cheap champagne. He'd paid cash for the same reason she didn't want to use her credit card for holiday gifts. The money was always withdrawn on Thursdays, she realized. Was he, at that very moment, humping some slut at the Waldorf? The weight loss. Wasn't it a predictable cliché that a man got in shape before dissolving his marriage, or when he took up with a younger woman?

Relationships are 90 percent perception. Her marriage, bright as the sun an hour ago, had plunged into a swamp of black gook. Should she feel upset, defensive, belligerent, or hopeless? Or all of the above? Until she sorted out her feelings and gathered information, Ilene had to present a calm exterior. "Pretend everything is normal," she instructed herself.

She picked up the phone and dialed Peter's office again. Jane answered. Ilene said, "Jane, it's Ilene. I'm so sorry I was rude to you before. Don't bother telling Peter I called."

Jane said, "The message was urgent."

"This Christmas, you deserve a full day of beauty at Georgette Klinger," said Ilene. "For all your hard work and dedication."

Jane, who usually received a half day of beauty at Georgette Klinger from Ilene, said, "I'm ripping up the message right now."

"And you won't mention my little episode?" said Ilene.

"What episode?" asked Jane.

Chapter 20

Monday, December 23
Midnight

"I thought you did well," said Frieda to Sam as they lay in bed.

"Just now?" he asked.

"Yes," she said, "but I was referring to the party."

The pre-Christmas dinner had been a success. Her guests left a couple of hours ago. Frieda went to work on the dishes and Sam put Justin to bed, as if they were a normal family. Once Justin was sound asleep, Frieda and Sam made love on her four-poster bed, Christmas lights wound around the posts and canopy like a starry ship. They'd never had sex on her bed before, or had a whole night sleepover. He'd been introduced to her family. As evenings go, this was a significant one for their relationship.

They'd decided that Sam should leave before Justin woke up. Frieda thought it might upset Justin to wake up and find Sam sleeping in his father's place. Sam was amenable, as always. He'd leave at 5 A.M. That gave them five more hours, of which they'd make good use. Frieda would have another day on minimal sleep. She was getting used to the REM-deprived buzzing in her brain. The physical demands of her relationship with Sam were like having a newborn baby. She felt exhausted, with sore breasts and a well-traveled vagina.

She said to him, "Party postmortem?"

"Okay," said Sam. "I like Justin."

Justin had appeared to like Sam.

Showing up twenty minutes late (a high drama entrance), Sam had seemed wary at first. Who could blame him, walking into an apartment full of strangers? Frieda rushed to Sam's side immediately, eager to introduce him around. Justin, who'd seen Sam's head shot in the *Playbill* for *Oliver!*, approached him before her sisters had the chance. He said, "You're Sam?"

And Sam said, "And you must be Peter. No? Then you're Betty. Ilene? Wait a minute. I've got it. You're the butler!"

Justin giggled appreciatively, and that was that.

Sam's arrival had drawn Frieda's sisters, Peter, and Earl into the living room from the kitchen. Frieda made the introductions. Sam shook hands around the semicircle of gawking people. Betty invited Sam to sit on the couch. He asked for a Scotch, which Peter supplied. Frieda said she had a turkey to baste. She headed back toward the kitchen. On the walk down the hall, she'd heard Justin say, "In your picture, you look a lot older."

Naturally, her sisters followed Frieda, leaving the men in the living room.

Once safely in the kitchen, Betty said, "He is so fucking hot!"

Frieda said, "I know!"

Ilene said, "He is, truly, a knockout."

Frieda said, "I know!"

"Very young," added Ilene. "He looks like a kid."

Frieda snuggled closer to Sam, remembering her sisters' praise. She said, "You and Justin played nicely together." Sam had given Justin a piggyback ride and let him jump from his shoulders to the couch (not allowed ordinarily).

He said simply, "Justin's a good kid." It was a benign statement, noncommittal. Frieda hadn't expected Sam to say, "He's exactly what I've been looking for in a stepson." But something more than "good kid" would have been appreciated. She reminded herself that marriage wasn't the goal. There was no goal. Only game.

Sam said, "Justin showed me his room. The cats were sleeping on his bed. They're named Black and White?"

"They're both Gray in the dark," said Frieda.

"And the turtles," said Sam. The tank was in Justin's room.

Frieda said, "What about them?"

"Named Sink and Swim?"

"There used to be a goldfish in the tank, too."

"Justin told me. The turtles ate it," said Sam. "What was the goldfish's name?"

"Lunch," said Frieda.

The couple lay side-by-side, bodies touching, holding

hands, looking at each other and the red, yellow, and pink lights around the bed. She asked, "What do you think of my apartment?"

"Big. Bright. Lots of pictures. Boxes for everything. A box for the remote controls. A box for pens, coasters, onions. Even this bed is a box, with the posts and canopy."

Frieda said, "I like things to be contained."

"I'll bet you'd like to contain me," said Sam.

She laughed. "I don't think they make boyfriend caddies at Pottery Barn."

"At some point, I'd like you to tell me about your stuff."

"Where I found my end tables? How I picked my china?"

He said, "You've accumulated a lot."

"I have."

"I haven't," he said.

Frieda said, "The night table on your side of the bed. Notice how the surface of the wood is pockmarked?" Sam nodded. "Every night when Gregg came home from work, he'd toss his keys on the night table, leaving the little marks. You're on his side of the bed, by the way."

"Great, so now every time I look at this night table, I'll see Gregg's indelible mark," Sam said. "You don't have to worry, Frieda. I won't forget what you've been through."

"That's not why I told you about it."

Sam said, "Sure it is."

They were silent for a minute. He said, "Are we still doing a postmortem?"

She nodded. "Start with Ilene."

Sam leaned up on one elbow and then kissed Frieda before saying, "She's not as beautiful as you are."

Ilene had long been recognized as the most beautiful sister, certainly possessing the lioness's share of style. Frieda said, "Thank you for lying."

"You're welcome," he said. "She was quiet, actually. Not what I'd been expecting. She gave good gifts. Can't think of the last time I wore a tie. We might be able to think of a use for it, though." Sam grabbed her wrist, and made eyes at the posts of her bed.

Frieda got up on one elbow, in the same position as Sam, and said, "Did you talk to her?"

He said, "Not really. She asked me a little bit about *Oliver!*"

"Did you talk to Betty?"

"Not really. She said she was sorry to have missed *Oliver!*"

"Both of them came into the kitchen and told me how intelligent and sophisticated you are," she said.

"Now who's lying?"

"What did you think of Earl?" she asked.

"Drunk."

"Besides that."

"He likes Betty," he said. "She likes him. When he made that toast, I thought she'd pass out with happiness."

After the turkey and stuffing, before the coffee and pie, Earl had held up his (sixth? seventh?) glass of wine and said, "And now, I'd like to discuss my traveling plans." He'd explained that his original schedule called for him to return to Chicago at the end of December, but he'd launched a campaign to remain in New York for an additional six months. He'd said, "I called my boss and told him, 'My work here is not done.' And he's given me permission to stay." Betty had jumped out of her chair and hugged Earl with abandon, in love or close to it.

Sam said, "I saw Peter and Betty talking conspiratorially in the kitchen."

"They're diet buddies. They were sneaking pie."

"Sneaking?" he asked.

Frieda waved it off. "What else did you see?"

"Ilene talked to everyone but her own husband. Peter had four Scotches. Justin gravitated toward Betty, but she didn't want to be crawled on in her new outfit. Earl called Justin 'kiddo.' "

"Did you talk to Peter?" she asked.

"Not really. He bought the soundtrack to *Oliver!*"

"So you're saying all anyone could think to ask you about was *Oliver!*" she said.

"That's the size of it."

"No one asked about your Norman Rockwell childhood in Maine?"

"They must be saving that for the next forced social encounter."

Frieda nodded. Her hand roamed the length of Sam's torso.

"I should have facilitated," she said.

"You were busy with the food and Justin," he said. "Besides, your sisters just wanted to get a look at me, not sit down and have a meaningful conversation. I got the vibe, especially from Ilene, that getting to know me would be a waste of time."

"She's just being protective."

"How is that protective?"

Frieda shrugged. "She's the oldest sister. She thinks my happiness is her responsibility."

"And she doesn't think you'll be happy with me."

"Don't get defensive," said Frieda. "She hardly talked to Earl either."

"Did you talk to him?" asked Sam.

"Not really," she said. "He told me he liked the apartment. That I had good taste in wine. He also said he was sorry to have missed your performance in *Oliver!*"

Sam said, "You should have told him the pockmarked-night-table story. I've sure he would have been deeply moved."

Frieda laughed. "You're an asshole."

"But I'm your asshole," he said. "I am undeniably, utterly, smittenly, your personal property. And you can tell Ilene that I'm not going anywhere. That she'll have to deal with me one of these days. And then she'll realize that a broke twenty-eight-year-old actor is exactly what you need."

"I'll pass that along," said Frieda, smiling at him, staring at his marvelous face.

He said, "As long as you look at me that way, I'll always love you."

"You love me," she said.

"I was holding off on saying it until I met your son," he said.

This confused her. "If my son had turned out to be awful, you wouldn't love me?" she asked.

He said, "I probably would've been able to pull back."

An honest response. Sam had been consistently truthful. She couldn't fault him for it. "I'm not sure I like that," she said.

"I said 'probably.' My love might have been an unstoppable force despite a monster child. But we won't know now because Justin is a good kid."

Sam pushed Frieda onto her back and started the rubbing and touching business that made her brain shut off and her body liquefy. In seconds, she would lose all reason. She stopped him and said, "Just tell me if you liked my family. Generally speaking."

He said, "You're all very close. It's intimidating to come up against that. Especially when I get the feeling you're the only one rooting for me." His hand was well under the comforter now, and she couldn't concentrate. Sam whispered in her ear: "And now, I'd like to discuss my travel plans."

Frieda said, "You'll be staying in New York another six months?"

"I'm leaving tomorrow for six weeks," he said.

She tried to sit upright, but Sam held her down. He said, "I have to go to Maine for Christmas. And then we're doing a Midwestern tour. It's decent money, and I'm contracted to do it."

Panicky, Frieda said, "Six weeks?"

"I told you when we met that I travel a lot."

"That was before I got addicted to you," she said.

He said, "You're not addicted to me."

"I am! Being with you is everything to me."

"Besides Justin," he said.

"Justin is beside the point," she said.

Sam said, "It's just six weeks. I'll be back and it'll be better for being apart. Think how great it'll be to see each other again. We'll talk every day while I'm gone."

"Tonight is our last night. We'll miss New Year's," she said. "Why didn't you tell me earlier?"

He said, "I knew you'd be upset."

She was upset. Terribly upset. She found herself anticipating the aloneness, knowing it well, the muted color and thorny texture.

Sam said, "You'll get back into work at the gallery. You'll spend time with friends. Justin has winter break. The weeks will pass. You'll hardly miss me."

"Are all your ex-girlfriends going, too?" she asked.

"Some," he said. "Look at me. You never have to worry about that. I am faithful like a dog. I've never cheated in my life. And I won't dare do anything to fuck this up."

She took a few deep breaths. He was leaving her. She thought of Dr. Bother, of her warning to be careful. That she was susceptible to emotional swings. Suddenly, she was in the midst of one.

He held her close. She said, "Where in the Midwest?"

Sam said, "Iowa, Illinois, Michigan. They love musical

theater in Michigan. They give us a cheese platter in the green room in Wisconsin."

"They do not."

"It's true. They cheese us up."

"I haven't told you I love you back," she said.

"I noticed."

She said, "I can't say it yet." She was too rocked by his news. The idea of losing him had brought up some Gregg stuff. She tried to push it back down, but couldn't.

Sam moved toward her and licked her lips. She could kiss him for hours, had kissed him for hours. She'd nearly come from just hugging. She found herself slipping into his kiss again. And the Gregg stuff did go away. For now.

She pulled back. "Oh, fuck it," she said. "I love you. You know I do. I've loved you since that first time we kissed at the gallery. You have me. I am at your mercy."

"I am on my honor," he promised, speaking against her cheek.

"You'd better be," she said.

In the morning, hours after Sam left, Justin plodded into her room. She'd had two hours of sleep. With Sam gone, knowing she wouldn't see him again for weeks, fatigue settled into her bones. She wouldn't open the store today. She'd put the original *Star Wars* trilogy on for Justin, and try to sleep over the sound of light sabers.

But first, the morning routine. Frieda got up, made Justin's breakfast, fed the cats, the turtles, watered the plants. Washed the dishes. Made Justin's bed, folded the laundry.

While he ate his Frosted Flakes, Justin said, "Mom. About Sam."

"Yes?" she said.

"He's a good guy."

Six Months Later

Chapter 21

Thursday, June 5
6:20 P.M.

"Where is he now?" asked Betty into the phone.

"Florida," said Frieda. "A few more weeks."

Betty absent-mindedly tugged at the waistband of her new Seven jeans. Actually, one could hardly call it a waistband. It was a hipband. The pants were so low-rise, her panties stuck out like a diaper when she sat down. She stood up, pulled the jeans as high as they'd go and sat down again, feeling that annoying tug downward. Dressing her size-10 body demanded at least an hour of her time every day. She'd actually used a stopwatch to calculate exactly how long it took to select an outfit, put it on, accessorize, do makeup, check herself out in the mirror, and obsess about how she looked. When she was twenty pounds heavier, at size 14, she would throw on baggy pants and a sweatshirt, and be done with it. Five minutes, tops. Betty had no idea what she used to do with the extra hour

169

a day she now spent dressing. Nothing productive. She probably ate French fries.

Frieda said, "You there?"

"Love my new body; hate my new jeans," said Betty.

"So tell Earl to fuck himself, and wear comfortable clothes," said Frieda. Her testiness was a new phenomenon, usually spiking the day Sam left for a tour, simmering for the duration of his absence, and softening upon his return. Betty kind of liked Frieda's new snappishness. Ilene had been through some personality adjustments, too, acting atypically sullen lately. Betty, meanwhile, basked in her own altered temperament. She'd become munificent. Socially confident. The friendliness was eye opening. People were easier to deal with when she smiled at them.

"Hey, Earl," said Betty. "Frieda says you should go fuck yourself."

Sitting in her office, his heels on the corner of her desk, Earl said, "Sounds like a terrible waste. And please don't curse, Betty."

Frieda asked, "He's sitting right there?"

Betty said, "Yup."

"Call me when you're alone." She hung up.

Betty, now off the hook, gathered her things. It was the end of the workday. The night manager was arriving shortly, and she had big plans. A surprise itinerary for the perfect romantic summer evening in New York. First, a stroll across the Brooklyn Bridge at sunset with a view of the South Street Seaport and the Statue of Liberty. On the

Brooklyn side, she'd take him to the Fulton Landing, where they could look at the glittering Manhattan skyline. A few cocktails at the floating River Café. And then the ferry back to the city, a slow churn across the East River. You couldn't sell New York City or romance harder than that. Betty wanted to give Earl every opportunity to tell her that (1) he loved her, (2) he was going to move to New York permanently, (3) he wanted to marry her, and (4) he wanted to start a family.

They'd been a couple for seven months. Betty didn't want it to end. She'd taken a few messages for Earl from Burton & Notham headquarters about his next move. They wanted him to set up audio-book booths at the Chicago flagship store as soon as possible. He hadn't said a word to her about his (their) future, even when she handed him the messages from his boss. But she was sure he was thinking about it. He'd been secretive lately, ducking out of the building for an hour here, a half hour there. Ring shopping, perhaps. Gert reported running into Earl in the diamond district last Saturday. When she asked him what he'd done that morning, he'd told Betty he was at his (their) gym.

Yes, shocking as it may be, especially to herself, Betty had joined a gym. She never thought the day would come when she became another a jerk-off marching nowhere on a treadmill. Yet she found herself at the New York Sports Club in Union Square three times a week, speed walking, pumping iron, and grunting. Betty was toned. Gert marveled daily at the transformation, how Betty's body got hard as her personality went soft. Betty fired Gert every time she made this observation. Yet Gert kept showing up for work.

Earl swung his legs off Betty's desk and asked, "What are you smiling at?"

Betty said, "I've gone soft."

He pursed his lips, hesitating. "In the head?"

"I can feel the spot," Betty said, massaging her cranium.

"Let's get out of here. My place. Room service," he said.

She raised her an eyebrow with what she hoped was sly seduction. "Tonight, I'm taking you on a date. Don't ask where. It's a surprise."

For a second, Earl seemed worried. Then he said slowly, "Okay, that's great. Yes."

Shit, thought Betty. The look on his face. The hesitation. What could that be about? Was it possible that her surprise plans were mangling his own? He might have something waiting in the hotel room. Like the box with a ring in it.

Betty said, "Forget it. The hotel sounds perfect."

He shook his head. "No, I'd like to go out. That's better. But we have to stop at my room first."

"Okay," she said. Heart leaping, knees quaking, ears ringing. "Do you want me to wait in the lobby while you run up?"

"Yes," he said, avoiding eye contact. "That would work."

They left the store, walking the three blocks to his hotel in silence. He ran up, and was back down in a minute. They took the number 4 train to the Brooklyn Bridge stop at City Hall.

The Brooklyn Bridge, 120 years old, one mile of suspension with tree-trunk-thick steel cables, two huge towers, a boardwalk-style footpath, was Betty's favorite New York landmark. They headed uphill, looking at those cables, walking into a spider's web. Betty was awed by the bridge's history, the dozens of bends-related deaths during and after construction. By the Roebling father and son, who'd engineered the Bridge, both died during or due to its construction. By the fact that elephants were led across the walkway to convince New Yorkers the cables could support foot traffic. The brick towers—one on the Manhattan side, one on the Brooklyn side—seemed like relics, monoliths of America's engineering infancy.

As they walked, Betty prayed Earl liked the view, her company, anything. He'd been quiet all day. Too quiet. At the Brooklyn tower, three quarters across, Betty said, "Take in the view?"

They stopped. One glimpse and Betty immediately remembered that the view from that spot was impressive in part for what was missing from it. She didn't want to get into a discussion about terrorism or to rehash their previously exchanged "Where were you when . . ." anecdotes. Nor did she want the ghostly backdrop behind her when (if) he proposed.

She said, "Windy up here."

A gust blew Earl's black hair back. Without it falling around his cheeks, his face was oblong, horselike. Betty had never noticed that before.

He said, "I'm going to Chicago next week."

She nodded. Betty suspected as much. She didn't want to face the rigors of a long-distance relationship. If she took Frieda as an example, it'd be an emotional tumult. Since Sam started his touring season, Frieda had agonizing cycles: She was elated when Sam was in town, flew into a panic when he left, tumbled into sadness while he was gone, hit a spike of anxiety immediately before his return, and then was maniacal at his homecoming. It'd been like that since Christmas.

Betty said, "You don't have to go. You can quit."

Earl frowned at that. "I'm not quitting my job."

"Then I'll come with you," she said, spreading out her options like a blanket on a bed.

The wind again. His horse face fixed on her. He said, "You shouldn't come."

Betty had sorted it all out. She could get a temp job or do consulting. Maybe Burton & Notham would set her up in Chicago. And maybe, after they were married, he'd want a job that required less city-hopping anyway. They could move back to New York. She said, "I'll do it to be with you."

Earl said, "I want to give you something."

This was it! she thought. He reached into his pants pocket, and pulled out a BLACK VELVET JEWELRY BOX. He said, "The last seven months have been fantastic, Betty. You've come so far. I'm proud to have made such an impact on your life."

Fingers trembling, she reached for the box. She nearly dropped it, sending it plunking into the East River below, but she scrambled to catch it. She laughed nervously at the slapstick, and then, slowly, she opened the bubbly lid. The sun was just setting. The sky behind her was pink, with a nice streak of orange over the refineries in Elizabeth, New Jersey.

The lid open, she stared at the box's contents and very nearly cried. "A brooch!" she said. "It's beautiful."

"It's made of jade," he said.

"I see that. And what kind of flower is this? I'm not sure I . . ."

Earl said, "It's in the shape of a forget-me-not."

"You're right," she said. "Blue jade, yes."

She leaned forward to give him a kiss, aiming for the lips, and landing, somehow, on his bony cheek. He said, "I wanted to give you a gift so you'll always remember me and what we accomplished together. When I first met you, you were horrible, Betty. Fat. Bitchy. A slob. And now, you're slim, neat, nice. You've completely changed. You're so much better now. You'll probably get a raise. You'll definitely get a boyfriend."

She said, "I have a boyfriend."

Earl shook his head. "Betty, you knew I was going to be a temporary thing. I told them in December, my work in New York wasn't done. Well, now it is, and I can leave with a sense of accomplishment."

"Your work?" she asked.

"You!" he said. "I told them it was about the booths. But I was thinking of you. My project. I couldn't leave you half-baked. I had to stay. I'm glad I did. But now, I'm moving on."

Betty said, "To do it again. With another woman."

"If the opportunity arises."

"Like you've done before?" she asked, a sudden chill in her bones.

He nodded. "Each time presents unique challenges," he said.

"What was the challenge with me?" she had to ask.

He said, "It took a while to break through your anxieties about sex."

A blow below the belt. She said, "You realize this bridge is famous for jumpers."

He laughed. "You would never."

"People get pushed off, too," she said.

Losing patience, Earl said, "Look Betty, you can't deny that you've had a good time. You can either remember me fondly for what we had, or hate me for leaving. But I'm going, regardless."

"So go," she said.

"I am."

"I mean now," she said.

He took the subtle hint, and started walking back toward Manhattan, leaving her without a kiss goodbye, holding a piece-of-shit fake-jade ugly brooch, for fuck's sake.

She hated him. From that moment forward, she despised Earl Long with all her heart, soul, kidneys, and lungs. With God as her witness, she vowed to get even with that man before she died, in some viscous, underhanded way. Betty might be slim. She might be neat. But she would never be nice.

With all the muster of her newly developed biceps, Betty heaved the jewelry box, brooch and all, as far as she could in the westerly direction of the Statue of Liberty.

Then she cried all the way to Frieda's house.

Chapter 22

Peter hadn't been to Aux-On-Arles since his five-year-anniversary dinner with Ilene. The French restaurant served the ultimate in haute cuisine, the prix fixe sampling menu costing a $150 per person. The crepe de chine curtains—off-white, eggshell or ecru, he wasn't sure, nor did he care—reminded him of that long-ago night when he and his wife rearranged their chairs so they could hold hands under the table.

He looked across his table tonight, way across, miles outside of handholding range, at his dinner companion. She was pretty. Her curly brown hair shined with megadoses of vitamin A, the tawny bare arms glowed from adequate lutein consumption, her eyes sparkled with high-concentrate beta-carotene. He'd never felt less attracted to a woman in his life.

Peter said, "Explain it again. I have to pay for dinner, plus your standard session fee?"

"That's right," said Peggy McFarthing.

"Since you're eating, shouldn't you pay for your own food?"

Peggy rearranged her napkin on her lap and said, "Peter, I wouldn't be here if I weren't working. This is your graduation session. It's both a celebration and a lesson on how to put your eating plan to practical use. Remember the adage: Humans used to have to hunt for food; nowadays, food hunts us. French cuisine is a particular challenge because of the sauces. And you were the one to suggest this restaurant. I've taken other clients to a Greek diner for the final session."

Therefore, he'd stewed himself in his own *pot au feu*. Yes, he'd suggested the restaurant. But for a specific purpose: Peter planned on bringing Ilene back here to celebrate his forty-five-pound weight loss, their upcoming eleventh wedding anniversary, and her raise of $10,000 a year (not much, considering that he'd spent $6,000 on nutritional counseling in the past seven months, at a rate of about $140 per lost pound). Peter never thought Peggy would expect him to pick up her tab. He would order a la carte, cheaper, by far, than the sampling menu. If she tried to get the prix fixe, he'd object. He corrected his posture in the high, straight-back chair with the thin cushion (all cushions felt thin to him these days), and contemplated making a run for it. Did he really need Peggy to instruct him on how to order a French meal? He eyed the breadbasket. The baguette was particularly tempting.

Peggy said, "I'm very proud of you, Peter."

"Thanks."

"No, I mean it," she said, draping a napkin over the bread, hiding it. "When you first came into my office, I didn't think you'd have the discipline—or the support system—to lose the weight."

He resented that remark, as he resented so much of Peggy's assumptions about his weakness (the napkin over the breadbasket, case in point).

"You thought I'd fail but you took the money anyway," he said.

"Perhaps spending the money was the motivation you needed to succeed."

He hadn't thought of it that way. The money was certainly a motivation not to gain it back. He couldn't stand to spend one more dollar on his vanity (don't think "vanity"; think "health," he reminded himself). He would have spent any amount of money to impress Ilene, but Peter hadn't gotten the feedback from her he'd hoped for; incredibly, his weight loss—dramatic, steady—was observed but uncommented upon by Ilene. He knew she noticed. How could she not notice? He'd had to buy an entire new wardrobe (that was another $5,000 right there), and he knew he looked sharp in his Hugo Boss summer-weight suits and his ironed Levi's. He'd taken to walking around in the nude, just to make sure she could see the difference. Her expression, upon sight of him, didn't waver. It was confounding to him that she kept her mouth shut about his weight loss, when she had not been able to stop harping on his gain.

He wanted to ask Peggy about all this, if she'd noticed, in

her other clients, whether a drastic change in one spouse's appearance affected a marriage adversely. But there was that sticky point in his dealings with Peggy. Discussing his marriage would cast light on her own—and whatever tensions existed there, in part, because Peter had fired Bruce, her husband, all those months ago. Therefore, his marriage was a taboo subject. Overtly, anyway. She alluded to it occasionally. That comment about his "support system," for example.

Peggy said, "Let's look at the menu."

Peter had been fingering the wine list. Alcohol was off limits, a "stop" class of beverage. The only kind of booze that could be consumed without offsetting his carefully calibrated carbohydrate intake was tequila. Mysteriously to him, the Mexican panacea was low-carb. And there was that piss-smelling low-carb beer from Michelob that was offensive in taste and sensibility. But they'd never serve that here, he thought mournfully.

He said, "Appetizer-wise, the goat cheese salad seems to be the way to go." He dearly craved the paté de fois gras with crisp toast wedges and pickles.

Peggy said, "Actually, it's a good standard policy to skip appetizers—and dessert, of course."

"So, then, we're looking at entrées," he said, happily envisioning a smaller bill. Two entrées only without cocktails, wouldn't cost more than a hundred bucks. He could live with that.

"I will get the prix fixe," she said. "And a few drinks."

God damn it. "It takes over two hours to get through the

sampling menu," he said. "And it wouldn't be fair to me, to have to watch you eat all those courses, and dessert."

Peggy said, "In the real world, your dinner companions will order things that are 'stop' foods. Part of the lesson here is learning to handle the restaurant environment, including what we call 'plate envy.' "

Grinding his teeth, Peter felt his blood pressure rising, the thundering palpitations of his heartbeat. He turned his eyes back to the menu and said, "Plate envy."

"Plate envy leads to what we call 'the wandering fork,' " she said. "When you take a forkful of your companion's rich, butter-laden selection, just to taste it. One bite of heavy fat and carbohydrates can lower resistance to the point of a breakdown. The restaurant environment itself severely lowers resistance: the idea that the meal is a special treat, that what you eat outside the home doesn't count. It's important to test your willpower, Peter. I intend to take only a bite of each course, leaving the food just sitting on the plate, to see if you can resist it."

When the waiter came, in a black tux, Peggy ordered the sampling menu as threatened, and a martini. Peter ordered roast squab, hold the l'orange sauce and wild rice. Peggy nodded with approval and actually patted his hand like a school marm. For his carcass of pigeon that would take him all of thirty seconds to inhale, he'd fork over $30, plus tax and tip. His non-carbonated water went for $8 a bottle.

The agony of ordering over, and their drinks having arrived, Peter said, "I appreciate everything you've done for me, Peggy."

She smiled and sipped her martini, which he could have grabbed out of her hand and poured down his throat.

They spoke about some of the social changes Peter would enjoy as a slim person. The attention from strangers. Increased respect from colleagues. Better treatment in stores and gas stations. Peter listened with half an ear. He'd heard it all before from Peggy. It was motivational speech number six.

He had to cut it off—the speech, or his head. "I am a changed man," he said when she paused to draw breath.

"You're half the man you once were," she said.

"The better half."

"Certainly healthier," she said, daintily nipping at the martini ("make it dry," she'd said to the waiter. "Ask the bartender to just *think* Vermouth while he pours the vodka").

Her first course arrived. An oyster stew. As she dipped in her spoon, perfectly oval nuggets of oyster flesh bobbed to the surface, glistening with cream, dotted with pepper. She took her first taste and said, "Ahhhh, ohhhh, my *God* this is good." Then she put down her spoon, dabbed the corners of her mouth, and placed her hands in her lap.

"Peggy, I've got to hand it to you," he said. "You are a lucky woman. You love your work."

"I do," she said, smiling.

"I can tell. It's obvious. You take a real personal pleasure in torture. You're a genuine sadist. You exist to inflict pain. Your eyes are glowing right now, do you realize? Watching me watching you eat is making you squirm in your seat. You're grinding your ass into that chair. You're getting off on this. My pain is sex for you."

Peggy listened to his speech without flinching. "I've heard worse," she said. "I'm tough because I care, Peter."

"You care about being tough," he said. "What amazes me is that you can be a dominatrix dragon-lady ball-breaker to your clients, and yet you expect practically nothing from your dilettante husband. He turns you into oatmeal. That day I spoke to you in Grand Central, you were a weepy little mouse. But in your office, you're the Calorie Nazi."

"Not calorie. Nutrition," she corrected. "The Nutrition Nazi."

A cheese-doodle smile sat on Peggy's face for the duration of Peter's venom spewing. She was holding back, he knew it, and even as he lashed out, he was bracing himself for her retaliation. He'd crossed the line, opened the door to a discussion of her marriage—and therefore, his.

She said, "I think all this is very healthy."

"All what?" he asked.

"Your venting," she said. "I've always believed you are an emotional eater, shoveling food into your mouth, swallowing your pain, instead of letting your negative thoughts and feelings out of your body. Venting at me is an excellent sign that you've learned how to express yourself. Let me ask you this, Peter. Since you started telling me what kind of sadist I am, have you thought of food? Have you looked at this bowl of stew? Are you in the least bit hungry?"

The shocking sideline stopped him cold. She was right, absolutely. But he couldn't admit it to her.

She drained her martini, reached across the table, and took his hand. "The truth is, I *have* been hard on you. I do have lingering resentment about Bruce's firing. And that's why I charged you significantly more than my usual rate per session. It was unprofessional of me, but not illegal. I've checked."

"How much more?" he squeaked out.

"That's all in the past," she said, waving it off. "We have to focus on the future."

From nearby, Peter heard a familiar voice—shrill, loud, and accusatory—blurting, "Did you hear that? She said, 'We have to focus on the future.' Their future!"

Peter spun around, but there was no need. Ilene was upon them, dragging a man through the restaurant. Bruce McFarthing. He hadn't seen Bruce since the day he was fired.

Ilene said to Peter, "I have been tracking you and this woman for months! I know everything, and I finally convinced her husband to follow you with me tonight."

Peggy laughed. Burst out laughing. She was a small woman. It was a large martini. Peter said, "You think we're having an affair?"

Bruce picked up Peter by his collar and tie, and punched him on the jaw. Peter flew back against his chair. The chair toppled over. Peter landed flat on his back, but not before grabbing the tablecloth with flailing hands. From the hardwood floor, Peter watched the rain of spoons, forks, stemware and stew. And bread.

Ilene screamed.

Peggy hiccuped.

Bruce cried. He actually cried. Peter stood up and said, "Bruce, this is ridiculous. I'm not having an affair with your wife. She's my nutritionist. I'm her client. We're eating together as part of my training."

Bruce wiped his eyes, and stared hard at Peter. He said, "Vermillion? Is that you?"

Ilene said, "Am I to understand that you . . ."

"I can't believe it!" shouted Bruce. "Peter Vermillion! You must have dropped, what, a thousand pounds? I wouldn't have recognized you if you'd sat on me."

Peter massaged his jaw and looked at the mess he'd made. And at the wait staff, nervously gathering to watch. And the other diners, both horrified and enthralled by the entertainment.

"Jesus, Peg," extolled Bruce, examining Peter. "You're good!"

"You actually thought I was sleeping with Peter Vermillion?" asked Peggy, a bit more serious now that the hilarity of her husband's violence had ended.

"If I'd known this was about Vermillion, I never would have suspected a thing. But this woman has been calling me for weeks, insisting you were having an affair. I blew it off, but she showed up at the apartment tonight, demanding that I come with her to catch the two of you in the act."

Peter said, "She never identified herself by name?"

"She did. Schast."

"She never identified me by name?" he asked.

Ilene said, "Your first name."

Peter said to his wife, "You didn't recognize *his* name?"

She said, "Why on earth would I recognize his name?"

"Because he worked for me for a year. Because I told you

at great length how hard it was for me to fire him. I've mentioned his name many times to you."

Peggy said, "Maybe the source of your emotional eating is that, when you do vent, you're rarely heard."

"Please shut up, Peggy, thank you."

Ilene said, "It does make sense now. You were seeing a nutritionist to diet. I thought you were seeing this woman, romantically, who happened to be a nutritionist, and the weight loss was for her. And I saw all those cash withdrawals from our checking account. I thought they were to pay for trysts."

"The withdrawals wouldn't have been as noticeable had I not been overcharged."

Bruce to Peggy: "You overcharged him? Sweet!"

Peter said, "And I wasn't dieting for her. I was doing it for you. For you. Always for you. Everything for you and your approval. Which I never fucking get. Instead of love and appreciation, instead of acknowledgment that I've done well or suffered to please you, I get accusations and humiliation. Plus, I'm sure, I have to pay for all these broken dishes." Peter glanced at the maître d', who nodded discreetly. "They cost a fortune, right? From France. Rare china." The maître d' frowned and lowered his eyes.

Peter could have started groaning and not stopped until Tuesday. He watched several waiters pile broken pieces of plates and glasses in the hammocks of their aprons. They worked quickly and quietly. The other patrons stopped staring and returned to their own meals with a story to dine out on here or elsewhere for months.

Bruce helped Peggy out of her chair—miraculously untouched in the fray. He gave her a tight, loving squeeze, and she returned it. Bruce smiled meekly at his wife, his face a palate of vulnerability that even Peter would have succumbed to. That famous McFarthing charm, at work again. Peggy smiled back up at him like she'd struck gold.

Bruce said, "Can you forgive me for being so stupid?"

"I do every day," said Peggy.

They kissed and left together.

Peter waved the maître d' over. He said, "I'm being charged for the full cost of the meals?"

"Well, you see, sir, we've already started preparing the food to order, and—"

"Doggie bag it. All of it. Including the basket of bread. And the water. And the lime in the water."

Ilene grinned nervously. He'd seen that expression before, whenever she knew she'd done wrong and had some reparation to make. She put a hand on his shoulder. She said, "Peter, I'm so sorry. I am proud of you. Can you forgive me for being so stupid?"

Peter said, "No. I can't."

Chapter 23

Monday, June 9
10:03 A.M.

Frieda liked the *New York Post.* She should read the *New York Times,* and often did, but she relished her gossipy tabloid. Unlike her child, her apartment, her gallery, her relationship, the *Post* was easy. Uncomplicated. The broadsheet made no emotional or intellectual demands. She could flip through the pages in seconds, scan, scan, scan, turn. Except when, on the odd morning, she was blindsided by an item. Like today, right there, on Page Six, she read that Gwyneth Paltrow was having a hard time dealing with the death of her father from cancer.

Gorgeous Gwyneth missed her father? *Boo fucking hoo,* thought Frieda. He lived long enough see his perfect daughter get an Oscar. He got to love his wife deep into their middle age. Gwyneth had decades' worth of memories of him. Justin, meanwhile, asked Frieda last night if his dad had had blue or green eyes. He couldn't remember, and it was hard to tell in photos. Not that there were many photos or videotape. Gregg had always held the camera. He was greedy that way. His voice was all over the video, narrating ("Justin, roll over. That's it, roll over. Nearly there, come on, kid. Frieda? Frieda, move that chair. Move the chair. Yes. Good. Back to Justin. Nearly over. One more push," etc.) But Gregg's face was rarely seen.

Frieda was alone in the gallery. She took a sip of coffee, a bite of bagel. She spotted an article in the *Post*'s health section: fascinating new research about the addictive properties of male ejaculate. According to scientists in England (randy bastards), seminal brine contained certain hormones and chemicals that, upon consumption (vaginally, orally, anally), gave women an endorphin-like rush of happiness. The greater their fluid intake, the happier women were. However, upon the sudden deprivation of said fluid, women sank into a withdrawal state that made them irritable, angry, and depressed.

That explained it, thought Frieda. She'd have to ask Sam to bottle a few samples next time he went away.

Whenever Sam left Brooklyn, Frieda thought about Gregg. Without the distraction of Sam's naked body in her bed, memories came alive. Gregg had been her life partner. They had been united in the struggles and joys of marriage, work, parenting. Sam's absences opened a gaping yawn of doubt. Was he just another man who vanished on her? Gregg left her, but only once. Sam disappeared again and again. Each time he left, she missed him like he'd never come back.

Granted, this was a particularly bad morning. Sam had been gone for a month already, not set to return for another fortnight. His phone calls had been erratic. The production was troubled. The director had quit after a few days, and Sam had to take the reigns. When he directed, he was single-minded, dedicated to the show's success, admirably so. But in his myopia, he'd forget to call. And when he did, he'd talk about the show for a second before making hang-up noises. The details of her life seemed miniscule, not worth describing, like she'd stood still since the last phone call and hadn't traversed the landscape of two long days. He seemed to assume that the relationship was frozen as of the date of his departure, and would defrost exactly as he'd left it upon his return. How could he know so little about basic relationship maintenance? Ilene's standard response to Frieda's complaints was, "I told you he was too young."

The phone. Dr. Bother asking to see her again. Justin was fine, doing well, she said. "He's worried about you," she said. Frieda made an appointment and hung up.

The phone. Betty, wanting to confirm the sister dinner date, and to know if Frieda had spoken to Ilene or Peter. She'd been unable to reach them for a couple of days. Frieda reported that she hadn't spoken to either one. Nor had she heard from Sam since Saturday. Betty said she had to go.

The phone, again. "Frieda?" It was Sam. "I can't talk long. I've got a rehearsal in ten minutes."

The potency of his voice. The immediate *whoosh* of bad air exiting her lungs. The jumper cables to her heart.

"Sam, how are you? Are you okay?"

"I'm fine. You?"

"Fine."

Long pause. What to say? Confess the truth, that she couldn't stand these separations? That she'd become as obsessive about his absence as she'd been about his presence?

He said, "The kid playing Oliver has bronchitis. We have to hold emergency auditions tonight. Local talent. It's going to be a nightmare."

Frieda said, "That's terrible."

"You have no idea."

She said, "Justin's summer break starts next week. I have him signed up for day camp, but that doesn't start until two weeks from now. I'm looking at a long stretch of Disney movies, computer games and whiffle ball. I promised to take him to Great Adventure."

"Should be fun," said Sam.

If Gregg were alive, she wouldn't have to shoulder unstructured weeks of parenting by herself. She missed Gregg nostalgically, mournful for the lifestyle of shared responsibility.

Frieda had tried to explain this to Betty (perhaps too soon after the Earl dumping). She said, "I think I'm using Sam as a distraction from my ongoing grief."

Betty blurted out, "Both of them are—were—a distraction."

Frieda said, "A distraction from what?"

"We all have to face our self-destructive tendencies at some point, Frieda," said Betty. "And your tendency is to let your biggest fear rule your life."

"What fear?" she asked.

"The fear of being alone," said Betty. Then she went on to postulate that Frieda knew this on some level, and had done herself the favor by choosing Sam. "The mood swings, the grappling with his absence. It's all a super-sized serving of what your subconscious has cooked. You've devised a test for yourself. You're failing miserably. But, one day, in the distant, unforeseeable future, it is possible that you might conquer your greatest fear and feel comfortable by yourself."

At present, fretting on the phone to Sam, Frieda was miles from conquest. She wasn't in the same time zone as the battlefield.

She said to him, "I hate this. I hate being apart. I think I may go crazy from it."

Long, long silence. And, after that, another helping of silence. With all her might, Frieda resisted speaking over the nearly inaudible cracking of the phone wire.

After an eternity, Sam said, "Relax."

"That's it?"

"When I get back, it'll be okay."

"I know you're occupied with the show, and you're very busy, while I'm sitting here counting the minutes. I understand it all. You might be good at long-distance relationships, but I can't get used to it. I'm tired of being alone." She drew a breath. "You promised me you wouldn't forget what I've been through."

"I haven't forgotten," he said. Muffling in the background. "Hold on a second."

She held. By a thread. He came back. "I've got to go," he said.

"Of course you do."

"We'll talk later," he said. "I love you, and I miss you. Just bear with me. Okay?"

"I don't know if I can," she said. "I need you here."

"I can't be there," he said flatly. "This is my job, Frieda. If I can pull this off, maybe I'll get another directing job. A better one. Do you think I want to be sweating it out in Florida, auditioning ten-year-old amateurs? Don't you think I'd rather be with you?"

She said, "I'm supportive. I want you to do well."

"I'm glad to hear that," he said.

They hung up a second later. She felt awful about the conversation. She'd alienated him. He would break up with her for sure. And then she'd be alone again. Her anxiety migrated across plains and hills. Miles and miles from the battlefield.

Chapter 24

Wednesday, June 11
9:45 P.M.

"I haven't been to the East Village in years," said Ilene. "Did you see that man? He had a metal spike sticking out of his cheek." And look, a gnawed chicken skeleton on the sidewalk. And smell that, the odorous homeless person on a grate. And over there, a tattooed mob of teenagers smoking cigars. Ilene felt a wave of nausea as she walked along Second Avenue. Sickness marched up her innards like a slow line of ants. She swallowed hard, and smiled as brightly as she could at her two sisters. Betty looked as bad as she felt. And Frieda would not shut up.

Frieda said, "Can someone please explain to me why Sam didn't call today?"

Betty and Ilene made eye contact. Ilene said, "Can we not talk about Sam for five minutes?"

The whole rant was pointless. So Sam, a twenty-nine-year-old with scant long-term-relationship know-how, couldn't manage Frieda, a woman with experience in abundance. This was surprising to Frieda? Beyond her comprehension? Ilene's only hope was that her sister would dump him finally, and move on to a relationship with potential. Her patience with Frieda's whining was nearing an end.

Her patience with everything was nearing an end. Peter had moved out of the apartment three days ago. Ilene hadn't told Betty and Frieda about it. If Betty heard from Peter on the diet-buddy hotline, she hadn't let on. It was foolish to keep it a secret, but she couldn't bring herself to admit that her marriage was over, even to her sisters. Or herself. It'd been just a few days. Ilene was sure Peter would return soon. She'd ask him to come home, but she didn't know where he was staying. Jane wouldn't tell.

The night before the incident at Aux-On-Arles, Ilene and Peter had made love with a white-hot passion. Ilene and Peter had been enjoying each other quite a bit, actually, in the months before the blowup. She was more attracted to the slim him. Also, she wanted to see what he was capable of. If he *was* having an affair, surely he wouldn't have the appetite or ability to satisfy two women on the same day. He succeeded at satisfying Ilene, each time. Regardless, she still thought he was cheating.

While he packed his bags to move out, Peter said, "You slept with me to catch me. Now all that great sex is tainted. I can't win with you."

He hadn't been losing when he came like a train. He didn't want to hear a word of it. So Ilene stopped defending herself. She sat on the edge of the bed and watched him put his new skinny suits into a garment bag. She had to lie down after a while, she was so inexplicably tired. She must have fallen asleep. When she woke up, he was gone—insulted, she was sure, that she'd drifted off.

The three sisters walked toward First Avenue. They intended to have their monthly sister dinner, but none of them was hungry. Betty suggested they go, instead, to Sidewalk Café, sit outside, watch the freak show, and drink until they passed out or threw up. Frieda was willing. Ilene nodded and smiled, game face on. She had never drunk to such excess. But it wasn't like she was going home to anyone. Might as well start.

"Ilene, give Peter a message for me," said Betty. "Tell him I know he's cheating."

"You know he's *what?*" she asked.

"He's not calling me back. Therefore, he's cheating on his diet and doesn't want to speak to me."

Ilene said, "I'll give him the message when I get home tonight. He'll be waiting up for me, snuggled in the comfort of our loving marital bed." She might be laying it on a bit thick. "Or watching TV in the reclining chair in an undershirt." Too thin? "Probably reading *The New Yorker* on the couch."

Betty said, "Sure he's not jerking off with *Penthouse* on the toilet?"

Frieda, showing admirable strength to lift herself out of her own obsession and ask about someone else's problem, said, "Any word from Earl?"

"Nope," said Betty. "And you will not speak of the Devil in my presence."

The sisters rounded the corner and Betty said, "Here we are."

The Sidewalk Café resembled a bombed-out shanty in Baghdad. The awning was falling off, the brick façade covered in graffiti. Betty found them an outside table. It was round, its wood crackling, green paint chipping. A splinter hazard. Ilene dusted the metal folding chair and sat, placing her Kate Spade purse in her lap. She'd keep her prized bag close to her belly, like a marsupial pouch, or risk losing it. Frieda sat next to Ilene, facing the street. Betty went inside to get their drinks. She returned with two pitchers of beer and three plastic cups.

The hops tasted and smelled like tin. The metallic aftertaste caused Ilene's inner ants to march upward, toward her esophagus. To keep them down, she practically chugged her beer. Impressed, Betty and Frieda followed suit. Within three minutes, Ilene was tipsy. She started on her second glass. Within three sips, she was drunk. Slowly now, she took a quick look around. At thirty-nine, she was the bar's most senior patron. Several of the other customers wore leather in June, and didn't appear to sweat.

Ilene said, "What's the agenda for tonight?"

Frieda said, "I promise to stop talking about Sam."

Betty and Ilene said, "Good."

"Right after I make one last point."

"Are there any points unmade?" asked Betty.

"About his infrequent phone calling . . ."

Betty said, "Do you ever call him?"

"I don't want to push."

"You should call him," said Ilene. "I bet he'll talk longer if you're paying for the call."

Frieda considered this. "True. Okay. I'll call him."

"Great, another thing you have to pay for," said Ilene. Drunk on beer, how pathetic. The ants were at rest. But her inhibitions were just waking up. "I'm curious about something, Frieda. In the eight months you've been together, has Sam ever paid for dinner?"

"Nine. It's been nine months," said Frieda. "And no. He hasn't."

"Has he ever left a tip? Paid for a cab? A movie ticket? The beer he drinks at your house? Has he ever chipped in for the baby-sitting? Bought you a gift?"

"He gave me a CD on my birthday," she said.

"From his own collection!" said Ilene.

"It was special to him. Autographed by André Previn," said Frieda.

"You could probably get ten dollars for it on ebay," said Betty.

Frieda swirled her beer; Ilene stirred the pot. "I'm going to crunch the numbers," she said, safely within her professional wheelhouse. "You spend about a hundred dollars for a local night out, going up to three hundred for a Manhattan date, like when you got the opera tickets or went to the Oyster Bar for lobster. You took him for that weekend in Quogue with Justin. You bought him a suit jacket. A bedspread. A pair of sneakers. A new kettle."

Frieda turned toward Betty, who said, "Don't look at *me*. I'm not feeling very generous about men these days."

Ilene wasn't either. She continued her crunching. "You've taken him out about three times a month, on average. Minimum monthly expenditure, including gifts, travel and entertainment: six hundred dollars. Over eight—forgive me, *nine*—months. You have paid a grand total of five thousand, four hundred—minimum—for the honor and privilege of having Sam Hill, thespian, in your life."

Frieda stared at her, dumbfounded. Betty seemed to be calculating in her head. Could that number be correct? Ilene hadn't planned any of this, but now that she'd stumbled onto the financial facts, she'd connected the dots until the picture took shape. To Ilene, Frieda didn't appear to be falling apart or overtly pained. She had to know that Ilene meant well, meant to protect her.

Ilene said, "I only bring up the money issue because you've been so miserable lately. Spending freely was one thing when you were happy and in love. The time seems right to consider the inequities in the relationship."

Frieda said, "I can afford it."

Indeed she could. Frieda *was* a wealthy woman. Gregg's estate was of a decent size, and there had been that very large life insurance policy. Frieda and Gregg bought their apartment for next to nothing and, in the explosive Brooklyn Heights real-estate market, the floor-through had tripled in value in five years. Sol Gallery made no money—lost some, actually—but Frieda had wisely bought the

Montague-Street property right after Gregg died, with money out of his family trust, eliminating her high rental costs and taking a sizeable tax deduction for her mortgage payment. Adding it all up—real estate, Justin's college fund, stocks, bonds, money markets, etc.—Frieda's net worth was about $3 million.

Ilene said, "I know you can afford it. Does Sam?" The implication was almost cruel. She instantly regretted it. "Let me take that back. Forget I said anything."

Betty said, "Frieda lives frugally. Some might say cheaply. There's no way Sam has any idea how loaded she is."

"He knows," said Frieda. "I told him."

"You *what?*" asked Ilene and Betty simultaneously. They'd been raised never to disclose personal financial details to anyone, except family.

"We were talking one night, about Justin," said Frieda. "Sam said it was a shame that Justin had learned to worry so early in life. I told Sam that at least Justin wouldn't have to worry about money, and it all came out."

"Sweet Jesus," said Betty.

Her bud of a theory blossoming into a black poison rose, Ilene wanted to nip the conversation short. But Betty said, "When did you tell him?"

"A few months ago."

"Before or after he said he loved you?"

"After," Frieda said. "Look, I see the money as just one more thing I have to offer. He gives me so much, the scales are even."

Ilene said gently, "What does Sam give you?"

"Love. Sex. A feeling that I'm not alone."

Even as Frieda spoke the words, Ilene could hear the leaking hiss of doubt in her sister's voice. Frieda had been complaining, ceaselessly, that his departures made her feel alone and untrusting of Sam's feelings. The lack of sex was self-evident. Ilene thought about Peter, and how he'd shown her love, been constantly available for sex, had always been there for her, in the bedroom, or at the end of the phone.

Ilene said to Frieda, "Enough for one night. But you might want to acknowledge—to yourself, at least—that Sam may not be a love god sent from heaven to save you. He's just a young man with lots and lots—and lots—of flaws."

"I agree," Betty said. "He's got problems. But, then again, the perfect man does not exist."

A shout from across the street. "Ilene! Over here!" A man, tall, slim, holding the hand of a small child. He waved at her, looking both ways before crossing First Avenue. The little girl ran to keep up with the man's long churning legs.

"Ilene! Hey!" he said, upon them. "You remember Stephanie?"

Ilene said, "Yes, of course. Hello, Stephanie. I'm a work friend of your dad's. Betty, Frieda, this is David Isen, a writer at *Cash*."

They all exchanged greetings. David reminded Frieda— didn't need to—that he'd seen *Oliver!* with her last fall. Betty recalled having met David on the street once.

Ilene was pleased to see her friend. David had made a quick recovery from his divorce. His usual amicable, easy-going demeanor was fully restored. If she were to confide in anyone about her separation from Peter, she would choose David. But he'd been out of the office, first on a business trip, and last week on vacation. She couldn't call him at home or show up at his apartment because his daughter was visiting from Vermont for a couple of weeks. The girl held firmly to her father's hand. Her eyes scanned the three women at the table distrustfully and with the solipsistic impatience of a seven-year-old.

David seemed a bit frantic. Overly excited to see them. He said, "Grown-ups! I've been adult deprived for days."

"What are you doing down here?" asked Ilene, wondering how and why he'd bring a child into this seedy neighborhood.

"We had dinner at the Second Avenue Deli."

Ilene looked at pretty Stephanie with her auburn hair and sparkly pink T-shirt. "That must have been fun," she said, inviting a response.

Stephanie ignored the comment. David sighed. He said, "She's been with me a week. Another week to go. We've seen every G-rated movie in the theaters. I've taken her to the Bronx Zoo, the Planetarium, Chelsea Piers. We've hit four museums."

"Dad, let's go," said Stephanie.

"I think she's bored," he said.

"Bored at museums?" asked Frieda with feigned shock and horror. She leaned forward conspiratorially and whispered, "I don't blame you." Stephanie, sensing that Frieda was child-friendly, smiled back. The presence of a child—an innocent—distracted them from the tense topic of Sam.

David said, "I made a huge list of things to do, and I'm trying to avoid TV dependency. But I'm running out of ideas. You can go to the park for only so long. I think she misses her friends. And her mom. I've tried to set up a play date with kids from her old school, but I haven't been able to reach anyone."

Ilene knew full well that Justin, too, was currently between school and camp and that Frieda struggled to keep him occupied during the day. That the two children were just one grade apart. For months, she'd been soft-selling David to her sister as the man she should be seeing, a golden alternative to Sam. This was a handcrafted ideal opportunity to arrange for her favorite sister and good friend to spend time together, help each other out, let the kids meet. It was a wide-open door, the flawless scenario, one Ilene couldn't have dreamed up in her wildest machinations. But—and it shamed Ilene to let such a dastardly thought enter her alcohol-addled brain; shamed her deeply, to the core, but the thought popped up nonetheless—she wanted David for herself. Not for a boyfriend (if anything, Peter's leaving made her realize how much she wanted to stay married to him). She needed David's attention in the uncertain months ahead. If David and Frieda started dating, she'd lose both of them to each other.

Betty said to Stephanie, "I bet you think boys are yucky."

"Please," said Stephanie. "That attitude is so kindergarten."

Betty raised one eyebrow and laughed. "Well, Stephanie, if you think boys are okay, I'm sure you'll like my nephew Justin. He's going into first grade, but is very mature for his age."

David turned abruptly toward Frieda. "Your son is free?" he asked eagerly. "We would love to set something up. How about tomorrow? Tomorrow morning? You live in Brooklyn Heights, right? We'll come to you."

Frieda said, "Are you really that desperate? You'd cross water for a play date?"

David said, "Do I have to beg?"

"I promised Justin that I'd take him to the Transit Museum tomorrow. It's right in my neighborhood, and you have to go underground to get there. I'm not sure Stephanie could stomach another museum. This one, though, has rows and rows of old-fashioned subway cars and a big city bus you can pretend to drive. No paintings or sculptures, though."

David said, "Stephanie loves trains!"

His daughter said, "That doesn't sound too boring."

Frieda and David exchanged phone numbers, a sight Ilene had longed to see for months. But now, it made her stomach clench, the ants marching double-time. Ilene actually felt herself gag.

Betty asked, "Are you all right?"

Ilene waved her off, and excused herself. She went into the bar, recoiled from the eardrum-splitting techno music.

She made her way toward the back of the bar, down a narrow stairway and made it into the ladies' room just in time.

After rinsing her mouth, she felt better. She was less drunk now. And hungry. Ravenous. She walked back upstairs to the bar and bought three bags of barbecue potato chips and three hard-boiled eggs. The only food on the premises. Oddly, the salt and protein were exactly what she wanted.

Ilene brought the food back outside. David had left, having instructed Frieda and Betty to say his goodbyes for him. Frieda tucked the piece of paper with David's phone number into the back pocket of her jeans. Ilene caught Betty staring at her. The look on Betty's face was suspicious, pensive. Ilene held out a bag of chips to Betty. "You want?" she asked.

Betty said, "I'll take an egg."

# Chapter 25

Friday, June 13
11:45 A.M.

Betty was three seconds from quitting her job. She'd been three seconds from quitting for days, and living in a constant state of disgust was taking its toll. On the plus side, she'd all but stopped eating. On the negative side, her svelteness was irrelevant, since her body—only too recently a source of pride and gratification—had been reduced to an unused, untouched mass of flesh.

She sat, as usual in the mornings, at the help desk on the ground floor at Burton & Notham, dealing with the customers. Every man reminded her of Earl Long in some small way. The color of his hair, the movement of his legs, the shirt, the eyes, the contours of his neck. Betty thought of Earl constantly (every square foot of retail space in the store had been defiled by his presence). She let the memories come. She couldn't pretend the relationship hadn't happened. The persistence of memory was overwhelming.

Valerie Frankel

That was why she wanted to quit. She had to get away from this place.

A man approached the desk. This one, thank God, was blonde, short. Not dark and lanky like Earl. He wanted to know if she could print out a list of titles that analyzed the culture dimensions and lasting social consequences of mid-twentieth century fascist regimes. Betty hated searches like this. She had to punch in a dozen keywords, scan hundreds of titles and read book descriptions in tiny type. He wanted her to do his library research. She was supposed to help with specific searches that directed a customer to the exact book he or she would locate and purchase right away.

When she had a list of fifty titles, she printed it out and gave it to the man. He thanked her, took the list, but didn't go away. He shuffled the pages, shuffled his feet. Loitered by the desk. Finally, he said, "I've seen you here a lot."

"I work here."

"I was wondering . . ."

"I'm married," she said dismissively.

He pointed at her hand. "I'm sorry. You don't wear a ring." Then he skulked off, rejected and embarrassed. Betty felt nothing. Not pity, power, revenge. Deflecting male attention was all in a day's work. Several times a day, lately.

Numb. That was her state. She hadn't masturbated or had a sexual fantasy since the scene with Earl on the Brooklyn Bridge. Now that she'd had a taste of where those fantasies could lead, she'd lost the appetite for them. Which was sad enough. What was worse: She was certain that if Earl Long called and said he'd made a horrible mistake, she'd take him back.

Gert appeared at the help desk, bright with silver and gold spangles. She held a dozen magazines, yellow Post-It Notes sticking out the top of each one. She dropped the stack on the desk.

"Some articles that might interest you," said Gert.

"Take them back to the magazine rack," said Betty.

"No."

"If you don't take them back, you're fired."

"Read them. For me," said Gert. "I've spent the entire morning on this project."

"What project?" asked Betty.

"The 'I Got Her into This, I'll Get Her Out' project."

Betty said, "For the last time, I don't blame you for what happened."

"I pushed you at him," said Gert.

"You did the right thing," said Betty. "How could you know that Earl would turn out wrong? So very, very wrong."

Gert would beat her chest with guilt for months, Betty knew. Her friend believed she was instrumental in destroying Betty's trust in men for the rest of her life. "The rest of my life," Betty chanted to Gert often, using the loathsome phrase with impunity.

Picking up the magazine on top, *Sports Illustrated*, Gert flipped to the marked page. She handed it to Betty and said, "Sarah Hughes. Gold-Metal winner, 2002 Winter Olympics."

"What can a sixteen-year figure skater have to say that is relevant to my situation?" asked Betty, irritated.

"Just read it," said Gert. "She talks about learning at an early age, through her experiences in sports, that failure is good. Failure is educational. Without failure in her life, she says she couldn't have succeeded in the Olympics. She thinks her appreciation of failure puts her at ease on the ice. She doesn't get nervous because of her Zen-like attitude. And, besides that—I know you'll like this about her—she's half-Jewish."

"The half with the bad hair," said Betty.

Gert placed the *Sports Illustrated* on the desk, leaving it open, and took the next magazine off the stack. *Glamour.* She found the page she was looking for. "Article called, 'It's Not You, It's Me,' about women who blame themselves when a relationship doesn't work out, even if it's not their fault. Some good quotes from shrinks about how comfortable it is for women to internalize their negative emotions instead of venting them."

Betty said, "I vent."

"Not healthfully," said Gert. "Not in a way that expends justifiable anger. Only in a way that further alienates you."

Betty said, "A little warning: If you read enough of those women's magazine articles, you start to sound like them."

Gert dropped the *Glamour* on top of the *Sports Illustrated.* She picked up *Cash*, Ilene's magazine. "Article called 'Corporate Penny Pinching and Ass Slinging.' How large companies are increasingly vigilant about nickels and dimes, checking employee phone records, expense accounts. Nice big section at the end about the extreme consequences for employees who got busted for abusing privileges."

Now that could be interesting, thought Betty. She took the magazine off Gert's hands, and started to read the article. Written by David Isen. The story was good. Inspiring.

Betty picked up the phone, and dialed Ilene's number at *Cash*. Her sister's assistant connected her to Isen's voice mail. Betty left a message and hung up.

She smiled at Gert and said, "Don't you have some phone records and expense reports to locate?"

Chapter 26

Monday, June 16
2:07 A.M.

Peter groped for his watch. It was on the coffee table somewhere. The room was black. He'd been asleep since ten. He
found the timepiece and pushed the illuminate button.
Jesus, only 2:00 A.M. Four hours of sleep this time. His old
slumber pattern had been to go to bed around midnight or
one, and wake up at seven or eight. Since he'd been living
at Jane's, sleeping on the couch, he'd gotten in the rut of
turning on the TV at eight, eating a high-carb snack (he
couldn't resist Jane's overflowing cabinets of 'stop' foods),
conking out to the blue glow at ten and waking up in the
middle of the night for good. Jane and her husband, Tim, a
genial contractor who couldn't have been more understanding about Peter's situation, seemed to be okay with
the loss of their living room. They hadn't told him to leave.

Peter checked his watch again. He was in for a long night
of insomnia. Flinging his comforter aside (Peter attentively

folded and stored his comforter and pillow in the hall closet each morning), he sat upright on the couch, rubbed his tired face, scratched his scalp. Standing took some effort. Then he walked the dozen paces in the dark to the bathroom. He opened the door, and flipped on the light.

The scream hit him before the light did. It took a few seconds for his pupils to narrow. His eyes adjusted, and he saw Tim sitting on the toilet, seat down, with Jane astride him. They were nude. Fucking. Peter shut off the light, closed the door, and backed into the living room. The sight of their two bodies stuck to his retinas, a hazy orange purple outline around it.

He found the couch, sat down, then lay down and pulled the comforter over his head. He hadn't realized just how tiny Jane was until he'd seen her bony naked back. Her waist: Tim's hands went all the way around. Peter was embarrassed by his intrusion. He couldn't deny feeling a rapid pulse in his groin. Too rapid? He clutched his chest and breathed deeply, sucking the limited oxygen from underneath the comforter until he felt lightheaded. He had to come up for air.

He pulled back the comforter. Even in the near darkness, Peter could make out the hulking shape of Tim Bambo, a towel wrapped around his waist, elbows on his knees, sitting on the coffee table next to the couch.

Once Peter had pulled the covers down to expose his entire head, Tim said, "Sorry you had to see that."

Peter, in his defensive posture, said, "No, it wasn't bad. In different circumstances, I'm sure I'd have enjoyed it."

Tim laughed politely at his wife's boss's joke. "The thing is, Peter, we haven't minded having you stay with us. For the week."

"Time to move on?" asked Peter.

Tim nodded. "Jane wouldn't have said anything because she cares about you."

"Because I'm her boss."

"You are her boss, and she also cares about you," said Tim.

Peter nodded. Odd to carry on a conversation in the middle of the night with a nearly naked man he'd seen humping not moments before. "Why would you go at it in the bathroom when you have that nice big bed?" Peter couldn't help asking.

Tim said, "That's none of your business, Peter."

Peter noticed the straightening of Tim's spine. He reflexively pulled the covers a bit higher under his chin. Peter said, "I'll find a new place to stay in the morning. A hotel, I guess. It'll be kind of lonely."

"Why don't you just go home?" asked Tim. "You've proven whatever you wanted to prove."

"Ilene doesn't love me," said Peter. The week of sleep deprivation and sadness threatened to spill out of his eyes. He could think of nothing more awkward than crying in front of Tim, a muscle-bulging prime cut of masculinity who'd probably never had a minute of marital doubt in his life.

Tim said, "You're not going to cry, are you?"

Peter said lamely, "No."

"She loves you," said Tim. "If she didn't love you, she

wouldn't have married you in the first place. You're not rich, handsome, famous, funny, talented, built or powerful."

"When you put it like that," Peter said. "How could she resist?"

"I guess you are kind of funny," amended Tim.

"I can't face her," said Peter. "I can't go back. I'm always the one who makes the big romantic gestures. She fucked up this time. I want her to get me back. To show me one bit of effort. Otherwise, this marriage is over."

"Okay, okay. Settle down," said Tim.

"The only problem is that she has no idea what I want from her. So I'll never get it."

Tim sighed. "I'm going to bed. I'm sorry I can't help you with this. Maybe Jane can."

"Jane has already done enough," said Peter. Jane sent Peter to Peggy in the first place. "I really appreciate your letting me stay," he added.

"You're welcome," said Tim.

"What's your secret?" asked Peter. "How do you and Jane stay so happy?"

Tim rose to his feet. From Peter's prone position on the couch, Tim was a colossus. "The secret of our happiness," said Tim, "is why you'd find us together in the bathroom at two in the morning."

A commitment to novelty? A passion that burns despite the cooling of years?

"You both have small bladders?" asked Peter.

"Pea size," said Tim.

Chapter 27

Wednesday, June 18
9:23 A.M.

Physical Effects of Spousal Abandonment
1. *Nausea (comes in waves)*
2. *Insatiable hunger (quells nausea)*
3. *Constipation/gas*
4. *Afternoon fatigue*
5. *Aversion to formerly appealing scents (rose and patchouli)*

The list could go on, but Ilene was too hungry to continue. At least her unrelenting appetite served to distract her from emotional angst. Who needed a husband anyway, when she'd found a new love? The morning muffin. She'd always been a bagel person. But last Wednesday morning, while perusing breadstuffs at the corner deli, her eyes locked on the muffin with the cranberry smile. It was enormous, a mother muffin that had swallowed her young, only to be swallowed by Ilene in turn. She got another muffin the next day. And the next. She was hooked. Savoring the heavenly bake of flour, sugar and cranberries had become the highlight of her day.

Ilene licked muffin crumbles off her fingertips, hummed tunelessly as she sipped her coffee. For the duration of her morning meal, she was happy. As soon as she wadded up the wax paper and threw it in the garbage, she was adrift. The confection was a temporary float. And, much as she would have wanted to, she couldn't eat muffins all the live-long day. She'd have to wait at least a couple of hours.

Work distracted her for longer periods, an hour at a time. But even the sanctuary of work was disrupted. *Cash* and *Bucks* were competitors. At nearly every editorial meeting, someone would say something about Peter's magazine. Ilene used to laugh and threaten to tell Peter about the criticism, or pretend to be a willing spy to see if *Bucks* was planning a certain story. But now, simply hearing the word *bucks* put her on edge. Often, she wore her sunglasses in meetings. Even in the evening. She wasn't sure if anyone noticed the change in her temperament, or the five pounds she'd gained in the past week. Or her mad dashes to the ladies' room to throw up. If any of her colleagues had, none mentioned it. She was safe with her secret for another day. And the days rolled along.

She wanted to talk about her separation, to somebody, anybody. But she hadn't. She just couldn't. That would be an admission that the marriage was over, and she steadfastly refused to let that thought take hold. She had been close to confiding in David Isen many times. He'd been there. But, like her, he kept his separation to himself for a while. He'd probably been waiting for Georgia to make things right, just as Ilene was waiting for Peter. If only he'd make the one big romantic gesture to prove he'd forgiven her. Until (unless) he did, she would do nothing. Making the first move would be groveling. Peter loved her (had loved her) for her strength. He would never respect her if she groveled.

The phone. David Isen, calling from his office. She said, "If you're calling about the google IPO—"

He said, "Your sister is here. Shall I bring her down?"

"Frieda's there?" To see David? Ilene shouldn't be surprised. She knew they'd spent most of the weekend together with Justin and Stephanie. The kids had clicked, too. Stephanie must have been sent back to Vermont already. With the child gone, Ilene suspected that Frieda and David would keep seeing each other, even without the excuse of play-dates. It was just a matter of time, Ilene was convinced, before Frieda saw David as the perfect man for her. Sam would fade away, just his name recorded as a footnote in the Schast sisters' romantic history.

Ilene said into the phone, "Bring her over."

David said, "Not Frieda. Betty's here."

"Betty?" asked Ilene.

"She needs some advice on a business idea," he said. "We're coming down." He hung up.

And within what seemed like seconds, Betty and David were in her office. Ilene did a double take whenever she saw Betty lately. Her baby sister had changed so much, not just in body size, but in style and attitude. She wasn't closed and defensive anymore. She'd become direct, confident. How she marched into Ilene's office, looked around, and sat in the chair opposite her desk without asking. Not that Betty had ever been timid. She just wouldn't have made herself as comfortable with such entitlement before.

Ilene said, "Betty! What a surprise! Why didn't you come to me with your business idea?"

David said, "Oh, she read my June article on corporate crackdowns and—"

Betty cut him off. "I'm going to get revenge on Earl Long by squealing on him."

"How underhanded and rotten," said Ilene. "Can I help?"

David said, "*I'm* helping."

Betty said, "Thank you, David."

"It's been my pleasure," he said. "And really, if you need anything . . ."

"I will call," said Betty.

Dear God, was David hitting on Betty, too? Was he a walking erection? Betty, to her credit, and Ilene's relief, showed no interest in David. Only in Ilene, whom she stared at openly.

After David left, Betty said plainly, "I've figured out what's going on."

Ilene's chest convulsed. "You've spoken to Peter."

"No," said Betty. "But I realized that he isn't taking my calls because he's afraid to let the cat out of the bag. The two of you have a secret, don't you? I've thought about what kind of secret a married couple would keep. And the explanation was only too obvious."

She knows, thought Ilene. "I suppose my behavior was the giveaway."

Betty nodded. "The way you picked at Frieda about Sam the other night. I might have found that cruel—honest, but cruel—until I factored in the new information and realized your attack on Sam was protective. And I couldn't help notice how you reacted to the alcohol. Plus your weight gain. It's all makes sense."

It does, thought Ilene. Instead of feeling mortified, Ilene was relieved not to have to say the words out loud, grateful that her youngest sister had done the hard work for her. She said, "I'm so glad you figured it out."

Betty said, "Frankly, I've been waiting a long time for this."

Ilene said, "You have?"

"We all have."

"Frieda, too?"

"Come on, Ilene. You can't say that you haven't wanted this yourself for years."

She could say no such thing. She might nag at Peter. She might have treated him badly on occasion. But Ilene loved him. She had since the moment she saw him sitting in the front row. How could she have fucked up so badly?

Ilene said, "I love Peter."

Betty said, "I hope *so*."

"We will make it work."

"Of course you will."

"Have you told Frieda?" asked Ilene.

Betty shook her head. "I didn't know if you wanted me to."

Ilene said, "I'll do it. Today."

Betty nodded and stood up. She walked around to Ilene's chair, leaned down and hugged her sister, tight. Ilene responded to the affection. She'd been missing that. She didn't think she'd touched another person in a week.

Betty said, "We will be right there with you, the whole way. Just like we were for Frieda."

Ilene just nodded against Betty's shoulder.

After a very long clinch, Betty pried Ilene's arms off her. She said, "I've got to get back to work. I brought this for you."

Ilene accepted the Burton & Notham bag. Ilene said, "Thanks."

Betty said, "Congratulations!" and showed herself out.

Ilene took the book out of the bag. Instead of *Divorce for Dummies*, she held a copy of *What to Expect When You're Expecting*.

She laughed. Talk about misunderstandings. Betty thought she was pregnant? Absurd! And all that time, Ilene assumed Betty had figured out that she'd been deserted. So her sister didn't know the truth. She'd taken Ilene's fatigue, nausea, ravenous appetite, weight gain and mood swings as signs of pregnancy? Ridiculous! After a half decade of trying, to succeed unwittingly at the worst possible time? It just wasn't feasible.

Then again, if Ilene were observing herself, she might leap to the same ludicrous conclusion. She and Peter had been doing it an awful lot before he left. She was, as a point of fact, quite late with her period. By two or three weeks. She assumed that she was skipping the month due to emotional stress.

Just to be absolutely sure Betty was wrong, Ilene slipped out of the building and ran into the Duane Reade on the corner. She bought the cheapest pregnancy test she could find, brought it back to work and locked herself in a bathroom stall.

She sat on the lid and read the box, front and back, side to side, up and down. She examined it for so long, she could have rewritten the instructions from memory. Ilene's heart pounded. What did she want the results to say? Could she face life as a single mom? Maybe Peter would come back if he knew she was knocked up. She could leak the info. No, no. Ilene wouldn't use a baby as leverage. That wasn't fair to her, the child, or Peter. He would have to come back on his own, without a word from her, or any knowledge about the baby. If there was one.

If there wasn't, well, it was just five minutes of mental exercise, contemplating an unforeseeable event that would have forever changed the course of her life in ways she couldn't possibly have imagined. Like Gregg's death had for Frieda.

Ilene liberated the pen-shaped test strip from its protective wrapping and held it in her urine stream for ten seconds. She waited the allotted three minutes before checking the two windows One line for not pregnant. Two lines for pregnant.

There, before her eyes, Ilene watched the second, fainter

line materialize slowly, patiently, in no rush at all. The unforeseeable event had happened. And the course of her life changed forever, in ways she couldn't possibly have imagined, while alone in a bathroom stall at work.

Chapter 28

Saturday, June 21
11:20 A.M.

Stephanie and Justin splashed in the tub together. Frieda, washcloth in hand, sopped up the overflow as best she could. David was kneeling at her side, holding another washcloth, scrubbing the paint off Stephanie's forehead.

David said, "At what age does mixed-gender bathing become inappropriate?"

"Eight?" said Frieda.

"I remember liking girls before then," said David. "I kissed a girl when I was six."

Stephanie said, "Dad, that's disgusting."

Frieda said, "Stop splashing, please."

Justin said, "It's just water, Mom. Chill out."

Giving up on both containing the overflow and scrubbing every drop of paint off her child's fingers, Frieda chucked her washcloth in the water, dropped a bath towel on the floor, and said, "Ten minutes."

Justin said, "Can I add hot?"

"No."

David gave up his washcloth, too. "I'll throw in the towel, too," he said. "You might think about using it to get that paint off the walls."

Stephanie said, "What paint?"

David pointed at the tiled walls around the tub. Diluted drops of red paint had created an eerie splatter pattern. David helped Frieda to her feet. The two adults left the kids and went into the kitchen to fill a bucket with Formula 409 and hot water. David took his choice of scrub brush like choosing his pistol before a duel, and they walked, armed and loaded with cleaning weaponry, to Justin's room.

David and Stephanie had arrived at Frieda's apartment less than two hours ago. They were a pleasant surprise for Frieda and Justin, who had no particular plans for that steamy Saturday. Apparently, Georgia had paid David her own surprise visit very early that morning, showing up at his doorstep with Stephanie, announcing that she was speaking on a panel at the annual organizers exhibit at the Javits Center. She'd originally planned on taking Stephanie to the show, but realized quickly that it was a bad idea, serving no one's interests. Georgia was sorry she hadn't called; the whole trip down to New York had been very last minute. But could David take Stephanie for the day?

One phone call and a taxi ride later, David and Frieda were making sandwiches in the kitchen of her apartment to take to Prospect Park for a picnic. Stephanie and Justin were playing quietly in his room. Curiosity pulled Frieda down the hall to discover that the kids had taken out the paint set (forbidden without supervision) and decided that Justin's wood floor would look better speckled. The spots were randomly ordered, sized, and shaped. The sight of them made Frieda see red, as well as blue, yellow, orange and green.

First, the reprimand. Frieda contained her anger fairly well. She was the first to admit that she had an obsession (nonclinical) with neatness. Usually, she became apoplectic when Justin created extra cleaning work for her. He was supposed to help her, not make her life harder. She used that motherly refrain upon seeing the spots, but not with her usual shrill vibrato. If David hadn't been here, Frieda would have gone ballistic.

Frieda dropped the bucket on the painted floor. She dipped her brush and scrubbed. David did the same. She said, "You know that TV commercial for bionic paper towels that shows a cute kid in a baseball cap spilling a gallon of orange juice on the floor, and when the mother sees what he's done, she shakes her head and smiles like she can hardly wait to clean up?"

David said, "I refuse to buy those paper towels in protest."

"Obviously, Justin did this to see how I'd react in front of you," said Frieda.

"Did you react differently?" he asked.

"Not really," she lied. "Somewhat," she revised.

David said, "I wonder if you'd treat me differently if Justin weren't here. If the kids weren't here, and we were alone."

A strange thing to say. She ignored it. "What should we do to them, punishment-wise?" she asked.

He paused his scrubbing to dunk his brush in the bucket. "I like 'no snacks,' meaning no sugary or salty substance, for a prescribed length of time."

"What? A day? A week?"

"For this," he gestured at the paint with his brush, "I'd give him the rest of the day. That'll hurt. Especially if we go out for ice cream. Which we will do. As soon as we finish and get them dressed," he said.

"What about Stephanie?" asked Frieda, instantly defensive. Her son hadn't acted alone.

He said, "No ice cream for her either—or we could all get ice cream, and say no TV."

"Yes, but then what will we do with them after dinner? Without TV, we'll have to entertain them ourselves."

"That is out of the question," said David, doing masterful work on a blue splotch. "Okay, how about this? We don't punish them, due to the mitigating circumstances, but we make them feel guilty and full of shame."

Frieda nodded. "Complain of back pain from scrubbing."

"The cost of having the floor cleaned professionally."

"The waste of a beautiful morning."

He said, "If we see people you know on the street, we will tell them what happened in very loud voices."

She laughed. "That is shameful." David's parenting style was so like hers. They both acted without fear for the child's future on the therapist's couch. After all, Justin was already on the couch.

Frieda said, " 'Due to the mitigating circumstances.' What did you mean by that?"

David didn't look up from the floor. "Justin knows your reactions. He doesn't know mine. He's on a fact-finding mission."

"I don't see why he'd care," said Frieda.

"He wants to know what I'd be like as his stepfather."

"That's crazy," said Frieda, scrubbing harder.

"They talk about it," said David. "Stephanie told me."

"We've known each other for only a couple of weeks," said Frieda.

He sat back on his heels, hands resting on his jeans-clad thighs. "Stephanie might be a bigger yenta than Ilene."

"Ilene has been pushing you on me for months," said Frieda.

"And you to me. She thinks she's subtle," he said.

They both had a laugh at that. David smiled at her, a dot of blue paint in his chin. He said, "You know, Ilene might be onto something."

Frieda stopped laughing. "You mean *up* to something."

David said, "You and me is a pretty good idea."

What was this? thought Frieda. David liked her now? She hadn't seen that coming. She certainly wasn't sending signals. David *was* good-looking, she supposed, but Frieda had always gone for quirkier types.

She said, "I haven't put you in a romantic context."

"You don't think scrubbing the floor, side by side, is romantic?" he asked.

Frieda said, "Scrubbing? Romantic? I don't think so."

David said, "I do."

Gregg's idea of romance was to surprise her with diamond jewelry. Sam's idea of romance was to remove her clothes with his teeth. David liked household chores?

He said, "Anything can be romantic with the right person."

"Well, of course," she said.

"Not only is scrubbing romantic," said David, "it's sexy."

"Now sexy," said Frieda.

"You should see yourself," he said.

Reflexively, she looked across the room at Justin's hanging mirror. Her hair was in a ponytail, curly strands sticking out like tentacles. Red paint was smeared across her nose. Her tank top was wet and soapy. Her shorts were stained, her bare legs covered with two days stubble.

"I don't see the hotness," she said.

"You and Georgia are a similar physical type," he said. "Curvy and cute."

Frieda wanted to change the subject. The children. Always safe territory. "Hey kids!" she yelled down the hall.

Two voices shouted back, "What?"

"They're fine," said David. "So are we. Together like this. You have to admit you've thought of what it would be like if we were a family, not just walking around in the shape of one."

"You know I'm seeing someone."

"*Seeing* is a bit of a euphemism," he said.

"Sam is coming back tomorrow," she said. "I'll see him then."

David said, "But he'll leave again. And again. I know how it feels to be left."

His wife had left him for another man. Frieda had heard the blow-by-blow. In fact, she'd gotten the blow-by-blow of David's entire life story. And he'd gotten hers. Whenever the kids were playing, or eating, or napping, they had told each other stories. They knew the names of each other's childhood pets, the first-hand-job anecdotes, the where were you when Reagan was shot, the Challenger exploded, the towers went down. They had shared and confided, as if the past revealed the teller's true character. Frieda wasn't sure. Maybe it did. They talked because they weren't having sex. Did that mean she and Sam had sex because they weren't talking? That wasn't fair. She and Sam *did* talk. Briefly. Between sex sessions.

"We're comfortable together," said David. "Our families mesh. We have social overlap. You're a strong, battle-tested woman. You're exactly what I'm looking for."

So she matched his shopping list. Technically, he matched hers, except she'd thrown out the list when she met Sam. David was the antithesis of Sam. He represented a Gregg-like reprise—a relationship based on friendship, comfort, security. She could easily put a frame around that. A nice, gold one, kids in clean, ironed clothes, standing in front of the handsome couple. She tried to put a frame around Sam. No use. Sam was impossible to contain. That might be the ultimate source of her anxiety about it, she realized suddenly.

Frieda said, "Comfort and social overlap aren't grounds for marriage."

"Who said anything about marriage?" he asked. "We can start slow. With dating. Sex."

"I haven't felt a big attraction on your part," she said.

"I was waiting for you to stop talking about Sam," he said. "You've mentioned him less and less, actually. Not once today. I took that as a sign."

Frieda said, "Prepare yourself for a triple-negative sentence structure."

David said, "Ready."

"Even if I don't talk about Sam, that doesn't mean I don't love him," she said.

"I made my move too early," said David. "I should have waited."

"Sam and I are not breaking up," she said.

"I didn't say you were."

Frieda didn't need this. They had two kids in the tub, a mess on the floor. And now she had to deflect David's advances, too? Frieda should be flattered that a man like him was tossing in his hat. He was, according to Ilene, perfect for her. And she did like him. But at present, she just felt pressure, not pleasure.

Frieda said, "I've got another sister, you know."

He nodded. "I like Betty a lot. She's very attractive. I've always thought so. But she's not a full-fledged adult yet."

Frieda considered his observation. "Perhaps not."

"May I make one suggestion, and then the subject is closed?" he asked.

"Go on."

"I suggest we kiss."

Echoes of what she'd said to Sam, months ago, the first day they'd met. Frieda started to shake her head, and then, stopped. A flat, boring kiss would put David off, and then he'd forget the whole thing. She readied her lips, mentally turning them into dry putty.

She said, "I'll allow it."

He leaned toward her, over the bucket of water. She leaned forward, on her knees. Just as their lips were about to make contact, the sound of wet kid feet came sloshing down the hall.

"He keeps calling me Luke," whined Stephanie from the doorway, wrapped in a pink towel.

Justin, towel draped over his head ominously, said to her, "Come to the dark side. It is your destiny."

"I know which movie we're watching tonight," said Frieda, and gathered Justin in her arms.

Later that night, after David and Stephanie left to meet Georgia, Justin and Frieda sat on the couch together watching *The Empire Strikes Back*. They shared a bowl of popcorn and a liter of diet ginger ale.

Justin was halfway on her lap, leaning back on her chest. Her free hand rested on his shoulder. For the first time in many months, Frieda could feel herself relax. She hadn't obsessed about Sam for hours. Hadn't really thought about him all day. They'd been so busy. Post cleanup, they went for ice cream, then the park, then Chinese, back home for cartoons. Their movements prevented David from hitting on her again. When he left, he didn't try to get the kiss she'd agreed to. She had to admit, she was disappointed he hadn't gone for it. Once the surprise of his advances wore off, Frieda liked his wanting her. What woman wouldn't? Her confidence was up. She felt admired.

Sam was returning tomorrow after five weeks away. Frieda had yet to do her legs.

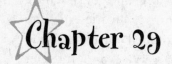

Chapter 29

Alone in her Avenue A apartment, Betty spread the evidence of Earl's petty thievery across her bed. She had dozen of pages, printouts, Xeroxes—the goods. And she was going to use them like a hammer, and nail him. Nail his ass to the ground. She cackled, loving the image: Earl Long sitting opposite the *uber* boss at Burton & Notham, her evidence piled high on the desk between them. Earl squirming in his chair, frantic to come up with an explanation for why thirty-two pay-per-view hotel-room screenings of *Anal Intruder* were billed as "entertainment, misc." on his monthly expense sheet.

Betty had been a busy, busy girl. The manager at the Union Square Grande Hotel hadn't been willing, at first, to give her copies of all of Earl's room charges for the eight months he'd stayed there. It took fibs ("Mr. Long needs a copy, and I told him I'd help him get it,") cajoling ("Come on, you know me! I've been here dozens of times!"), deception ("Does this look like the face of a liar?"), and, ultimately, bribery ("Thirty percent off any best-selling hardcover for the next twelve months"). In the end, she got the dirt. Betty and Gert also combed through phone bills, petty-cash vouchers, and car service and Internet charges, looking for flagrant abuses.

In their research, Betty learned several fascinating tidbits about the man she'd wanted to spend the rest of her life with. Earl had a secret sexual fetish, quite pedestrian, for leather boots (he'd used the company charge to set up an account at hotfoot.com.) She should have known. On their very first shopping expedition, he'd been insistent about those high-heeled boots at Daffy's. He also had a thing for sunglasses, having purchased twenty different pairs in six months, describing them as "protective construction gear" on his expense reports. The biggest shock of all: He had a three-year-old son in Chicago. Repeat calls to the 312 area code had been placed from Betty's office phone to a woman named Stella Bridle. Betty called Ms. Bridle and found out about Earl's "love child," as Stella described him.

Of course, the discoveries galled Betty. But what ate at her the most was Earl's confidence that he would get away with everything. He'd done little to cover his tracks. He must have assumed Betty would be too embarrassed about being dumped to expose him. How he'd underestimated her. She could hardly wait to blow the whistle, long, and loud, and to the tune of "Another One Bites the Dust."

Betty gathered her incriminating papers and slipped

them into a sturdy plastic binder bought especially for her project. She put the binder under her mattress, lay back in her bed, and plotted her next move. When would she alert the powers that be about "the puzzling expenses she discovered quite by chance and felt duty bound to report"? She wanted maximum impact. Timing was key. Revenge was a dish that people of taste preferred to eat cold. Could she wait for the cool? Or should she act now, while her anger was red hot?

After the initial post-dump weeks of numbness, she'd come alive again in anger. Hatching the revenge plot was a massive turning point. She'd been having sexual fantasies again, too. Interestingly, they featured leather boots. She felt the urge coming on, and turned down the lights.

She'd just gotten started when the buzzer sounded, jerking her upright on the bed. She tried to ignore it, but the intercom beeped out a staccato rhythm to get up, get up, get up. Betty buttoned her pants, pressed the intercom and asked who it was.

"Betty! Thank God you're home. It's Peter! Can I come up?"

Peter? The man who hadn't returned her phone calls in weeks, the father of her future nephew/niece? What the hell was he doing on the Lower East Side, late on a Saturday night? She buzzed him in, and quickly straightened her bed, checked her clothes. She looked around the rest of the apartment. It was untidy, but not a complete disaster.

Knock on the door. Betty opened it and saw a strange man on the threshold. "Jesus, Peter. I didn't recognize you for a second there. Come on in."

Betty had lost only about half the weight Peter had. She

didn't look too different—the same, but slimmer. But Peter! His face used to be bloated and round. Now it was angular, his dark eyes wider and hungrier. His hair seemed thicker, his hairline lower. Smile wider. He looked fresh and collected in a tan summer suit. A big change from the sloppy, sweaty butterball in too-tight navy jackets. Ilene must love this, to be married to the same man, and get a whole new body to play with, thought Betty.

Peter walked in, looked around nervously. "You look flushed. Are you okay?"

"I'm fine. Just exertion. From cleaning."

"Cleaning?" he said dubiously. His eyes swept the apartment. "I haven't been here since Ilene's moving day."

Over eleven years ago. "It hasn't changed much," observed Betty. When the apartment was handed down from oldest to youngest sister—Ilene moved in with Peter the same month Betty graduated from college—Betty had had little money to redecorate, and Ilene hadn't taken much of her furniture with her anyway. As soon as she settled in, Betty added her own touches. She threw a building-block quilt on the sleigh bed, a Navaho blanket on the black velvet couch. She hung tassels from the dresser knobs. She also brought in a purple iMac, a large bookshelf, a hand-painted lamp she found at a Village thrift store, a rag rug, some gauzy, off-white curtains. She hadn't added anything or made any other changes in years. It was as if she'd been frozen in time—stuck, decoratively speaking, in her early twenties. Her stuff had aged, though, just as she had. The quilts and curtains had been brighter when they were new.

Betty said, "So. Congratulations are in order."

Peter looked horrified. "How can you say that?"

"Isn't that what most people say?" asked Betty.

"Most people say they're sorry to hear it," said Peter. "Separation is not a cause for celebration."

Separation? Peter had left Ilene? In her condition?

"You *shit*," said Betty.

"You've only heard her side of the story." He defended himself, still standing in the middle of the living room.

"Actually, I haven't heard her side either."

"She hasn't told you?" he asked. "I thought that's why you were calling me all the time. To yell at me to go back."

"I don't yell," she said. "I use snide undertones." Betty quickly calculated when he'd stopped returning her calls. "Do you mean to tell me that you left two weeks ago?"

"Thirteen days," he said. "I lived with my assistant for a week. I've been staying at the Marriott in Times Square for the past week. It's just too lonely. I can't bear it." He sat down on the black couch, completely dejected. "I can't believe she hasn't told you about this. Does she care at all about our marriage?"

Betty realized with a start that Peter didn't know Ilene was pregnant. Ilene hadn't told Betty that she was separated, and she hadn't told her husband about the baby. Come to think of it, maybe Ilene wasn't even pregnant. Betty had assumed her erratic behavior was due to pregnancy, but it could be explained by the breakup. Sort of. Betty didn't know what to think.

She said, "You have clothes, luggage?"

"At the hotel."

"You've wandered a long way tonight."

He sighed heavily, the tonnage of a tractor-trailer. "She doesn't love me, Betty," he said.

The phone rang, saving Betty from having to respond. She held up her index finger, said, "Wait one second," and picked up the receiver on the desk.

"Hello?"

"Betty," said the phone. "It's Ilene."

"Ilene," said Betty. Peter's head shot upright. He jumped to his feet and started frantically waving, mouthing, "I'm not here."

Ilene said, "I need to ask you a favor."

"Anything," said Betty. Peter was pacing now, nervously excited to be connected, by proxy, to his wife.

"If you speak to Peter, please don't tell him I'm pregnant."

"So you *are*, then."

Pause. Ilene said, "Yes, I am. But I haven't told Peter yet. I want to surprise him with the good news. I want to tell him at just the right moment."

"When?" asked Betty.

Peter looked at her and silently repeated her question. *"When what?"*

Ilene said, "I've got it all planned. I'll tell him next weekend. We're . . . we're going away, to Montauk. It's our eleventh wedding anniversary, and we're just so much in love, I thought it'd be the perfect time to tell him how lucky we are."

"Good thinking," said Betty.

"So you won't tell him?" asked Ilene. "In fact, maybe you should stop trying to reach him. He'll call you. Okay?"

Betty said, "Okay."

"Thanks."

"Ilene?"

"Yes?"

"Take care," said Betty, trying to transmit concern without giving Peter a reason to freak out.

Pause again. Betty sensed Ilene wavering, deciding. Then she said, "I will," and hung up.

Peter stared at Betty like a man on a deserted island, starving for news of his wife. Betty didn't know what to say. She couldn't explain her sister's behavior. Why all the secrets? Betty would have to think that one through carefully. But not now, with Peter here.

He said, "Did she mention me?"

"She's pretending everything is normal," said Betty.

"Our separation is too insignificant to talk about."

"Bullshit, and you know it," said Betty. Ilene must be drowning, thought Betty, isolating herself during the biggest crisis of her life. Until Ilene confided in her, Betty would do what she could to help Ilene indirectly. For starters, she would keep a close eye on Peter.

Peter rubbed his temples. "I have never been so bone-cracking tired in my life."

Betty said, "Pick up your stuff at the hotel tomorrow and move in here. You shouldn't be alone. The couch pulls out. It's more comfortable than it looks."

He mustered a smile. "I won't stay long."

She nodded. "You'll be home soon. Things will work out with Ilene," she said. "But first, let's make you feel better right now."

"Not possible."

She walked into the kitchen area of the living room (basically, a sink, oven, and refrigerator tucked into a corner). Opening the freezer door, she reached inside and pulled out a pint of Ben and Jerry's Coffee Heath Bar Crunch. She had bought the pint on the way home from work the day after Earl dumped her, and she'd planned on eating the whole thing that night. But when she sat down to commit the act of self-destruction, she just couldn't do it. Stopping herself was a defining moment for Betty. Ever since, she'd looked at the full ice-cream container as a symbol of strength. She vowed to leave the pint in her freezer forever to remind her to stay strong.

But considering Peter's predicament, her ice-cream-as-heroic-symbol theory seemed silly. Purposefully abstaining was just as wrong-headed as mindlessly shoveling. She should think of ice cream the way a normal person would, as a special treat on a hot summer night.

Betty took two spoons out of the dish rack, and handed one to Peter. "As your diet buddy, I advise you to eat this."

"You look so much like her," he said.

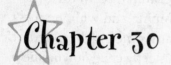

Chapter 30

Sunday, June 22
9:00 P.M.

"Sorry I'm late," said Sam when he showed up at Frieda's apartment.

He was supposed to arrive an hour and a half ago. He said he'd be right over after he straightened up his apartment and went through his mail. Frieda had told Justin that Sam would be there soon, well before bedtime.

Justin had said, "Is David coming over, too?"

"Sam has been away for over a month," she said. "Aren't you excited to see him?"

Her son shrugged. "He'll never be my father," he said.

Sam had been assuming a role closer to brother than stepfather. He had taught Justin how to faux fight (pretending to throw a punch, recoiling from a phony blow). They played computer games together. They watched horror movies. But they hadn't bonded in a parent-child way. How could they, when Sam was away so often?

For that reason alone, Frieda had been determined to keep Justin awake until Sam arrived. She gave him a late bath. She turned on the TV, any channel he wanted. At 8:45, though, Justin had started whining and whimpering that he wanted to go to bed. On any other night, Frieda would have been overjoyed to put a sleepy child down. She reluctantly agreed and tucked him in. Justin was out as soon as his head hit the pillow.

Sam buzzed fifteen minutes later. During that quarter hour, Frieda had fumed. Wasn't the whole point to find a man who could be a father for Justin? A husband for her? And what had she gotten for herself? A man who seemed unwilling or unable to be either. A flash of her "no goal in dating" philosophy popped into her head. Just a flash, though.

Frieda looked at Sam as he stood in the doorway. She hadn't seen him in five weeks. He was tan, the bronze skin making his eyes look darker. He needed a haircut. She'd seen him in those shorts a million times. Didn't he have any other clothes?

He said, "You look good," smiling at her.

She said, "Come in."

Sam stepped into the apartment. He grabbed Frieda and started kissing her, pulling her close. At this point in their reunion ritual, the physical contact would make her swoon and melt against him. Wordlessly, they'd head for the bedroom. In short order, any confusion about Sam would be replaced by magic, passion, a certainty that he was hers, that she would endure any test to spend one more hour with him. But tonight, with his arms around her and his lips on her neck, she was too mad to let herself go.

He could feel it. She was stiff as a plank. "I'm sorry I'm late. I got a call from an agent. A real agent, unlike the loser I have now."

"In California?" she asked.

He paused. "In New York."

"On a Sunday night."

"You think I'm lying?" he asked.

"My relationship with you is defined by waiting," she snapped.

He backed off. Dropped her out of his arms like a load of dirty laundry. "I'm not going to rush an ICM agent off the phone," he said.

"You missed Justin," she said.

"I can spend the day with him tomorrow."

"He has camp tomorrow," she said, exasperated.

Silence. Big, glacial Maine-sized silence. All the while, Sam stared at Frieda questioningly. She sighed with disgust. Gritted her teeth. She could not take the black hole of silence. She had to fill it, or be sucked in by it.

"You have never bought me a present," she said.

He squinted at her. "What are you talking about?"

"I don't think you understand what it means to be in a committed relationship."

Sam resisted the challenge, and walked past her into the kitchen. She followed. He poured himself a glass of water from the sink and sat down at the table. She sat down, too, the chair farthest away from him. He drank. Put the glass down on the table. Picked it up. Drank. Put it down. Action to bide time during one of his Catholic New England lapses of mental synaptical spark. A Jewish guy from New York would have blurted out ten different defenses by now, told her he loved her twenty times, run out and come back with flowers, dropped to one knee to beg for forgiveness and understanding. But not Sam. He had to think. Frieda simmered in wait, every passing second bringing her closer to boiling.

Finally, he said, "I know what commitment means."

She waited an ice age for that? "Everything about our relationship is on your terms," she said. "When we see each other. When we talk. You're just living your life, and seeing me when I fit into your schedule. How can I believe that what we have is real? That we have more than sex? You have to do more for me. If you can't, or won't, why should I bother?"

The expression on his face was heartbreaking. She wondered if anyone he cared about had ever spoken to him with such animosity. The opposite of kindness and affection, the two things they'd promised always to give each other.

He took a while to respond, of course. Then he said, "I don't do enough for you? I put my hands all over your body. I worship you. I clean your apartment, I play with Justin, I listen to every word you say."

"You like doing those things," she said.

"You want me to do things I don't like?"

Now she was confused. "Of course not."

Sam pushed his chair back. It scraped on the floor. He folded his arms across his chest defensively. "Why do you think I stop loving you when I'm out of town?" he asked. "Why does your insecurity throw my commitment into question?"

She said, "I don't feel it. You say the words, but they don't sound sincere. Like you're just saying your lines."

"Our relationship is not a performance," he said.

"You just aren't convincing," she said.

"What about you?" he asked. "All you send my way is doubt. You've got it twisted around, Frieda. I'm committed to you. You're the one who's holding back. And now I know why."

"What do you—"

"You've been holding back since the very beginning," he said. "Do you realize that the first thing you asked when I walked in here is why I don't buy you gifts?" he said. "I don't like being broke. I hate it. I want to make money, to stop having to travel so much. I'm working as hard as I can for all that. But you don't care about what I'm trying to do. You only complain about what I don't do."

He was getting angry, defensive. But then she thought about it: Had she ever asked him about his work? Or had she only resented his job because it took him away from her?

She tried to sound supportive. "I want you to make it."

"You want a man who's already made it," said Sam. "Someone who can buy you gifts and stay in New York. A man who'll run when you snap your fingers. Someone you can corral or contain."

"That's an overstatement," she said. "I don't want to put you or anyone in a box."

"I imagine you don't," he said. "You've already buried your husband in one."

Frieda's jaw dropped. Had she heard correctly?

"Get out," she said, tears forming.

He softened instantly, and came toward her. "That was awful. I shouldn't have said that. I didn't even think it, but the words came out. I'm sorry, Frieda," he said.

She'd wanted him to speak without thinking. Look what it got her. She said, "You should go."

"Do you really want me to leave?" he asked.

Frieda was too rattled to answer. Her emotions were a tumble. He'd said it clearly: He felt like she was trying to trap him, which would be the equivalent of death. Obviously, Sam was intimidated by the demands of a single widowed mother. He wasn't up for it. He was too young, inexperienced. Ilene had been right all along.

Resolved, Frieda led Sam back into the living room. As they walked, he said, "You worry that all we have is sex. I don't believe that. You know it's more. I grab you upon sight because sex with you is the greatest thing I've ever known. And I want the greatest thing ever as often as possible. I know you do, too. You can't want to give that up."

He was scrambling. His eyes were scanning her face, searching in a panic for the softening he was used to. Frieda showed him nothing. In his uncertainty, she felt a surge of power. She was older, wiser, and she suddenly had the perspective to see what she needed for herself and Justin.

Sam stood in the doorway. For once, he was waiting for her to speak.

She said, "You're right."

"I am?"

"I have been holding back since the beginning." She hadn't wanted to see the end, from the beginning or at any point along the way, but here it was. "I can't see us going forward."

His eyes turned from brown to black. "That's it?" he said.

She nodded.

"I wish I'd been wrong," he said before kissing her on the forehead and leaving. She quietly squeezed the door shut.

Three Months Later

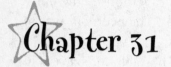

Chapter 31

Thursday, September 11
11:45 P.M.

"This is it," said David Isen as he ushered Frieda into his apartment. They were returning to his place on their first official *date*-date. It had started in a cozy booth at Le Bernardin. Then orchestra seats at *The Producers*. And finally, the back seat of a taxi to his place. David paid for everything, had planned it all, and arrived at the restaurant with flowers. That was six hours ago. The roses (red) had long since lost their perk. Frieda had lost hers, too. She was sleepy from the wine at dinner and tired of carrying around two dozen roses all night (she had to cram the bouquet under her theater seat). Frieda wanted to go home. But David insisted she come up for one last drink.

"These need water immediately, if not sooner," she said.

He pointed toward the back. "Kitchen, that way."

She wandered through the loftlike living room, with its wheat-colored couch, soft wool carpeting, glass coffee table, low-hung and acceptably framed abstracts on the sand-colored walls. His bookshelves were well stocked. She walked down a long hallway past a cavernous home office crammed with computer equipment. The bedroom was to the left.

She finally found the kitchen. The table-for-six, eat-in room had enough counter space to fillet an antelope. And cabinets! It took her a full five minutes of opening and closing doors to find a vase that could handle long stems. The vase itself was crystal, the prisms of light making tiny rainbows. A wedding gift, she figured.

David's West Village apartment was bigger than her brownstone floor-through, she estimated. Had to cost a fortune. He appeared in the doorway of the kitchen, smiling as the sounds of Ella Fitzgerald floated down the hall.

Frieda filled the vase with water and said, "Nice place you got here."

"It was a rush purchase. I bought it not long after Georgia and I split up," he said. "I like it, but I'm not married to it. I'd move. Out of borough. I'm not a Manhattan snob."

She took that in. As usual, he was pushing. She'd held him off for a few months, since the breakup with Sam. She had to get over that before she could consider dating again, she'd said. They continued to see each other a few times a week as friends. David took her out to restaurants. He had a sophisticated palate and Frieda enjoyed dining with him. He always ordered wine. Never Scotch. And he never got drunk. She didn't think they'd ever killed a whole bottle between them. After dinner, he would put her in a taxi and accept a chaste kiss on the cheek. He'd say, "If you want to use me to get over Sam, I'm available."

That job was slow going. She lost hours of sleep thinking about Sam, things they'd done, things she'd said. She almost called him a million times. Within days of the breakup, she'd reconsidered everything she'd thought. Had her reservations been real or imagined? How could she turn her back on the greatest passion she'd ever known? Had she Learned Nothing from Gregg's Death? Certifiable bliss was to be clung to at all costs, even if what came with it wasn't the perfect fit.

Ilene, meanwhile, told Frieda that passion didn't last. It was scientific fact. "Once the lust goes, you're left with a guy who disappears for weeks at a time and has no money," said Ilene.

Frieda countered with, "But it was love at first sight. You of all people should understand."

Ilene said cryptically, "Love at first sight may not mean love everlasting."

That day, Frieda had received a direct-mail package from Sam's theater company. He'd put her name and address on the mailing list when they'd first hooked up, nearly a year ago. No Sudden Movements Players were returning "triumphantly!" to City Center in October to present a fully staged revival of *Guys and Dolls*. On the cover of the brochure was a picture of Sam, smirking in Damon Runyon regalia: wide-brimmed hat, sharkskin suit with wide lapels. The picture was fetching. He looked funny and handsome and happy, and she wished she were still in a relationship with a man whose face was on the cover of a vivid four-color direct-mail package.

Inside, she read that he was starring as Nathan Detroit. An asterisk next to his name. She read the footnote at the bottom: Sam Hill was represented by International Creative Management. Well, he'd gotten a good agent. Frieda was happy for him. His improved status only meant that he'd have to travel more, she figured. And what if he became a big success? Why would he want to have anything to do with her? Her destiny had been set when she'd become a mother, become a widow. His life was just unfolding. Frieda realized that letting him go, however much she'd been regretting it, was the right thing for him. She folded the brochure into smaller and smaller squares, and then threw it away. She picked up the phone and called David. She agreed to go on a real date with him, and she would possibly sleep with him, since she was very vulnerable right now.

David had jumped at the chance, and wanted to take her out tonight. God, he was easy. Frieda put on a new dress from Banana Republic and took the subway to Le Bernardin (no clue how he'd gotten a reservation on such short notice). The roses. *The Producers* (no clue how he'd gotten tickets on such short notice).

Arranging the roses, she looked across the kitchen counter at David. "Justin seemed to like it that I was going to see you tonight," she said. Actually, he'd been whiny about her leaving.

"You're great with Stephanie," he said. "I didn't mention

this at dinner, but Georgia has been offered a job at a consulting firm in New York. Something she set up at the Javits convention in June. If all the pieces fall where they're supposed to, Stephanie might be back in New York in a couple of weeks."

"How will you get her into a school?" asked Frieda, all too aware of the competition to secure coveted slots in New York's private schools.

David said, "I'm good with short notice."

"I noticed," said Frieda.

"In theory," he said, "if we got married, she could go to Justin's school on their sibling policy."

"Theoretically," said Frieda. "Wouldn't that be a story in *New York* magazine, the lengths people go to for a spot in a private school?"

"Or we could get married for real," he said. David came toward her. She braced herself. He was going to kiss her now. She'd already decided to have sex with him. It'd been a while for Frieda, over four months since the last time she and Sam were together. Frieda didn't expect to feel the same explosive chemistry with David. But how bad could it be? He had an excellent body. As soon as they got down to business, she'd forget about her nerves and think only of nerve endings. Maybe she'd forget about Sam.

David was one step away. She turned toward him. He reached out. And took her hands. He held them in his own. Kissed her knuckles. Little pecks. He said, "We could make a family, the four of us. The kids get along so well."

This was not the time to talk about family or the kids or

private school. Or marriage. Frieda said, "You haven't shown me the bedroom yet."

"We need to talk for another minute," he said.

"Enough talking, David," said Frieda. "We talk and talk and talk. I'm ready to stop talking."

He said, "I'm nervous."

She flashed back to the first date with Sam. No dinner, no expensive wine, no show, hardly any conversation. Just Scotch in his dumpy apartment. It'd taken him mere minutes to get her naked. He had much more confidence than David.

He searched her face. He wanted to know that it was okay to be nervous. That it would go well. Frieda said, "It's okay to be nervous, David. It will go well."

"I want it to," he said.

"Why wouldn't it?" she asked impatiently. He continued to clutch her hands. They were getting slippery. Fatigue was settling into her shoulders. If he didn't act like a man and make a move in the next three minutes, she was out of there.

He said, "I haven't been with anyone since Georgia left."

She'd said the same thing to Sam about his being her first since Gregg. Sam had been patient. Frieda found David's need for reassurance tiresome, a turnoff. Sam hadn't been turned off by *her* insecurity.

Frieda said, "It's just sex, David." Sex had been her sun and moon with Sam.

David smiled. "You're right. We have so much more than sex."

She said, "Maybe we have sex, too."

He led her to the bedroom. Besides the tasteful platform bed and black chenille coverlet, the room was sparsely decorated with a night table, swan-necked chrome lamp, and built-in bookshelves. David excused himself to the bathroom. She half expected him to emerge in something a little more comfortable.

While he was gone, she scanned the bookshelves. No novels in sight. He came out of the bathroom exactly as he'd gone in, except she could smell the Listerine on his breath from across the room.

She said, "What's with the war books?"

He said, "They fascinate me."

"What do you get out of them?" she asked.

"Stories. A history of the world," he said. "History really does repeat itself."

She nodded. He sat on the edge of the bed and she joined him. He kissed her on the lips, and it was okay.

She sat up to take off her shirt. Once it was over her head, she turned to check David's reaction. She looked hard at his eager face. After just a second, his features started to blur. An overlay rest upon them and Frieda realized with a jolt: David was Not Sam. He would always be Not Sam.

David pulled her down and rolled on top of her to begin his groping in earnest.

Frieda closed her eyes. She was able to respond to David's attentions. But the idea that history repeated itself kept intruding into her thoughts.

Chapter 32

Friday, September 12
4:30 P.M.

"Feet in the stirrups," said Dr. Regina Habibi. Ilene had been coming to Regina, a raven-haired Pakistani, at the St. Luke's-Roosevelt gynecology department for twenty-plus years. Together, they'd shared many intimate moments. Regina had been Pap smearing Frieda and Betty since adolescence. She'd delivered Justin. Attended Gregg's funeral.

Ilene put her feet in the metal stirrups, and slid down to the end of the table. "I know I should have come sooner," she said. "Don't give me any shit about that, please." This was Ilene's first appointment since taking her EPT test. "I'm still not sure I want to have it."

Regina ignored her. The nurse acted as if she hadn't heard a word, adjusting the light properly, preparing to give Ilene's crotch the third degree.

Ten minutes of poking and probing later, Regina snapped off her gloves and asked the nurse for another pair. The doc said, "Have you been drinking alcohol? Smoking ciga-rettes? Taking recreational or prescription drugs?"

"No," said Ilene. "I'm not stupid. Just in denial."

"You've gained twenty pounds since your last appoint-ment," said Regina.

"All in the last three months."

The nurse handed the doctor a tape measure. She stretched the tape down Ilene's belly, from belly button to the top of her pubic bone. More palpating of the uterus (blessedly, external). "Do you know the date of your last period?" asked Regina.

"No," said Ilene. "I was only getting my period every six weeks anyway. Sometime in the spring? Late spring?"

"You're about four months pregnant," said Regina. "We'll need to do more tests to pin down a due date. And I'd advise you to slow down with the eating. You should have gained five pounds at this point. I want to do blood and urine testing. You're over 35, so we should do an amnio next week. You need to start taking prenatal vita-mins immediately."

"You're being curt," said Ilene, sitting up.

"I'm cross with you," said Regina. "You've been trying to get pregnant for six years, and then, when you finally do, you're blasé and irresponsible. Don't get up."

The nurse wheeled in a large machine with a computer monitor and keyboard. Regina turned it on and started punching keys and fiddling with the mouse. Ilene adjusted her gown, and moved back so her ass wasn't hanging off the end of the table.

"I didn't come in for so long because I didn't want to get a speech," she said. A bald lie. Ilene could take speeches. She didn't want to have to explain why Peter hadn't come with her. Why she was still considering an abortion. Three months had gone by and no word from Peter. She didn't know where he was, or what he was doing. He had no idea she was pregnant. And the thought of being a single mother was so repellent to Ilene that she couldn't commit her mind to the pregnancy. On the other hand, she knew this was her last chance. If she didn't have this baby now, she could forget motherhood, single or married, forever. And, of course, she had to consider the financial picture. On just her salary, could she afford childcare, diapers, baby furniture and gear, eventually school, camp, piano lessons?

Ilene said, "If I had an abortion at this stage, would it hurt?"

Regina said, "You'd be put under. Wouldn't feel a thing."

"Hospital stay? Would insurance cover it?"

"What does Peter think?" asked Regina. She picked up a plastic wand, put a condom on it, and smeared K-Y jelly on the condom.

"You're not putting that inside me," said Ilene.

"Brace yourself," said Regina.

The nurse pushed Ilene's knees apart. She felt every inch of the plastic wand enter her. It was the most action she'd seen in months. Regina wiggled it around, hitting some spots.

"I have to pee," said Ilene.

"We need a full bladder," responded the doctor. The

nurse turned down the overhead lights. "What do Frieda and Betty think?" asked Regina.

Betty always called, every couple of days, to see how Ilene was feeling, but she didn't press her on why Peter never answered the phone, or why Ilene still hadn't told Frieda. Ilene rushed her off the phone, put off or canceled plans. She'd postponed the monthly dinner again and again. Whenever Frieda called, all she wanted to talk about was Sam and/or David. Ilene was grateful, actually, for Frieda's self-absorption. Playing the role of advice giver was comfortable and familiar. The idea of turning to Frieda and Betty for help made her feel strange, out of control.

If she decided to abort, Ilene had already scripted a weepy miscarriage account to relay to Betty. She'd swear her baby sister to secrecy. Betty would agree. She might not believe the miscarriage story, but she was trustworthy enough to keep her doubts to herself.

Ilene said, "Frieda and Betty want what's best for me."

The doctor continued to fiddle with the mouse. Mumbling meaningless numbers to the nurse, who spooled inky black squares of paper as they churned out of the printer.

Regina said, "Heart beat normal, organ size normal, spine, skull measurements normal."

"You can see all that?" asked Ilene.

"Want to take a look?" asked Regina.

Ilene hesitated. She remembered looking at Justin's sonogram pictures and being awed by them. But if she dared to peek at the images of the action in her own uterus, she wouldn't see a fetus. She'd see a closing circle of options, like tightening the drawstring of a velvet pouch. If Peter were here for this, he'd be standing over the doctor's shoulder, pointing at the screen, asking, "What's that? What's this?" Wanting to keep every printout. Framing them. Saying, "as long as it's healthy," but desperately wanting a baby girl to name Daisy. In their optimistic days, years ago, when they'd started trying, they'd talked about such things. Names, genders. Ilene could imagine Peter crying at this moment. Ilene would roll her eyes in mock disgust at her big, fat, sentimental husband. But Peter wasn't fat. Not anymore. Nor was he with her anymore. She was alone on the table, alone in this moment, even with a fish swimming around inside her uterus.

Ilene closed her eyes, not wanting to catch a glimpse of the monitor, and said, "Can you tell the sex?"

Regina dug the wand a bit deeper, searching for a new angle. She said, "I can't say with absolute certainty. Eighty percent sure."

"Go ahead," said Ilene.

Regina said, "It appears to be a girl."

Chapter 33

Friday, September 12
6:30 P.M.

"It's a girl," said Jane. "She says she met you at the *Financial Times* media luncheon last week. Lisa something."

Peter was in a hurry, throwing folders and a pack of gum into his briefcase and slamming it shut. "I don't have time to talk. Ask her what she wants."

Jane said, "She wants to schedule a lunch. I think she'd be happier with dinner."

Another one. Amazing how they came out of the woodwork when news of his separation traveled across the transom of finance journalism. Peter had barely said a word to anyone about his marital situation, but people in his office knew he couldn't be reached at home, and that faxes and packages should be sent to his temporary address on Avenue A. Jane, Peter suspected, filled in the blanks. Random phone calls from young women started coming in.

He had to admit he liked the attention. So much so that he sought it out. He never used to go to media events, cocktail parties, or award ceremonies. But these days, when the invitations hit his desk, he was quick to RSVP. Not that he'd do anything with these women. They wanted to use him. What was in it for him? Sex? He was nowhere near that point. One particularly frustrating aspect of the separation with Ilene was that their sex life at the end had been fantastic. Like when they first got married.

Ready to go, Peter checked his desk one last time. Was he forgetting anything? His eyes fell on the empty space where the wedding photo used to be. Jane's idea. She'd hidden the picture, removed the sad reminder. He picked up his briefcase and left his office.

Before he could extricate himself completely from the world of work and get downtown to meet Betty for dinner, Jane said, "Where's the fire?" With her small-boned hand, his secretary pointed at the chair next to her desk. He hesitated. He wasn't up for a chat with Jane. But he sat as instructed. Since seeing her naked, he didn't have the balls to refuse her anything. He'd trespassed on her in the most personal fashion. He owed her, big time, and part of his payment was to listen to whatever geyser of wisdom spouted from her lips.

He said, "I'm already late." Check the watch, look pointedly at the desk clock. Straighten the tie.

"Another date with Betty?" she asked.

"It's not a date. We've having dinner and then going to a movie."

"Dinner and a movie," said Jane. "And then back to her apartment to sleep on the couch?"

"Only you would make assumptions. Betty's my sister-in-law. That's practically incest. You've got bonking on the brain. Much as I admire you and wish ardently that more women were like you, in this one instance, you are wrong," he said.

"I don't think you're sleeping together," said Jane. "I *do* think it's strange that you choose to live in her tiny apartment. Wouldn't you be more comfortable in a hotel?"

Peter sighed. This was exactly what he'd wanted to avoid. "I don't have an ulterior motive. I just like the company."

Jane nodded patiently, condescendingly. "Betty is, what? Thirty-two?"

"I guess."

"How old was Ilene when you got married?"

"I can see where you're going with this," he said. "Betty and I are friends. We have a lot in common. Can't a man and a woman simply be friends?"

While he protested, Jane opened her desk drawer. She pulled out a framed photograph. The wedding picture. He hasn't seen it in months. "Look at this," she said.

He looked. Peter and Ilene, staring at each other, grinning goofily. In a love as roiling and deep as the ocean. The happiest he'd ever been. How had things gone so wrong? Ilene's hair was darker then. Her skin pinker. She was glorious. He had an ill-fitting tux, a sheen of sweat, bed head. What had she seen in him?

Jane said, "You can't tell me that Betty today isn't the spitting image of Ilene eleven years ago."

He handed back the picture and stood to go. "I'll be in early tomorrow. We've got a staff meeting at nine. Before you leave, call the senior editors and remind them that lateness will not be tolerated. And I expect researched story ideas, not vague notions."

Jane tucked the frame back into her drawer. "Yes, sir," she said. "Is there anything else? Sir?"

"Your annual review forms are on my desk," he said. "Please fill them out. And say something bad about yourself for once. Personnel might catch on."

Jane said, "I'm recommending a fifteen percent raise."

"Recommend ten," he said, "and leave it on my desk to sign."

With that, Peter made a dash for the elevator. He refused to contemplate what Jane was suggesting about Betty. The sisters might look alike, but their personalities were completely different. Even if looking at Betty did evoke memories of a young Ilene, Peter would never touch his sister-in-law. He wouldn't dare. She'd be horrified. Even more abhorrent, she might not be horrified.

The whole issue gave him palpitations. He knew he'd have to move out of her one-bedroom at some point. Betty hadn't fired a "leave now" warning shot like Jane and Tim had. But Peter knew he wasn't good for Betty. She was content to spend every evening watching videos with him. She was a beautiful young woman. She needed to go out.

Peter strode out of the building, into the September heat. Still felt like August in the city. He loosened his tie, remarking to himself as always that he sweat so much less than he had last summer. He walked across Madison Avenue, along 45th Street, toward Grand Central. As usual, he stopped at Hudson News—the big one, to watch if anyone picked up a copy of *Bucks*.

He couldn't resist flipping through a copy himself, turning immediately to his story on price gouging in the personal services industry. He'd written a nasty screed on the arbitrary billing practices of personal trainers, nutritionists, private chefs, and interior decorators, including a first-person sidebar about Peggy McFarthing. He hoped to God that she went out of business because of it. He hadn't gotten a phone call from her lawyer, not that she had any basis to sue him. He'd described his own experience. No slander in that. He sent a dozen copies to Peggy's office with a note, thanking her for all she'd done for him. He chuckled to himself, thinking of her reading his description of her as "a brittle scarecrow."

"Excuse me," said a lilting female voice.

Peter looked up from his article to see a woman—make that a WOMAN. Blonde ponytail swinging high on her head, tight stretchy bike shorts, a midriff-baring T-shirt that revealed a tan, crunched-to-concrete belly. Skin that practically snapped with dewy freshness. He guessed she was twenty-one. Twenty-three, tops.

Peter stepped out of her way, clearing a passage to the magazine racks. To his amazement, she picked up a copy of *Bucks*. She flipped to his article. She saw him staring, and noticed that his magazine was opened to the same page.

She pointed at her magazine, and then at his. They laughed. Together. Like old, dear friends. She said, "I'm a personal trainer. This article is the talk of New York Sports. Some customers have come in demanding flat fees."

"You don't say," Peter marveled, loving the idea that a bevy of hard female bodies in skimpy spandex leotards were evoking his name and prose, even to revile him. Perhaps the harem of spinning instructors would try to pile on top of him in protest.

She said, "A lot of trainers are pretty pissed off about it. But I think it's good."

"Really?"

"Yeah. It's wrong to charge some old geezer three times as much for an hour just because he's willing to pay it."

"Yeah," he agreed. He'd agree to anything she said just to watch her talk. When she spoke, she bobbed her head up and down, telegraphing "yes, yes, yes" with each syllable.

"A lot of the male trainers do the same thing, jacking up the price for old ladies."

"That is pathetic," he said.

"I'd never do it," she said. "I have this one customer? He's divorced from his wife, and he's really lonely. You can tell, because all he does is talk about getting in shape to meet women. He's asked me out a couple times, and I keep telling him that I don't date clients. He asks about other girls at the club, too. I don't have the heart to tell him that none of the other girls would date a guy that old, even though he's in pretty good shape. I tell you, there's nothing sadder than a hard-up, lonely, divorced older man."

Peter nodded along (yes, yes, yes) for the duration of her confession, picturing her bending over a glute builder, some stooped, gray-haired granddad looking on. Peter didn't want to ask, but felt compelled: "How old is this geezer?"

"Ancient," she said.

"In years," he asked.

"I'd have to guess," she said.

Please don't say forty, he prayed. "Go ahead."

She stopped nodding suddenly, and said, "How old are you?"

"Thirty," he said. "You thought twenty-five, right?"

She laughed. So did he. Together. They were *such* dear friends. She said, "Okay, I'll tell you."

Please don't say forty, he prayed harder. "Yes?"

"He's at least fifty."

"Fifty?" Peter practically shouted the number with relief. "And he's hitting on twenty-year-olds? You *should* charge him double just to teach him a lesson."

"It's more fun to make him do a hundred military-style pushups," she said, bobbing her head.

He liked her so very much. He held out his hand. She shook. "I'm Peter," he said. "Peter Vermillion."

She mouthed his name to herself. "You're the guy who wrote this article?" she asked, reverence in her voice.

He tried to be humble. "I wouldn't have admitted it. But you're such a scrupulous woman."

"Pleased to meet you," she said. "I'd better be going."

She was leaving? "Wait," he said. "You haven't told me your name. We could talk again, over drinks or dinner."

The blonde trainer smiled radiantly, head bobbing yes, yes, yes, while she said, "No, no, no. I can't go out with you, Peter. Even at thirty, you're still way too old for me. And you seem like the kind of guy who wants a relationship. I don't do that. I hook up."

Before he insisted he didn't want a relationship, Peter figured he should find out what she meant. "Hooking up?" he asked. It sounded painful.

"Going out in groups of girls, and picking up groups of guys, taking them back to someone's apartment and having safe-yet-casual sex," she said. "I think I'm leaning toward lesbianism, anyway. And even if I were attracted to you, I couldn't do much about it until my labial piercings heal."

"Labial piercings," he said.

"Four of them. Two on each side. Very tasteful. Refined," she said, nodding yes, yes, yes.

Peter checked his watch, straightened his tie, cleared his throat. He said, "I'll be going now."

She smiled again, bobbing. He couldn't keep himself from glancing at the crotch of her bike shorts for visible signs of hardware. He replaced the magazine on the rack and walked off toward the subway, trying hard not to imagine what a labial piercing looked like. He also tried hard to forget something she'd said, but the phrase "hard-up, lonely, divorced older man" rang in his head.

Chapter 34

Saturday, September 13
7:00 P.M.

Betty arrived right on time. She was embarrassed to be so punctual. Punctuality meant only one thing: that she had nothing better to do on a Saturday night than baby-sit her nephew.

Frieda welcomed her with a hug. "Justin is in a mood," she warned.

Betty had seen his moods. "I can handle it," she said. Betty's strategy with her nephew's crankiness was to ignore him completely. It worked amazingly well. When Frieda tried to crack a bad mood of Justin's, she hovered, cajoled, eventually got angry, which, plain as day to Betty, only worsened the kid's temperament.

"Come in back," said Frieda. Betty followed her into the bedroom. Her sister fussed with her black cocktail number. "We're going to some magazine party," said Frieda. "David said it'll be a bunch of bond wonks pounding dirty martinis."

"Fun," said Betty, settling in on the bed to watch her sister finish dressing.

"David gets invited everywhere. Sam and I never went to parties. We never spent time with other people," said Frieda.

Betty said, "Every time you say something positive about David, you throw in a comparison to Sam. You and Sam never spent time with other people because you couldn't tear yourself out of bed. How is the sex with David, by the way?"

Her sister struggled to latch a string of pearls around her neck. Betty got up to help. She stood behind Frieda, in front of the full-length mirror. After securing the clasp, she looked at their reflection. Betty was taller, darker. Her hair straighter. But they were sisters, anyone could see that.

Frieda said, "Sex with David is fine."

"Fine?"

"We've only done it a few times. It takes a while to get used to each other's bodies," said Frieda.

"It took you and Sam about two seconds," said Betty.

Frieda applied blush. "You never liked Sam," she said. "You never supported the relationship."

Betty hadn't gotten to know Sam well enough to dislike him. "I wasn't sure Sam was right for you. I'm not sure David is either. But what do I know? I mean, it's hard to know what's right when you're on the inside of a relationship. It's impossible from the outside."

Frieda said, "You miss Earl."

Bingo. Betty had successfully worked through her apathy, and her antipathy toward the bastard Earl. Now that her raw emotions had been cooked all the way through, she found herself missing him, wanting to go back to the morning he walked into her office and turned her life upside down.

Frieda said, "David told me something odd. About Ilene. He said that people at *Cash* are saying Peter left *her*. Can you believe the viciousness of office gossip? To make up a complete lie and spread it around?"

Ilene's secret wouldn't keep. Frieda would be the last to know. Betty said, "How does a rumor like that get started?"

"David said it comes from people at *Bucks*. They're saying Peter is shacked up with a much younger woman in some Lower-East-Side hovel."

"What does Ilene say?" asked Betty, wondering how staffers at *Bucks* knew what her apartment looked like.

Frieda said, "I haven't breathed a word to Ilene. She'd be furious. David said she's been working like a dog on some big bankruptcy story and barely interacts with anyone at work."

Betty hated hearing that. So now she'd cut herself off from her colleagues, too. Betty had been pushing Peter to contact his wife, to make up with her. But he was waiting for Ilene to make the first move. He said he'd waited this long, he could wait a while longer. It was a stalemate, Betty in the middle, keeping Peter's location a secret from Ilene, and Ilene's pregnancy a secret from Peter.

The whole cloak-and-speculum business was starting to wear on her nerves. Betty felt locked in their conflict, unable to break free, but not quite wanting to, since, if she were unencumbered with secrets and a house guest, she'd be duty bound to battle her own demons. The plastic folder with the goods on Earl remained under her mattress. She wasn't ready to mail it, thereby letting him go. He mistreated her. He manipulated her. He was a liar, a cheat, a swindler, and a jerk. But he made her pulse race. That had to count for something. Maybe it counted for everything.

Not for Frieda, apparently. She'd switched from sex to security in a blink. Betty watched Frieda primping, wrestling with her curls so they fell just so. She seemed content. Betty wanted to ask Frieda how she'd let go of Sam so easily, whether she still thought about him. Betty could not stop thinking about Earl.

Changing the subject, Betty said, "What's Justin's problem tonight?"

"He's pissed off that I'm going out," said Frieda, finishing her face and spritzing Obsession. "I better go. I'll call you."

"If you want to stay at David's tonight, I'll sleep over," volunteered Betty.

"Thanks," said Frieda, "but I'm definitely coming home."

"With David?"

"Don't know."

"You'd willfully pass up the opportunity for some of that fine, fine sex?" asked Betty.

"I'll tell you what," said Frieda. "If I do bring him home, you can have sex with him."

"Don't think I won't," said Betty.

*   *   *

Ignoring Justin took a lot out of Betty. She needed suste-
nance, so she made popcorn in the microwave and put it in
a large bowl on the living-room table. She ate a handful,
pushing the bowl an inch closer to Justin. From his nest of
pillows on the couch, he looked at the popcorn, but didn't
dive in. Betty continued to nibble, making exaggerated
yummy sounds, inhaling the butter scent, waving nosefuls
of it into her face.

Justin could only take so much. Finally, he edged forward on the couch and started eating. A few mouthfuls
later, his mood broke. Justin and Betty tossed kernels into
each other's mouths, and ended up whipping the corn at
each other's eyeballs as hard as they could.

More popcorn ended up on the floor than in their stom-
achs. Black and White wandered over, eating what they
could. Black started choking and then puked, which made
Betty and Justin laugh.

The absent-mindedness of popcorn eating loosened Justin's
lips. "No one will ever be my dad except my dad."

"Your mom knows that," said Betty. "But it would be
nice to have a stepdad, don't you think?"

Justin said, "I liked it better with Sam. When he wasn't
away, he spent every night here with me. He never made
Mom go out."

"Grown-ups need to go out," said Betty.

"She can go out with me," said Justin, completely missing the point.

Betty said, "She needs to go out with a man. Your mom
has always had boyfriends. She doesn't feel happy unless

someone pays attention to her in a special way." There. That had to make sense, even to a six-year-old.

He seemed to absorb the information, pausing motionlessly as his hard drive of a brain spun and processed the data. "I'll pay special attention to her."

"No, no. You're not getting it. I'm talking about grown-up stuff. You probably don't understand."

"Are you talking about sex?" asked Justin.

"Let's stick with 'special attention,'" she said, not sure what the proper perimeters were on this conversation.

Justin said, "Not all grown-ups care about that. I bet my teacher doesn't."

"You'd be surprised," said Betty.

"You don't seem to care about it," he said. "You never have boyfriends, except that long-haired guy at Christmas, but just that one time. Mom said he dumped you. Sorry about that."

"Good riddance," said Betty.

Justin continued. "If you don't want special attention, then you're like a kid. That's why you're here. You'd rather be with your own kind."

She shook her head. "Your logic is flawed," she explained. "I'm a fully formed adult who makes rational decisions, weighs risk/benefit ratios, and then acts accordingly. I've decided that special attention isn't worth the pain it can cause. I'm an adult, ruled by reason. A child is ruled by desire, like your mom. By that analysis, she's more childlike than I am."

Justin stared at her, unblinking. She said. "Did you get that?"

He said, "You lost me."

"Which part?"

"I don't know what *logic* means," he shouted. "I'm only six!"

She laughed. "Sometimes I forget," she said, grabbing him and giving him a squeeze. He sat on her lap, and they ate popcorn out of each other's hair.

He said, "Sounds to me like you're playing hide and seek. You're good at hiding, but you're supposed to let yourself get found."

Betty asked, "Are you still in therapy?"

He shook his head. "The insurance ran out."

"Good," she said. "You've clearly had enough of that already."

Chapter 35

Tuesday, September 16
10:30 A.M.

"What brings you here today?" asked Denise Bother. She wore a smart sweater set, cotton, breathable, purple. It reminded Frieda of orchid petals.

"I'm worried about Justin," replied Frieda. "He asked his first-grade teacher, a twenty-eight-year-old woman, if she needed sex. Or 'special attention from a man' was how he put it."

"That doesn't sound alarming," said Dr. Bother. "Many first graders are curious about sexuality."

"He resents it whenever I leave the house," said Frieda. "He whines constantly. He's clingy."

Dr. Bother crossed her legs and rested her interlocked hands on top of her knee. She said, "Let's put Justin aside for a moment. How are you doing?"

"Great. Good," said Frieda.

She was. The school year in full swing, Frieda was settling into a daily routine. Summers were endless, especially the weeks between camp and school. Fall was finally here, and Frieda felt centered, steady enough to hang around a bit at drop-off to chat with the moms, exchanging stories about What I Did This Summer.

One mom, Sandy, had asked her, "Are you still dating the actor?"

"Oh, no," said Frieda. "I'm done with him. We broke up a few months ago."

Sandy said, "You'll find someone else."

Frieda said, "I already have. David is an award-winning financial journalist. He works at my sister's magazine." She laid it on thick. "He's a recently divorced dad, but alimony and child support aren't a problem for him. Money isn't a problem for him." Frieda watched Sandy's eyebrows go up. "He's got blue eyes, brown hair. Six feet tall. A marathoner." She could get into this, bragging about David as if he were her prized bull at the fair.

Sandy said, "You sure can rope them in."

Frieda said, "I've been fortunate."

Sandy said, "He sounds like a keeper."

"You mean Sam wasn't?" Frieda asked, forgetting for a minute that she was supposed to be madly in love with David.

Sandy had given her a puzzled stare. Then she said, "Well, congratulations. David sounds perfect."

David was letter perfect. So why wasn't she perfectly happy?

*　　*　　*

Dr. Bother said, "If you're doing so well, why did you call for an emergency appointment? Don't waste my time or yours by saying this is about Justin."

"I'm afraid of being alone," said Frieda.

"You're human."

"The man I've been seeing . . ."

"Sam," said Dr. Bother.

"Sam and I broke up," she said quickly. "I'm with David now. He's been my friend for a while. We can talk for hours. He fits into my life. He loves Justin. His daughter, Stephanie, is moving to New York. If we get married, she'll be Justin's sister, and we can get her into Packer. David says he wants to get married anyway. But this school situation has pressed the issue. The wedding plan may seem rushed. But I can tell we'll have a good life together."

"You describe him as a friend," said Dr. Bother.

"We've been lovers for a couple of weeks."

"How's that part of it?" asked the shrink.

"Nice," said Frieda. "Fine."

"Friendly?"

"Very."

"Why did you and Sam break up?" asked Dr. Bother.

Frieda tried to come up with a pithy answer. "It wasn't working," she said.

Dr. Bother nodded knowingly. Smugly. "The passion died?"

"No, actually. If anything, it got more intense."

"You stopped loving him?"

"No."

"Did he stop loving you?"

"No."

"He didn't get along with Justin?"

"They liked each other," said Frieda.

"You fought often?" asked the shrink.

Frieda shook her head. "We hardly ever fought. Only about my frustration with his travel schedule."

"Was he emotionally withholding?"

"No. He said I was."

"Did you resent his financial situation?"

"No."

Dr. Bother was silent for a minute. "I don't understand why it wasn't working."

Frieda blurted, "Neither do I. The pressure just built and built. He was gone so much. My sisters made me wonder if he was using me. Justin didn't seem so enamored of him. But I still love him. It's just like it was before. I can't stop thinking about him." Oh, shit. The tears again. What was it about this couch? Frieda reached for the box of Kleenex. "I made a terrible mistake!" she wailed.

"You're here to talk about how to fix it," prompted Dr. Bother.

She shook her head. "I can't fix it. I'm here to learn how to live with it."

"Why can't you fix it?"

"I acted terribly the night we broke up. I was dismissive and condescending. I must have made him hate me. Besides, he's doing so well without me. It's almost as if our breakup was what he needed to succeed. I can't step back in and be his bad-luck charm."

The timer bell rang. "We have to stop," said Dr. Bother. "We should schedule another appointment. And I'd advise you to hold off on marrying David."

Frieda stood, relieved to tell someone the truth about how badly she missed Sam. The relief was so monumental, Frieda decided that unburdening herself was all she needed to do. Now, she could move on. She could let him go.

Frieda said, "I'll call you for an appointment."

Dr. Bother said, "We can make one right now."

"I've got to run. I'll call you," said Frieda, lighter than she'd been in months. Ready to see David in a whole new light. Ready to embrace a life with him.

The doc smiled. Knowingly. Smugly. "One last thing," she said.

"Yes?" asked Frieda.

"Comfort and security are appealing," she said. "You should know. You've been there with Gregg. You'd better ask yourself how badly you want to go back."

Chapter 36

So it'd come to this, thought Ilene, paging through the short stack of legal pages. The packet had been messengered from Peter's office this morning, with a handwritten note.

> *Ilene,*
>
> *First step, legal separation. One year from the date of the countersigned document, we can file for uncontested divorce, no lawyers needed. Notarize. SASE enclosed.*
>
> *Happy birthday,*
Peter

Ilene's fortiethth birthday wasn't for another month. She'd let Peter's August birthday, his forty-first, blow by unacknowledged. She dragged her fingers over the raised seal of the notary stamp by Peter's signature. This was the grand romantic gesture she'd been waiting for?

When she found the envelope—her assistant had placed it prominently on her chair, instead of in her IN box—Ilene's heart skipped a beat. The *Bucks* logo, Peter's handwriting. He'd finally contacted her. She picked up the package and sat down. Drawing a breath, she opened it. It wasn't, she saw immediately, an impassioned plea to let him come home. Ilene started reading the documents, her skin prickling with shock. At that moment, her assistant stuck her head in to ask if Ilene needed coffee. Ilene was certain that her assistant had been the one churning the gossip mill. The whispering had gotten loud enough to reach her boss's office.

Mark responded to the news with an e-mail. He asked her what she was going to work on next, "that is, if you think you can handle a big story right now," he'd written. "I can put you on Bank Notes if you'd like to take it easy for a while." Bank Notes was a front-of-the-book section of short items. Two-, three-hundred-word boxes on employment news, minor mergers and sell-offs. It was the low-rent section of the magazine, strictly relegated to associate editors and junior writers who were hungry enough to toil over glorified blurbs. Bank Notes stories were way (WAY) beneath her. Ilene send Mark a reply, suggesting she do a lifestyle feature on the hidden expenses of divorce. She hadn't heard back yet.

Her assistant repeated the offer of coffee. Ilene told her to go away, close the door, and leave her the fuck alone.

She said "the fuck" with enough emphasis that her lip bounced off her teeth, sharpening that *f* to a knifepoint. Her assistant—the poor girl was as dim as a porch light—scurried away like the rat she was. In seconds, Ilene could hear her murmuring on the phone. She bent her head to study the separation papers.

Ten minutes later, she heard a gentle tapping on her door. She ignored it. David Isen slid her door open anyway. He sat down in the chair opposite her desk. He was smiling, beaming. Her separation was a happy event for him? He was no longer the only one with a failed marriage on staff?

Ilene said, "What's with the grin?"

He said, "I'm bursting."

Bursting with sympathy? "Don't do it in here," she said. "I just had the carpet cleaned."

"I'm supposed to keep my mouth shut. And I will. I'm relying on your powers of deduction," he said. "At dinner with your sisters the day-after-tomorrow, Frieda is going to shock and amaze you."

This was about Frieda? Ilene didn't know if she should feel relieved or insulted. She said, "The suspense will have to kill me until then. I'm too busy right now to talk." She gestured to the door.

David laughed. He laughed! He was bursting with the giggles, apparently. He said, "I'll go. But first, I want to thank you for introducing me to Frieda. You'll know just how grateful I am in a couple of days."

As soon as he was gone, Ilene stuffed the envelope into

her purse and ran out of the office. Peter's signature had been notarized that morning. Not to be outdone, Ilene would get her countersignature notarized this afternoon. And she wouldn't just pop the papers into the SASE. She'd send them certified mail. Overnight certified mail. She'd spend the extra $20, and then messenger Peter the receipt.

She got the papers notarized at the newsstand in her building lobby and walked the dozen odd blocks to the post office at Third and 54th. It was an old one, built at the turn of the century. The last century. Stone mosaic floors, thirty-foot ceilings, a hanging chandelier, a long, winding circular staircase to the second-floor balcony, which overlooked the teller action below. A prime example of Old World opulence. Ilene walked up to a young man in an immaculate uniform (security), and asked, "Excuse me. Do you know where I can get a letter certified?"

"Information desk," he grunted.

Rude prick. She'd almost let herself get swept up by the grandeur of the setting and the crispness of his uniform. But she was still in New York, and that meant waiting. The information desk had a line. From there, she was directed to another line.

She got on it, and watched the seconds tick by on her watch. She was fidgeting so much and with such aggression, she bumped into the man ahead of her on line.

He turned profile to accept her apology. Then, he spun all the way around to look at her.

"Ilene, hello," he said.

"What in the?" she said. "Sam Hill, hello to you."

The impoverished actor man stood before her, wearing cargo pants, a down jacket and old sneakers. She realized with a sinking stomach (already a pixel-width from nausea) that she'd have to talk to him for the duration of the wait, or ignore him with such focus and silent volume that she might have to flee the post office. Which she simply could not do. She'd have to stand her ground and talk to him.

Ilene said, "So. How've you been?"

Sam said, "I've been all right. You are pregnant?"

Did it show? She was only four months. He hadn't seen her for a while, so her weight gain would seem dramatic. "Yes. But I'm not out with it yet. Waiting for the amnio." That was the correct response. If she decided to terminate (the window was still open), she would blame it on the bad test results.

He said, "Congratulations."

"Hmmm," she said, nodding. "I'm surprised to see you."

"I bet you never wanted to see me again."

"You don't seem surprised to see me," she said.

He shrugged. "Small city."

He bore into her eyes. His were bottomless, a dark chocolate sea. She found herself staring, trying to find his pupils.

He said, "Don't get lost in there."

She blinked and looked over his shoulder. "You can take a step," she said. The line had moved forward an inch. "We should get to the teller window by some time next week."

He stepped ahead and said, "I don't have much time. I

ran out of a rehearsal at City Center to do this, and had no idea it would take so long. We leave for London a week from Friday to do a two-week run of *Oliver!*"

"We?" she asked. Had he hooked up with yet another chorus girl?

"We, the entire company," he said. "I'm here—on this stagnant line—to renew my passport. I hadn't realized it had expired. I have to send it certified mail to the Passport Bureau in Washington today, and pay a huge fee, to get a new one in a week."

"The fee must hurt," she said, snarkily. Bad girl. She'd never survive the wait on this creeping line if she couldn't be civil. "I'm sending legal documents, too." She flashed the package, not giving him a chance to read the Marriage Bureau address.

"How's Peter?" asked Sam.

"He's well."

"How's Frieda?"

Brave of him to ask. "She's doing great. She's seeing someone, a fantastic man."

"He must be incredibly rich to meet your approval," said Sam with an even smile.

"I fixed them up," she said. "And he is quite comfortable, actually."

Ilene thought she saw a ripple in the sea of his eyes, but his expression remained the same. He *was* a talented actor, she thought.

He said, "I'm glad she's happy. If she is."

"Oh, she's happy."

"How the hell would you know?" he asked with sudden venom.

Ilene felt a tap on her shoulder. A large woman, black in a blue dress, said, "The line is moving."

Sam took a step backward. Ilene moved the six inches toward him. She said, "Frieda is my sister. I've known her for thirty-six years. You lasted, how long? Nine months?"

He smiled, slow, enjoying this. "You put the doubts in her head. About money. About my commitment."

Ilene said, "You have no idea how miserable she was when you left town."

"She was miserable to be apart because of how happy we were together," he said. "She'll never be that happy again."

Ilene scoffed. "You don't know that."

"I do," he said. "Her feelings matched mine. Frieda and I talked about it all the time. We'd never been as happy before. We won't be again. You are to blame."

"Move along," said the woman behind Ilene.

They strode two paces ensemble, right, right, left, left, Sam backward, Ilene forward, as if they were dancing. "Frieda isn't a puppet," said Ilene. "She's got her own mind."

"You . . ." he laughed in wonderment, it seemed. "You have no idea how persistently manipulative you are. I know how you operate. Asking the leading question, making the casual observation. And if you can't control the situation, you pretend it doesn't exist. You barely acknowledged me—or Betty's boyfriend—at that Christmas party, except to check me out and then dismiss me.

You made me feel like a speck. This is how you treat the man your sister's in love with?" He paused and watched her reel at the affront. "From the look you're giving me right now, I'm guessing that no one has ever treated you as rudely as you treated me," he said. "I consider it an honor to do so." He bowed. A grand low dip with the swing of an imaginary hat. He straightened up and stepped backward into the empty spot behind him without looking.

Agile, showy bastard, she thought. "If I had any guilt about influencing Frieda about you, it is gone. Thank God she's with David."

"David?" asked Sam. "Not that Ken doll you brought to *Oliver!*? He's not right for her."

"He's stable, reliable, and treats her like a queen."

"She's not excited about him," he said. "She couldn't be."

Ilene said, "After what Frieda's been through, she needs stability."

"Wrong!" he said definitively. "Frieda needs excitement. Desperately. Especially after what she's been through."

"She was with Gregg for nine years. He was stable and reliable."

"Exactly!" he said. "You're only making my point."

"You *are* making his point," said the woman in the blue dress.

Ilene turned behind her to glare, and the package slipped out of her grasp and hit the stone floor with a splat. Sam picked it up before she had a chance.

He read the address on the envelope and his eyes shot

wide open. He handed the package back. Now he'd feel sorry for her and stop his tirade. For the first time, she welcomed the pity.

He said, "If you'd been paying attention to your own relationship instead of interfering with mine, neither one of us would have been dumped. I'm glad Peter's divorcing you. He deserves better."

Sam turned around, just in time to step to the front of the line and up to the open clerk's window on the right. Blue Dress said, "You should mind your own business."

Ilene turned around, face pinched with frustration and indignation. She spit, "You're one to talk."

Seconds later, Ilene moved to the available window on the left. She turned over her package. In the corner of her eye, she saw Sam leave. She concluded her mailing and left.

That was the first time Ilene and Sam had exchanged thoughts and ideas. Swiftly, he'd deflated and insulted her. She was impressed. He was right, of course. She'd barely thought of him as anything but an inappropriate boy to be dismissed. But Sam was more of a man than Ilene had previously assumed—more intelligent, observant, articulate, handsome (couldn't deny those eyes), and pissed off. Quite a conversation, she thought.

It would not be their last.

Chapter 37

Thursday, September 18
3:13 P.M.

Betty held the bomb in her hands. She was still undecided about whether to drop it, or to put it in a drawer and let it collect dust.

Her office door was closed. She needed the precious privacy, as if she didn't get enough of that on her own time. Peter was around, of course, but he'd been spending a lot of evenings at the bar on the corner. Drinking himself into the courage to send the separation agreement to Ilene, which he'd messengered yesterday. Betty was against it, but Peter muttered something about wanting to move on with his life before he became a hard-up geezer.

Inspired by Peter's initiative, Betty had brought the plastic binder to work. She put it in a large Jiffy bag. She used the company scale and postal meter. She addressed the envelope to the human resources department at headquarters. But for some reason, Betty couldn't walk down the hall and drop it in the outgoing mailbag.

The phone rang. The ring was long, meaning the call came from inside the building. She picked up.

"Be strong, girl," said Gert.

"Huh?" asked Betty, puzzled.

"Fluff your hair," said Gert.

Betty did it reflexively. Then there was a knock at the door. Gert said, "Good luck," and hung up.

Betty put the phone down and said, "Come in."

She should have known. He said, "Is this a good time?"

Earl. The shock of seeing him made her drop the bomb in her lap. "A good time for what?" she asked, recovering enough to put the package in her bottom desk drawer before he could see it.

He pushed back his long hair. It was a bit shorter, but the gesture was all him. She couldn't deny that he looked great. Butterflies flew around in her throat and chest. They felt heavy, though, sticky. "I just flew in from Chicago," he said.

"And boy are your arms tired."

"There's a problem with the audio-book booths?" he asked.

"Not that I'm aware of," she said. They were doing fine. Sales of audio books had increased tenfold, as projected. The *uber* bosses were happy, the customers were happy. Everything was keen.

He said, "I got a call to come here and fix the booths."

Betty hadn't made the call. Was it the night manager?

Or, Betty wondered, had it been someone else? Someone with teased blonde hair who quoted articles in *Psychology Today* about lowering dangerously high levels of the stress hormone cortisol by articulating feelings of regret, hurt, and anger?

Betty said, "You got a call to fix the booths, then go do it."

Earl sat down instead. He smiled shyly. She looked across the table at him, the man who'd opened her up with his hands. She could not speak. Those sticky butterflies were clogging her throat. Betty's cortisol levels weren't going anywhere but up. Earl said, "I have a confession to make."

She didn't want to hear it. "An apology?"

He said, "I think about you every day."

"Me, too." She did. Why lie?

He said, "This is a first for me."

"Missing someone?"

"Yes," he said.

"You've never missed your son?" she asked.

That got him. She thoroughly enjoyed his stricken expression. He said, "I have an arrangement with his mother that prevents me from spending a lot of time with him. Honestly, I don't know him well enough to miss him."

Betty said, "How disassociative of you."

Earl said, "Whatever you've found out about that situation, you can't possibly understand the nuances. I'd like to tell you the whole story, but that'll take a while. And we have other things to discuss."

"The weather?" she asked.

"I want to start over with you," he said.

Betty said, "But your work here is done." When she said "here," she pointed at her chest.

"I want to start over as equals."

"You don't want to control me anymore?" she asked. "I'm no longer your *project?* You've stopped wanting to improve me, to shepherd me into the world as a slimmer, better dressed and therefore more valuable member of society?"

He said, "You have every right to be angry."

"I don't think I can handle equality, Earl," she said. "It's too much pressure for me to have to think for myself. I might wear the wrong shirt, or eat the wrong food. I might watch a bad movie and like it. I might even have friends or family who annoy you."

He waved his hands, encouraging her to keep it coming. "Go ahead," he said. "Get it all out."

"You see?" she said. "You're already telling me what to do."

Earl leaned forward, elbows on her desk. She leaned back. As far back as she could. She reminded herself of all the lies he'd told her, all the cheats on his expenses. That cheap brooch.

He said, "As I recall, you liked it when I told you what to do in my hotel room."

Her heart flopped a tiny bit. He was right. It had been thrilling to be controlled sexually. Submission stripped away (as it were) her self-consciousness about her body and inexperience. He was masterful; he made her feel safe. One would think being dominated would inspire the opposite reaction—unsafe, vulnerable. But not for Betty. Once she sank into the role (it took a while), she dissolved in the palm of his hand.

She said, "I faked every orgasm."

Earl sighed wearily. "I've had enough," he said, standing. "If the audio-book booths aren't broken, I'm going to my hotel. Union Square, same place. I'll be there all night. If you want me back, or want me at all, even for one night, I'm available."

Earl moved from sitting to standing, his body revealed to her inch by inch. The sight made her waver. One more night of him wouldn't hurt her psyche, would it? She was about to say, "Wait," when the phone rang.

She picked up. "Yes?"

"It's me." Peter. "Will you be home tonight?"

"Maybe not," she said, looking at Earl.

"Why not?" asked Peter.

"Can't say."

"Please cancel your plans," he begged. "Ilene sent in the countersigned separation agreement already. It's over. She didn't ask me to tear it up."

"Shit," she said. Earl scowled. He hated it when she cursed. "If you didn't want her to sign it, you shouldn't have sent it to her."

"You can tell me how stupid I am all you want. Even that would be better than being alone tonight," Peter said. "I'll get a movie. Anything you want. And booze. Just name it."

Earl's hair hung against his cheeks in the way that used to make her swoon. He drummed his belt buckle with his fingertips impatiently at the insult of being kept waiting by the woman who'd once jumped at his word.

The belt buckle drumming did it. Broke the spell. For the first time, Betty saw him as just a guy. Not a magician with flying fingers. Not a heartless villain. He was just some guy she knew once. No one of consequence. Not anymore.

Betty said into the phone, "*Braveheart.* White Russians. And get pot, too."

"Great!" said Peter. "Thanks, Betty."

She hung up. The phone rang again.

"Do you need to be rescued?" said Gert.

Betty said, "No."

She hung up. To Earl, she said, "I've got plans tonight with a man who might not be as exciting as you, but he's kind and sweet and desperately in love." She didn't explain that Peter was desperately in love with her sister, of course.

Earl raised his eyebrows. "A video date? Alcohol and pot? You'll get the munchies and eat the wallpaper."

She said, "If you'd ever condescended to visit my apartment, you'd know that I don't have wallpaper. And *Braveheart* is a brilliant film. A much higher caliber that, say, *Anal Intruder,* which is probably what you'll watch tonight." She paused. "And, by the way, fuck you, piece of shit, asshole, for saying anything about my eating habits. Dick. Head."

Her former lover, the man she once wanted to marry, shook his head and grimaced at her like he'd been force-fed rotten meat.

He said, "One day, you'll see that our past is just the first chapter of our story."

She said, "Having listened to the first chapter, I'll pass on buying the book."

Betty would not contact him. She wouldn't waver again. She'd given him the power in the relationship, and now Betty wanted to grab it back. Every time she'd worn uncomfortable clothes for him, ordered a salad when she wanted pasta, stopped herself from cursing, waited hours for him to call her on a weekend, abstained from alcohol, put on makeup, or prayed he'd come back, Betty had screwed herself. And if screwing Earl meant screwing herself, well, she could do that on her own anyway.

Betty said, "Before you go—and *do* let the door hit you on the ass on the way out—I have something for you."

She reached into her bottom desk drawer and pulled out the hefty envelope with the proof of his misdoings. She handed it to him, and said, "This was *my* project. I was excited about it because it kept me connected to you. I'm not excited anymore."

Chapter 38

Thursday, September 18
11:15 P.M.

Drunk, stoned, in a dimly lit room, with a pretty woman's head on his lap. Peter reviewed the situation and was pleased to find himself in it. He was especially impressed by one thing, though: His dick was not in the least bit hard. Not a single blood cell was within stiffening distance.

Peter and Betty were on the couch of her living room. The movie was nearly over. The bottle of Kahlua empty: A resin-stained roach in the ashtray. He looked around the room. The tapestry hanging on the wall, the cheap Indian print sarong used as a slipcover. The distressed (not on purpose) furniture. The scene was a flashback to college. If he were to act like he had back then, he'd be all over Betty, feeling her up, trying to revive her from her alcohol- and pot-induced slumber.

He touched her hair. It was thick and black, like Ilene's, but not as shiny and well tended. Ilene kept herself immaculately groomed. He'd always appreciated that, the care she put into herself, the courtesy to him that her legs were always smooth, moisturized and exfoliated to petal softness. He'd told her early on that he wasn't offended by body hair. He assured her that he would love her furry. She said she would never insult him by coming to bed with stubble. Of course, Peter enjoyed the smoothness.

He'd sent the separation papers for one reason: to get her back. Convoluted logic, true. He figured that the reality of their situation, presented in the form of legal documents, would make her see that this standoff had gone too far. When he received *her* package with the overnight mail receipt, he was devastated. He had to leave work immediately, glad to have the errand of picking up some pot.

When Betty got home, he was waiting on the couch, already one drink and half a joint away. He let her take off her jacket and said, "I'm a statistic."

"You'd be a statistic if you stayed married, too," she said.

"Can we put on the movie now?" he said.

Braveheart. He'd never seen it before. For the first half hour, he kept thinking of a joke. He had to tell Betty.

"I can't concentrate until I let this out," he said, pausing the action, "A Scottish guy. Goes up to a bonnie lass and says, 'Aye, lass, look under me kilt.' "

Betty said, "I like your brogue."

He said, "The lass says she can't do it, but the Scot insists. Finally, she looks under his kilt and says, 'It's gruesome!' The Scot says, 'Look again. It's gruesome more.' "

Betty laughed. She said, "You're gruesome."

If anything, he'd shrunk somewhat. The movie was full of boils, spit, death, and blood. He was touched. Especially by the disembowelment scene at the end. Made him tear up.

Betty was sagging on the couch. He asked if he should help her to bed. Instead, she put a pillow on his lap and rested her head upon it. He braced himself for the erection to come, but it didn't. His bladder felt okay. He relaxed and watched the credits roll.

It was a nice position to be in. Peter felt warmly toward Betty. If he'd ever thought about transferring his affections from Ilene to her sister, he couldn't possibly consider it now. He may have lost a wife, but he'd gained a true friend in Betty. He was so grateful for that, he nearly cried. It would be safe if he did. She was asleep and wouldn't hear it.

He let a sob escape. She shifted slightly and said, "I'm awake," she said. "Go ahead and cry if you have to."

"I just might," he said.

"This is a top-five tender moment for me," she said.

The credits finished and the VCR kicked automatically into rewind. The TV screen turned blue. Betty said, "Just for the record, I never put my head on Gregg's lap."

Peter thought about Gregg at the end. The tenderness Frieda showed him in the hospital. The ravages of Gregg's illness, images that haunted him still, and would forever.

Betty said, "Did you notice that Gregg never doubted that he'd beat the cancer. That he'd be the exception, the miracle case."

"That was his personality," said Peter.

"But it wasn't," she said. "Gregg was a pessimistic hypochondriac."

"What were his options? Concede defeat?" asked Peter. "He might have been keeping a strong front for Frieda and Justin's sake."

"Frieda told me early after the diagnosis that she couldn't live without Gregg," said Betty. "Maybe that's the takeaway. The life lesson. That no matter how much you love someone, how dependent you are on him—or her— even if you believe you can't live without him, you can. You will. Even the deepest connections may be temporary by design."

Peter realized Betty was stoned and therefore contemplative. She was trying to rationalize the way things had played out for her so far. He was also high, but he didn't believe that all connections were temporary. He'd made a commitment to Ilene for life. And even if—when—the divorce went through, he wouldn't stop loving her.

Peter said, "I'm going to have to move out at some point," he said. "This apartment is too small for two people."

"I know," she said. "We should look for a bigger place."

Chapter 39

Friday, September 19
7:34 P.M.

"I have an announcement to make," said Frieda at the sister dinner, the first since June.

What a difference three months made. The women sat at the corner table at Pepe's, a Mexican place on Atlantic Avenue around the corner from Frieda's apartment, where presently David baby-sat Justin. Her son hadn't wanted her to go. He'd been impossibly clingy, and Frieda had to peel him off her leg. David had done his best to bribe Justin into complacency with Gum by the Foot and a Nintendo Game Cube. Justin rejected the bribes. He didn't want a Game Cube. He wanted his mommy.

Frieda dug into the Pepe's red-hot salsa with a freshly baked corn chip. A chip of crunchy perfection: triangular, the size of her palm, puffy in the middle, crispy on the edges. Frieda bit into it, savoring the flavor of corn, tomato and lime. If only the perfect man were as uncomplicated a combination of flavors.

David had been impatient with Justin's mood. He said, "He's acting like a brat."

Frieda jumped to defend her son. "He's tired. He's hungry. He's overwhelmed."

Justin cleaved to her side and said, "David will never be my father." An echo of the night she and Sam broke up, when Justin had said, "Sam will never be my father." The statement had maximum impact that time. But not now. Frieda had had nearly enough of Justin's dismissals of these potential "father substitutes." She'd never pitched the "replacement concept." Not once.

Frieda said to her son, "So what?"

David and Justin both looked at her funny. "So what?" asked David.

"David won't be your father," she said to Justin. "You're absolutely right. Your father is dead. So is my husband. I'm trying to be happy anyway, and so should you." She turned to David. "As you shouldn't expect too much from Justin. He didn't fall in love with you at first sight. He needs time to let it develop. He might need a long, long time. He may never love you."

Frieda knew she wasn't talking about *Justin's* feelings. Her son and David stared at her as if she'd just landed on their planet. She grabbed her keys and jeans jacket. She said, "I've got my cell," and bolted. Out the door, into the Brooklyn night, free at last. One year ago, she'd felt the same exhilaration while walking toward Sam's apartment. Now she felt it again, as she speeded away from her own. David was planning to move in as soon as he could sell his place.

The atmosphere at Pepe's was festive. Piñatas hung from the walls, which were bright with strings of jalapeño-shaped Christmas lights. Red and green. The walls themselves were painted mesa yellow. The bottles on the mirrored bar wore mini-sombreros. Pepe's boasted Brooklyn's finest and largest selection of tequila: Forty-four varieties, many of which had the word *Diablo* or *Loco* on the label. The music: think Speedy Gonzalez cartoons. The pitcher of margaritas they'd ordered was nearly gone, and they hadn't been served one of the five entrees they'd ordered. Ilene had begged off the hard stuff. She sipped a Corona. Had been nursing it like a newborn babe.

Betty and Frieda made up for Ilene's sobriety by hammering their drinks. Ilene made up for her sobriety with gluttony. For every one salsa-laden chip Frieda or Betty ate (and they were not being ladies), Ilene shoveled in at least two. She was chowing *down*. Frieda hasn't seen her in a while. Had to be a couple of months (how had that happened?). She was astonished to see how much weight Ilene had gained.

Licking the salt off her glass, Betty said, "Announcement?"

Frieda knocked back the remainder of her drink and poured another, the dregs of the pitcher sliding into her glass. She said, "David and I are getting married!"

Frieda's sisters were silent. She added quickly, "It'll be at City Hall. On Friday afternoon. Just to make it official. We'll do a real ceremony and reception in a few months."

"Congrats!" said Betty finally.

"I know it seems rushed," said Frieda. "We're hurrying for Stephanie. Her mom is moving back to New York, and Stephanie can't get into a school. But if we get married . . ."

"It's like a green card marriage," said Betty. "But for school admission. A hall-pass marriage. Only in New York."

Ilene said, "How romantic."

"This is a real marriage," said Frieda. "We've been close friends for a while, and we both want the same things for our children. We share interests, values, status. He's wealthy and can provide for our future. He's accomplished, talented, handsome."

Ilene took a sip, a tiny one, of beer, and said, "Do you hear yourself? You sound like you're reading from a catalog called *The Perfect Man*."

"I sound exactly like you did when you were pushing him on me all year," said Frieda. "It took a while, but now I agree with you."

"Do you really?" asked Ilene, leaning forward, her newly chubby belly pushing against the table.

Betty said to Ilene, "You don't seem surprised."

"David gave me advance warning," she said. "Just hints. I figured it out on my own."

"And?" asked Frieda.

"And the thought of you marrying David makes me sick," said Ilene. "Nauseated. I may have to excuse myself. Seriously, I may become violently, spectacularly ill at any moment."

Betty said, "Bathroom's that-a-way," and pointed toward the back.

"What the hell is wrong with you?" asked Frieda. "David is your friend."

"I've been thinking about Sam Hill lately," said Ilene. "A man who, I assure you, is not my friend."

At the mention of his name, Frieda felt her throat catch. She'd been fighting him out of her head every day. Frieda said, "I've made my peace with that. I spoke to Justin's therapist about it, and I've successfully let him go. He was too much for me, really. I was frazzled from the intensity of it. We're moving in different directions. Life is much easier with David. It's level, stable."

"Unexciting?" said Ilene.

"Maybe *you'd* like to make an announcement, Ilene," said Betty suddenly.

Ilene turned toward Betty. The movement seemed to make her woozy. Frieda said, "What is going on here?"

Ilene nodded. "I do have an announcement to make. A couple of them." Ilene turned to Frieda. "Last week, I had an amniocentesis to determine if the baby I've been carrying for the last sixteen weeks has a chromosomal abnormality. If the test had shown a problem, I would have aborted. But even if the results were positive, I was still unsure about seeing it through because—here comes announcement number two—Peter and I have been separated for the last three and a half months. I didn't find out I was pregnant until after Peter left. It's a legal separation. The paperwork has been filed."

"Jesus H. Christ," said Frieda.

"You mean, *Jesucristo*," said Betty with a Mexican accent.

"You knew about this?" asked Frieda to Betty.

The youngest sister said, "I knew about the pregnancy. The Peter stuff . . ." Betty trailed off.

Frieda was stunned. She'd been oblivious, so wrapped up in her own drama, the turf war over her heart (a battle that hadn't been won or lost; everyone just dropped his or her weapons and went home). Meanwhile, Ilene had been in torment for four months?

"What can I do for you?" Frieda asked Ilene. "I'll be your Lamaze partner. I'll take you to doctor's appointments. I'll teach you to breast-feed."

Ilene said, "I haven't told you if I'm keeping it."

Betty said, "You wouldn't do that without telling Peter. He's wanted a baby for so long."

Frieda said, "Peter doesn't know?"

"Peter and I haven't spoken to each other in months," said Ilene. "Our marriage has been terrible for nearly two years. I blame Gregg."

"Gregg?" said Frieda. "What did he do to you?"

"He died," said Ilene. "Peter and I had opposite reactions to the death. He wanted to be closer to me; I wanted to pull away from him. I got the idea in my head that he was going to have a heart attack and die. And he refused to acknowledge the risk, or tolerate my fears. We started arguing. Tiny things would start huge fights. We all but stopped sleeping together. I was afraid to become a widow. I thought it was the worst thing in the world, to be in your shoes. And look at me now. A single mother in the making."

"I had no idea," said Frieda.

Ilene said, "I thought that if you could start over in a new marriage—recreate your life with someone like Gregg—then Peter and I could go back in time, too. I've only recently sorted this out. It was wrong for me to impose on you. I'm sorry."

Frieda glanced at Betty to see how she was taking all this. Her younger sister poked at the salsa with her chip, listening passively.

Ilene went on. "I don't want to be a single mother, like the woman in my office with twenty wallet pictures of her kids, and blouses that are always blotted with seltzer," she said. "I can't imagine being as devoted to another person as you are to Justin. I'm not fit to be a mother. I'm too old. I won't have a clue. The child will grow up to be a serial killer. I'm sure of it." She paused, and then finished: "Factoring in all of that, I've decided to keep it anyway. Her."

"A girl!" shouted Frieda.

"They gave me the map of her chromosomes," said Ilene. "You actually can see the two X's."

Frieda jumped up and hugged Ilene. If Frieda were to have another baby, she'd want a girl. But she probably wouldn't. A family of four was large enough even if they would have Stephanie only every other weekend, Wednesdays, and some major holidays.

Betty said, "You must tell Peter. You need to talk to him."

Frieda said, "Leave him out of it. Let's leave all the men out of it. Ilene, come live with me. We'll raise our kids together and never speak to another man. Except Justin."

Ilene said, "You're furious that I didn't tell you."

"I'm livid!" said Frieda. "But I'll cut you some slack. I'm sure you had your reasons. I'd like to hear what they were. No rush. Some time later. Tomorrow."

From her hug position, Frieda looked at Betty. "What about you?" asked Frieda. "Any announcements to make?"

Betty shook her head. "Not me," she said. "My life is uneventful and not worth discussing."

"Enough hugging," Ilene said to Frieda. "I'm prone to pregnancy-related spasmodic gastric eruption, remember?"

Frieda gave her one last squeeze and took her seat. Three waiters paraded out of the kitchen with sizzling-hot plates.

One Week Later

Chapter 40

Friday, September 26
10 A.M.

In the past week, Ilene had told her pregnancy/separation story to her sisters, friends, acquaintances, coworkers, boss, doorman, dry cleaners, the checker at the supermarket, and every cabdriver she'd taken a ride with.

Who else was there to tell? Since uncorking the plug to Frieda and Betty, Ilene had been overflowing with her news. She told everyone who'd listen, and several people who pretended to listen. Some who didn't listen at all. The basic speech: "I am both pregnant and separated. I know, I know. Me, a single mother. Hard to believe. The future will bring change. Sacrifice. Hardship. But I'll deal with the challenges as they come. I have no idea what will happen. And, for once, I have no plan."

In fact, "I have no plan," had become her mantra of liberation. Ilene gained strength from saying it. She'd always struggled to keep her life orderly, her days plotted. In giving up the struggle, she'd tapped a secret spring of inner peace and vitality. She decided to float on it, and hadn't drowned yet.

Like most of her pursuits, liberty was to be approached in a specific way. But not with a plan. It was an anti-plan. Ilene took to consciously breaking her routine. She stopped buying the newspaper at the bodega in the morning, and started picking it up at the deli in the evening. A small, seemingly insignificant alteration, but it forced her to walk a different path, one that might take her who knows where. She'd been coming in to work later, leaving earlier. What would they do? Fire a pregnant pre-divorcée? Mark was so embarrassed by her plight that he would leave the room whenever she walked in. A week ago, she would have felt conspicuous and alienated. But now, she loved the power his embarrassment gave her. She could say or do anything she wanted, with no apparent consequence. She'd been contemplating quitting *Cash* anyway, and pursuing a career as a radio talk-show host. She had a lot to say on the trendy subject of life's second act.

Today was Frieda's wedding day. Her betrothed sister had been busy all week dealing with lawyers, getting prenups squared away, telling Justin the big news (that hadn't gone well), buying a dress (not a gown; she'd get one, though, for the real wedding in a temple? Church? Frieda and David hadn't decided about that yet). Frieda had found the time, though, to listen to Ilene's story in detail, from discovering Peter's ATM withdrawals to the disastrous confrontation at Aux-On-Arles, then the pregnancy test, and the separation agreement.

Ilene left out the part about running into Sam at the post office, although that conversation did more to turn her head than anything else. Sam Hill had been absolutely right. If she'd minded her own marriage, she would still have one. If she'd left Frieda alone, her favorite sister wouldn't be marrying a man she wasn't excited by. From now on, Ilene vowed to mind her own business and search for excitement, wherever she might find it, in the healthy, responsible way of a future parent.

Excitement *was* important. Of course it was! When she'd decided to stop seeing her plight as, well, a plight, she'd realized that change was thrilling. She was exhilarated by what parenthood would mean. She'd gone all the way around the barn with it, and finally, Ilene was excited for herself.

She checked the clock. Ilene was to meet Frieda, David, Justin and Betty at City Hall, One Centre Street, at 2 P.M. for the ceremony. The time was approximate. The way Ilene understood it, there was a holding pen room for the wedding principals and their parties. Each bride was given a number, and she had to wait her turn. Frieda had been advised to give the whole ceremony—from getting a number to leaving as husband and wife—a couple of hours.

Ilene took a personal day. David had, too. *Cash* was buzzing about Ilene's pregnancy/separation and David's surprise wedding. She was sure the gossip would travel along the business journalism wire to *Bucks*. Peter probably hadn't heard yet. If the news had reached his office, and he still hadn't contacted her, that just said it all, didn't it?

She shook the thought out of her head. "Kibosh negative thought" was the fourth tenet of the anti-plan (after "No planning," "Mind own business," and "Seek excitement"—not that she'd made a written list; that would be so old school).

Tenet four had been a challenge. The most persistent negative thought, especially on this day, was getting harder and harder to suppress. Ilene lay in her bed, trying to milk another few minutes of rest out of the morning.

When she closed her eyes, Ilene saw Sam Hill.

Her lids sprang open. She shook her head clear and said out loud, "Frieda and David *will* be happy. This is what she wants. Mind your own business."

She repeated those sentences while bathing (not showering), eating eggs and bacon (not a muffin), dressing in slacks and a cotton shirt (not a skirt and blouse), drinking green tea (not coffee). She sipped too quickly, slightly burning her tongue. She closed her eyes from the minor pain. And saw Sam Hill.

Ilene said, "Sam Hill is gone. Frieda says she doesn't want him, and that's good enough for me."

Ilene turned on the TV. She turned it off. She flipped on the computer, checked e-mail. Signed off. She picked up the phone and put it down. "I will not interfere with Frieda's life," she said. "She is capable of making her own decisions."

She made her bed and reorganized her underwear

drawer. She cleaned out her night-table drawer. She started to alphabetize the CD collection. She plucked a handful of jewel boxes off the shelf. A CD fell on the floor. She picked it up, looked at the cover.

And saw Sam Hill. Literally. She held the cast recording of *Oliver!* Peter had insisted on buying. She was glad Peter purchased it. He had a spine. He stood up to her. He'd genuinely enjoyed the show and wanted to keep a reminder. Ilene held the CD, a reminder to her of how badly she'd acted that night, how dismissive of Sam and intolerant of Peter. She'd pushed David on Frieda when they'd come to watch Sam. She was ashamed of herself. She looked again at the photo of Sam, in red beard and wig, as Fagin. His eyes couldn't be costumed, though, and they were fantastic. Frieda had told Ilene that Sam stared into her eyes the entire time they made love. Position allowing.

Ilene checked the back of the CD. Underneath the song list, she found an address, phone number, and website info for No Sudden Movement Players. "I will not interfere," she said.

She picked up her phone and dialed. While it rang, she looked at her ceiling and said, "Hear me, God. This is the last time, I swear."

"No Sudden Movement Players," said the female voice on the other end.

"I need to contact Sam Hill immediately," she said.

"Who is this?"

"I'm a top Hollywood agent," replied Ilene.

"The one from ICM?" asked the girl. Sam had an agent?

wondered Ilene. Maybe he wouldn't be broke forever after all.

She said, "I'm from CAA." Did CAA still exist? Ilene had no clue.

"I'll have to take a message for Sam," said the receptionist. "He's flying to London today."

Shit and double shit! He'd told her at the post office about this trip. Ilene said, "When is his flight? Can I reach him at home?"

The voice said, "I'm sure he's left for the airport by now. The plane leaves in a few hours. With security checks and—"

"Which airline?" asked Ilene, grabbing her purse.

The voice hesitated. "I'll tell you the airline and the flight number, if I can send you my head shot."

"I'd love to see it. I can tell from your voice that you're a very talented woman."

The very talented voice said, "Virgin Atlantic, flight number five sixty-seven. Departs Kennedy at two."

Ilene hung up. She grabbed her purse, zipped down the elevator and grabbed a cab.

"Sam!" screamed Ilene as she raced down Concourse C, rounding the corner into Gate 45. She waved her arms over her head, catching the attention of everyone in the airport.

"SAM HILL! WHERE ARE YOU?" she shouted. She scanned the crowd of people waiting for their turn to board his flight. She ran up and down the rows of chairs in a panic. She had to find him. He had to be here.

Knowing she couldn't get to the gate without a ticket, Ilene had ordered hers by cell phone on the way to the airport. Once she got to Kennedy, she used her credit card at the e-tickets machine, got a paper boarding pass, and hurried to security. She had to relinquish her prized pair of manicure scissors ($25), her tortoise-shell handled nail file ($15), and her Swiss army knife ($100). She could redeem the items on her return, or try the airport lost and found. She was in too much of a rush to listen to all the details, so she mentally kissed her grooming tools goodbye.

She beelined to the gate. Ilene hadn't run like that since the sixth grade, when she swore off moving at a pace that would make her glow. She was glowing with a cause now, and not ashamed of it.

"SAM HILL!" she shouted again, as loudly as she could. Raising her voice higher than she had since the seventh grade, when she swore off calling undue attention to herself in an unseemly fashion. "WHERE ARE YOU??!!"

A fat, bald, pockmarked man came up to her. He said, "You're looking for Sam Hill?"

She said, "You know him?"

The man said, "I'm Lars Altuna. The artistic director for No Sudden Movement Players."

"Where's Sam?" she demanded, grabbing his ugly polyester jacket lapels and pulling him toward her.

"I'm right here," said Sam, coming up alongside Lars Altuna.

Ilene exhaled. "You have to stop Frieda from marrying David." She checked her watch. "In one hour."

Sam blanched. "She's going to *marry* him?"

"Not if we get there first," said Ilene.

He said, "Now you like me?"

"Who I like doesn't matter."

"Is this because of the post office?"

"Yes, it is," she said. "And now we go." She tugged his sleeve.

Lars Altuna tugged on the other. "Not so fast, Sam," he said. "We have a show tomorrow night in London. You're contracted to do it. If you don't get on the plane, you're fired. You'll never work in this town again."

Sam said, "I barely work in this town now. Let's go, Ilene."

Ilene said, "You're not fired." She dug in her purse and pulled out a plane ticket. She said, "This a Virgin Airlines ticket in Sam's name, leaving New York tomorrow morning at six, arriving in London at noon. He can be at the theater by two. He'll do the show tomorrow, and he'll get tonight with Frieda before he disappears for two weeks and makes her crazy again." She drew breath. "Sam, give me your ticket for today's flight."

They exchanged tickets. She found the luggage claim check stapled to it and shoved it into Lars Altuna's hand. She said, "Lars, pick up Sam's bags in London and take them to the hotel for him." She pulled a couple of twenties out of her wallet. "For any inconvenience."

Sam and Lars stood motionless and watched Ilene work. She was the queen of planning. Too bad she was giving it all up. Or maybe she could simply stop evil plotting and use her powers for the greater good.

Lars said, "Works for me."

"This is a first-class ticket," Sam said of his seat for to-morrow's flight.

"They didn't have any seats in coach," she said.

"How much was it?" asked Sam.

"Never mind," she said. "Two thousand dollars."

"You spent two thousand dollars to reunite me and Frieda?"

"Plus the five hundred for my Virgin ticket to get to the gate, and another two hundred for miscellaneous expenses."

Sam whistled. "Almost three thousand dollars? That's one-seventh of my annual income."

"Ack!" bleated Ilene. "Don't say that out loud. It hurts my ears. I never want to hear it again."

They exited the airport and got a taxi. In the backseat, Sam said, "The night we broke up, I said something terri-ble to Frieda. She might not forgive me. She might marry David anyway."

Ilene said, "You take direction?" He nodded. "We show up. You look at her with your eyes. Say as little as possible. She really gets off on the pensive, laconic Maine treatment. And kiss her. She also gets off on your lips. Although they seem a bit thin to me. It might be best not to make a big speech. You two did most of your communicating without words anyway."

"It's a plan," he said.

She cringed. "Don't say that word."

Chapter 41

Friday, September 26
Noon

Betty called in sick. She didn't have any personal days left. She'd used them up in Earl's hotel room. She'd been lying in bed for hours. The thought of this marriage made her tired. How did Frieda do it? David was, inarguably, a catch. What was it about her sister that drew men? Betty couldn't draw a man with a pencil. She hated herself for the jealousy, but it had crept into her head and wouldn't leave.

Things had become strained with Peter, too. In the week since their *Braveheart* screening, he'd been remote. He'd been looking at apartments—one bedrooms and studios. She told him that he should just go home, back to Ilene, where he belonged. But he insisted on getting his own place, determined to leave yet another Schast sister to her own devices.

Earl, meanwhile, had dropped off the face of the Earth. Betty's steely resolve had lasted only one day before she called his hotel. She tried his cell. She paged him. No response. Maybe he'd been killed by a mugger. Or eaten by a pack of feral dogs. Or been bound, gagged, and manacled at an S & M club. Hit by a bus, run over by a subway, or (the worst possible option) fallen in love with a good woman who had turned him into an honest man. The question—where *was* he?—compelled her to call and page, again and again. It was a humiliating exercise.

She stopped calling when the receptionist at his hotel told her he'd checked out. Gert couldn't have been more relieved to hear the news. She told Betty to forget Earl, to push Peter out of the nest ("he's cramping your style") and date a bunch of men so she wouldn't get too attached to any one. Start saying "yes" to the guys who hit on her at Burton & Notham. Gert said she should whore around for a couple of years. Frieda, who eventually got the details on the Return of Earl suggested the same thing. That Earl had been an initiation by fire. She'd passed the test, and had some easy, fun flings coming to her. With her "new hotness" (Frieda's words), Betty would have loads of men to choose from.

Ilene steadfastly refused to have anything to do with plotting Betty's next romantic steps. She kept telling her baby sister to just "let it flow" and "take it as it comes." Betty, who'd had problems with the old Ilene, was starting to despise the changes in her sister. At least the meddling Ilene was involved and seemed to care. This new free-range philosophy, to Betty, seemed chicken. She'd always counted on her big sister to make a declarative statement about everything.

Betty threw back the covers. Only two hours until the ceremony, and she had things to do. She showered and picked through her closet to find something to wear. Something colorful. She chose a red wrap shirt Earl had picked out and black jeans. A City Hall ceremony wasn't formal. She'd go casual.

She needed to buy a gift. She had no idea what to get. It wasn't a traditional wedding. The couple hadn't registered. They each had a whole apartment full of furniture and dishes. Neither David nor Frieda needed any material objects. Still, Betty wanted to bring something nice for the bride and groom.

What would please Frieda? wondered Betty. She'd asked several times, but Frieda only wanted to discuss Ilene. Betty suspected the focus on Ilene was a way for Frieda to avoid thinking about this wedding. Frieda might spend the rest of her life finding ways to avoid thinking about this marriage.

Frieda said to Betty yesterday, "Ilene is headed for a nervous breakdown. She's acting like a religious convert. She actually said that confessing had set her free."

"So she's converting to Catholicism," said Betty.

"Worse," said Frieda. "The Cult of the Anti-Plan."

"Don't worry about her," said Betty. "For a pilgrim, she's pretty tough."

"No one is that tough," said Frieda.

Frieda pointed out that the Schast brother-in-laws had been wiped out of the family by cancer: Gregg by the disease, and Peter in its aftermath. Frieda told Betty she would love to see Peter to tell him how sorry she was about the separation. She tried to call him at work, but Jane said he wasn't available. She'd left a message. No return call. Frieda had always had a soft spot for Peter, especially because of the way he'd treated Justin.

Suddenly, Betty knew exactly what she would bring to Frieda's wedding. A gift that would make Frieda happy. And it might do more for the Schasts, too. But how to arrange it, without raising suspicion?

Betty picked up the phone and dialed.

"Peter Vermillion's office," said Jane Bambo.

"It's Betty."

"He's out to lunch," said Jane.

"I want you to tell him that the Mayor's Office called. They're holding an emergency press conference to announce that Mike Bloomberg is buying the New York Stock Exchange. He's offered to pay two million dollars a seat. Tell Peter that one hundred seat holders have already agreed to sell. The meeting is scheduled at two, but not at the usual pressroom. Reporters are to go to the sixth-floor lobby at One Centre Street to be checked in by security. Oh, and the list is by invitation only. No substitutions."

"He'll never believe it," said Jane.

"Convince him," said Betty.

"What are you up to?"

"I'm making my first attempt to meddle in other people's lives," said Betty. "It could end horribly. It might ruin what should be a day of love and rejoicing."

"Does this have anything to do with Ilene?" asked Jane.

"Yes," said Betty.

"Getting them back together?"

"At least in the same room."

Jane said, "When Ilene wanted something from me, she used to give me gifts."

"What did she give you?" asked Betty.

"A day of beauty at Georgette Klinger."

Betty said, "I'll get you *Making Faces* by Kevyn Aucoin for thirty percent off the cover price."

"Throw in *The New Joy of Sex* at thirty percent off, and we've got a deal," said Jane.

Chapter 42

Friday, September 26
2:33 P.M.

The holding pen was crowded, but, thankfully, the city had supplied enough chairs. Frieda counted ten wedding parties in the room. A few of the brides-to-be wore all-out, white sequined and beaded gowns, veils, trains. The matching grooms were in tuxes (one black, one green and one purple). Some of the groups were large (ceremonies were limited to ten witnesses), but the majority were parties of two, the husband and wife, husband and "wife," or "husband" and wife (the latter two categories were having same-sex commitment ceremonies, recognized by the State of New York as legally binding). At present, Frieda's wedding party consisted of herself in a lavender dress, David in a gray suit, and Justin in chocolate smudges and lollipop smears.

"The candy was a mistake," said David.

Frieda knew there'd be a wait, so she'd brought a bag of

sweets to occupy Justin. He'd consumed the goodies in the first ten minutes, and was now running up and down the length of the room, jumping and smacking the walls to leave ever-higher chocolate marks on the beige paint.

She said, "Maybe we should come back another time."

David said, "This isn't a crowded restaurant. We're here to get married. It shouldn't be much longer."

The clerk opened the door and yelled into the crowd, "Now serving couple number seventy-eight." Frieda and David were number 80.

Justin ran by. David and Frieda watched him, their heads swiveling. "I've never told you 'I love you' back," she said.

"That's okay," he said, "When you're ready."

David said he'd fallen in love with her in days. Nights, actually, the ones spent out to dinner, talking about their lives. She found this assertion unbelievable, but then reminded herself that she'd fallen in love with Gregg, and then Sam, in minutes.

She said, "If I asked you to walk across the room and touch the wall with your left foot to prove your love, would you do it?"

He didn't answer. He stood up, walked across the room, kicked the wall with his left foot and returned. He said, "I'll do it again if you want me to. I'll do anything within reason. I do draw the line at murder and robbery."

"What about vandalism?" she asked. "Public nudity?"

"I have been naked in public, and liked it. So I can't reasonably object to that," he said, and started telling her a story about a summer at Martha's Vineyard.

She half listened. The other half of her mind replayed the night she and Sam broke up. She had tried to corral Sam, to leash him to her side. And now that she had a man who would bark like a dog if she asked, she wished she'd stuck with the one who trusted her enough to leave her on her own.

Frieda smiled and nodded at her fiancé, seeing his mouth move but not hearing the words. Whenever he kissed her, she thought of pencil erasers. When he felt her up, she imagined a baker kneading dough. When they fucked, she saw Gregg. His ghost. She watched him hover near the ceiling, looking down at them, nodding in approval, his phantasmal mind-meld sending her the message that he could rest in peace knowing that she and Justin would be taken care of by a reliable man like David.

She'd never seen the ghost of Gregg when she was with Sam. With Sam, she never saw or thought about anything except what they were doing to each other.

"Where the hell are Ilene and Betty?" she asked suddenly. "Oh, I'm sorry for interrupting."

"Don't apologize," said David, taking her hand and placing it on his heart. Sam used to take her hand and press it against his hard-on.

David looked over her shoulder. "Here's Ilene now," he said.

Frieda turned to look. There was her pregnant sister, elbowing her way through the crowd. Justin was with her, leading her by the hand to Frieda and David.

Frieda jumped up and grabbed her sister. "You're late!" she said.

"I had to pick something up," she said.

Out of the corner of her eye, Frieda saw sugar-high Justin slapping a man's leg. She looked up toward his face, and her breath caught. Sam Hill. She rubbed her eyes. Had to be hallucinating.

"Hello, Frieda," Sam said, smiling. "You look good."

Ilene put her arm around Sam's shoulder. "Look who I found!" she announced.

David stood up and pecked Ilene on the cheek. He reached out to shake Sam's hand. Frieda didn't move. She just stared. He looked glorious, of course. His hair, a mad-scientistish riot. His eyes, fixed on her, were shimmering. His skin, clear and vibrant. She'd forgotten how beautiful he was, the intensity of their molecular attraction, the chemical lure to press herself against him.

David said, "What are you doing here?"

Ilene said, "I was invited!"

"I was talking about him."

"I ran into Sam and thought he might want to congratulate the bride," said Ilene.

Justin ran off again, smacking chocolate fingerprints on the walls. "Where did you run into him?" asked David.

Ilene smiled. "The airport. JFK. I pulled him off a flight to London."

Frieda and Sam listened to this exchange, not breaking eye contact the entire time. "Is that true?" asked Frieda.

Sam kept staring. He didn't speak right away. After a beat of ten, he said, "Yes."

"And you want to congratulate me?" she asked.

He opened his mouth, but didn't talk. He looked at Ilene, then back at Frieda. Up at David, down at his feet. Finally, he said, "No."

Ilene said, "Sam, you might be overplaying the terse Mainer."

The clerk opened the door and called for number 79. David said, "We're next."

Justin bounced back, this time, pulling Betty toward their group. Betty gripped the arm of a confused-looking thin man in a beautifully tailored blue suit. It took a moment for Frieda to realize it was Peter.

"What is Justin doing at the mayor's press conference . . . ?" Peter muttered until he spotted Frieda. Then David. Then Sam. When his eyes lit on Ilene, he reeled backward, clutching his heart, colliding with a groom.

The groom, green tux, said, "Watch it, jerk-off."

"I'm sorry," said Peter.

The bride said, "You promised. No one gets whacked on my wedding day."

"You just got lucky, asshole," said the groom.

Lucky Peter turned back to the Schast party. He exclaimed, "I've been deceived."

"In a nice way," said Betty, steadying Peter.

Peter massaged his chest and sized up the situation. "Was this a conspiracy, or did you act alone?" he asked Betty.

"I did it on my own," she said proudly.

Peter said to her, "What did you hope to achieve? That Ilene and I would take one look at each other and see what complete fools we've been? That we're made for each other? That my heart aches to look at her because she's so beautiful? That she would realize she loves me and needs me, too? Is that what you expected?"

Before Betty could speak, Ilene said to her, "Peter couldn't possibly think I'm beautiful. I've gained twenty pounds."

Peter said to Betty, "I don't care about that. Her weight gain is due to emotional eating anyway. I'm glad, actually. It's proof that she's been upset about the separation."

"Can you two please talk to each other?" said Betty. "And Ilene's weight gain isn't about emotional eating. She's . . ."

Ilene held up her hand. "I'll thank you to stop there," she said to her youngest sister.

Justin, meanwhile, took Frieda's hand and squeezed hard. He looked droopy, about to crash from his sugar frenzy. She said, "Are you okay?"

Her son said, "I don't feel good."

Sam said, "He's turning green. I'll take him to the men's room."

David said, "I'll take him. He's my stepson."

Justin said, "Rock, paper, scissors."

David and Sam agreed. Together, they said, "One, two, three, shoot!"

Sam said, "Shit. Best of three?"

"I won," said David. "*I'll* take Justin to the bathroom. *I'll* marry Frieda. *I'll* be friends with Ilene. And you will disappear from our lives forever."

Sam asked Frieda, "Is that what you want?"

Frieda was too stunned by the turn of events to answer. She groped for coherency, but failed to come up with anything. Sam said, "Okay then," and walked away, maneuvering around brides and grooms. He stopped a few feet from the exit, waiting for something. Frieda thought, *Look back. Look back.* He didn't look back.

He did turn around and run toward her, leaping over white tulle trains and satin-shod feet. He grabbed Frieda in his arms and kissed her hard on the mouth. He gripped her ass with one hand, and snagged her hair with the other. Frieda swooned against him, holding him as tightly as she could. As soon as her hand touched the skin of his neck, she was gone. It was heaven, bliss, walking on air, a passion of fire and majesty. How could she have considered marrying David for one second, when a kiss from Sam made her feel like this?

"Get a room," said the green-tux groom.

Coming up for air, Sam said, "I think we should get back together."

She said, "Excellent idea."

"But if you marry David, we'll have to break up for good."

The clerk opened the door and yelled, "Now serving couple number eighty."

"That's us," said David. "Sam, I thought this about you when I saw you onstage: You've got great timing."

The clerk called back. "Number eighty. Does anyone with ticket number eighty want to get married?"

Frieda looked at Sam. She said, "Should we?"

Sam said, "Should we *what?*"

Ilene said, "Actors are supposed to take risks."

"Show some nuts, man," said Betty.

"Sam has nuts?" Justin asked.

Peter said, "We're about to find out."

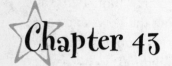

Chapter 43

Friday, September 26
3:33 P.M.

"By the powers vested in me by the City of New York, I pronounce you husband and wife. You may kiss," said the judge.

He leaned in to kiss his bride. The touch of her lips was sweet and satisfying, like returning home after years in forced exile. She seemed to like it, too. She sighed, the sound rippling through his memory, setting off a physical chain reaction that he couldn't derail.

His bride, feeling the intrusion on her thigh, whispered in his ear, "Save that for later."

The family gathered around them, laughing, backslapping. Betty whistled through her teeth. He had no idea she could do that. It was an ability he'd long admired, and this raised Betty in his already sky-high esteem. Justin gave him a high five with such velocity that it caused genuine pain. He didn't mind. Nothing could bother him now.

David stayed for the ceremony, which was brave of him. He was a decent guy. No wonder Ilene had made him her friend, why Frieda had agreed to marry him. Betty and David stood next to each other during the vows exchange. As the group filed out of the judge's chambers, he heard Betty say to David, "You're on the rebound, so it's perfect. I'm looking for casual. The relationship equivalent of cut-offs and a tank top."

David said, "I need some time."

"Oh," said Betty. "I understand."

"Will a week from Saturday work for you?" he asked.

Justin seemed unfazed by the turn of events. "What happened to the nuts?" he kept asking, and then he'd laugh hysterically (Betty had explained to him what *nuts* meant, in this case). Frieda told Justin he could have a Snickers bar from the vending machine if he shut up. The kid complied.

News of Sam's 6-A.M. flight to London didn't please Frieda. She said, "You're leaving *tomorrow* morning? For two weeks? How am I going to get through it?"

"You'll make it," promised Sam. "You know I'm coming back."

That seemed to satisfy her. For the moment. The wedding party exited City Hall onto Centre Street, a half block from the entrance of the Brooklyn Bridge. Sam, Frieda, and Justin decided to walk over it, back to Brooklyn. David and Betty shared a cab uptown.

"Alone at last," said Ilene. The woman of Peter's dreams. His new bride as of eleven minutes ago. His old wife as of eleven years ago. The judge had agreed to marry them, even though they hadn't filled out the paperwork, after they explained the special circumstances. They'd done enough paperwork already.

"What can I do for you?" asked Peter. "Want me to marry you a third time? I'll do it. Let's get back on line."

Ilene laughed. He hadn't heard her laugh in what felt like years. He wanted to make love to her until they were both as raw as hamburger meat.

"The time we've been apart," she said. "It was useful."

He agreed. If he hadn't been away, he wouldn't have known that he could function without her, which, counterintuitively, made him want her even more.

"It really was an arrow to the heart, seeing you standing there, next to Sam Hill of all people," said Peter.

Ilene's face had filled out. The sharp edges had a pretty curve to them now. Her skin was pinker from the effort of carrying the extra weight. Her hair seemed thicker, shinier. He had to touch it. The only thing that could possibly make her more beautiful? Peter said, "Brides should have flowers. I want to get some for you. What kind do you want?"

She took his hand and placed it on her rounded belly. "Daisy," she said.

"Just one? Can't I buy a bunch? Many bunches?"

She shook her head. "This is Daisy," said Ilene, pressing his palm into her stomach. "We'll meet her in January. Or February."

It took a minute to register. But when he understood what his wife was telling him, Peter felt instantly blessed, closer to God, flawless and ideal. He was a perfect man. Not because of who he was, what he did, his successes, accomplishments. None of that mattered. Peter felt like a perfect man for one reason only: The perfect woman was smiling at him.

He smiled back.

AVON TRADE... because every great bag
deserves a great book!

Paperback $13.95
ISBN 0-06-056277-3

Paperback $13.95
($21.95 Can.)
ISBN 0-06-056012-6

Paperback $13.95
ISBN 0-06-053437-0

Paperback $13.95 ($21.95 Can.)
ISBN 0-06-053668-3

Paperback $13.95 ($21.95 Can.)
ISBN 0-06-056075-4

Paperback $13.95 ($21.95 Can.)
ISBN 0-06-008545-2

**Don't miss the next book by your favorite author.
Sign up for AuthorTracker by visiting *www.AuthorTracker.com*.**

Available wherever books are sold, or call 1-800-331-3761 to order.

ATP 0204

Don't miss these other smart, witty stories by

VALERIE FRANKEL

0-380-80542-1 • $13.00 US • $20.00 Can

"Charming and highly entertaining.
A must read for anyone
who has a sister."
Candace Bushnell, author of *Sex in the City*

0-06-093841-2 • $13.95 US • $21.95 Can
"Valerie Frankel knows how to
create a wicked, sexy story."
Ottawa Citizen

AVON TRADE...because every great bag deserves a great book!

Available wherever books are sold
or please call 1-800-331-3761 to order.

VF 0204